'But that's awful!' Jess Budd exclaimed in dismay. 'Two little sisters, taken away from where they were settled and sent to separate children's homes! Why ever have the billeting people done that? I thought they must have decided to leave them with you after all.'

'I hoped so too. It's several months now since their father's ship was lost, and as I'd heard nothing else ...' The telephone line crackled and a train steamed by, drowning Mr Beckett's words. Jess tutted in exasperation, but she knew she was lucky to be able to ring up the billet in the village of Bridge End, near Southampton, where her son Keith had been evacuated, to speak to him once a week. Most parents back in Portsmouth had to rely on hastily scribbled letters or postcards to know how their children were faring out in the country.

'I'm sorry, Mr Beckett, I didn't hear that,' she said when the train had passed. 'You'd think the Post Office would have more sense than to put a telephone kiosk right beside the railway in the middle of Portsmouth! It's bad enough that we're on a main road ... What were you saying about Stella and Muriel? Have they actually gone?'

Lilian Harry's grandfather hailed from Devon and Lilian always longed to return to her roots, so moving from Hampshire to a small Dartmoor town in her early twenties was a dream come true. She quickly absorbed herself in local life, learning the fascinating folklore and history of the moors, joining the church bell-ringers and a country dance club, and meeting people who are still her friends today. Although she later moved north, living first in Herefordshire and then in the Lake District, she returned in the 1990s and now lives on the edge of the moor with her two miniature schnauzers. She is still an active bell-ringer and member of the local drama group, and loves to walk on the moors. Her daughter and two grandchildren live nearby.

Visit her website at *www.lilianharry.co.uk* or you can follow her on Twitter @LilianHarry.

Also by Lilian Harry

A Child in Burracombe

LILIAN HARRY

ORION

An Orion paperback

First published in Great Britain in 2017
by Orion Books
This paperback edition published in 2018
by Orion Books,
an imprint of The Orion Publishing Group Ltd,
Carmelite House, 50 Victoria Embankment
London EC4Y 0DZ

An Hachette UK Company

1 3 5 7 9 10 8 6 4 2

A CIP catalogue record for this book
is available from the British Library.

ISBN 978 1 4091 6732 7

Typeset by Deltatype Ltd, Birkenhead, Merseyside

Printed in Great Britain by Clays Ltd, St Ives plc

www.orionbooks.co.uk

This book is dedicated to the readers whose letters, cards and emails have touched me so deeply over the years. The husband, caring for a wife living with cancer, the son whose mother has just died with Alzheimer's, all those struggling with difficult lives who have nevertheless managed to find time to write and tell me what my books have meant to them. The many who lived through the years of the Second World War and have written of their memories; those who were evacuated, bombed out of their homes and even lost their own families; those who worked as nurses or in munitions, who took on other war work or served in the Armed Forces; and those whose service was on the Home Front. And, in my later Burracombe books, those who have told me stories of their own lives during the 1950s, and sometimes provided inspiration for events in Burracombe itself.

It has been a privilege to play some small part in the lives of all these readers and the many others that I know are there, carrying my books home from bookshop or library or downloading them on to their e-readers (something undreamed of when I began to write over forty years ago). Thank you all.

Acknowledgements

It is impossible to acknowledge by name all those who have helped, encouraged and furthered my writing career since I wrote my first walking article in the *Worcester Evening News* back in 1973 (calling myself 'Wayfarer'). I cannot even count how many editors, copy-editors, proof-readers and others have spent their working days doing their best to make sure my books are presented to the readers in the best possible way. To all of those, I send my grateful thanks.

But there is one person who has remained constant in all this time, and that is my literary agent, Caroline Sheldon, who has been a staunch friend and unfailing support for the past thirty years.

Thank you all – and especially Caroline.

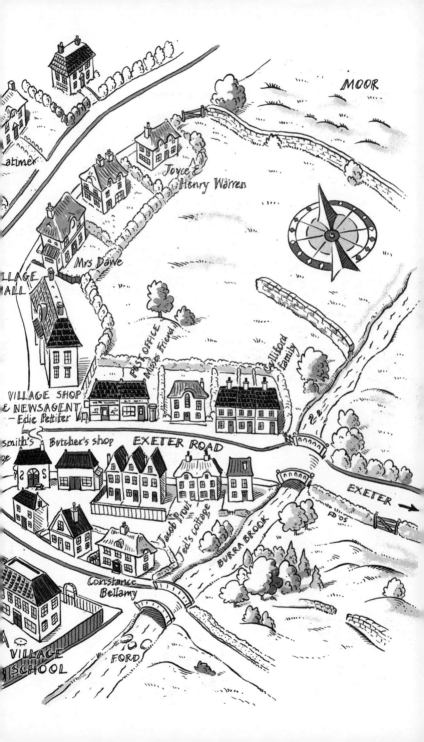

Part One

Part One

Chapter One

April Grove, Portsmouth, February 1943

'But that's awful!' Jess Budd exclaimed in dismay. 'Two little sisters, taken away from where they were settled and sent to separate children's homes! Why ever have the billeting people done that? I thought they must have decided to leave them with you after all.'

'I hoped so too. It's several months now since their father's ship was lost, and as I'd heard nothing else ...' The telephone line crackled and a train steamed by, drowning Mr Beckett's words. Jess tutted in exasperation, but she knew she was lucky to be able to ring up the billet in the village of Bridge End, near Southampton, where her son Keith had been evacuated, to speak to him once a week. Most parents back in Portsmouth had to rely on hastily scribbled letters or postcards to know how their children were faring out in the country.

'I'm sorry, Mr Beckett, I didn't hear that,' she said when the train had passed. 'You'd think the Post Office would have more sense than to put a telephone kiosk right beside the railway in the middle of Portsmouth! It's bad enough that we're on a main road ... What were you saying about Stella and Muriel? Have they actually gone?'

'I'm afraid so,' he said, his voice sounding thin and wispy over the crackling line. 'A woman came from the billeting office and told me to have everything ready for them, and she took them away yesterday. I tried my very best to persuade her to leave them with me but it was useless. She said it was "unsuitable".'

3

'Unsuitable?' Jess repeated. 'But how could it be? It was suitable enough before their father, poor Mr Simmons, was drowned. And they'd been with you for eighteen months before that.'

'She said the situation is different now they're orphans. Until then, their father had the last word in what happened to them, but now ... they come under a different authority, you see.' He sounded dejected, and Jess felt suddenly sorry for him. Poor old man, she thought, living alone in that great rambling vicarage all these years with no one but his housekeeper for company ... Having evacuees to stay had given him a new lease of life, you could see that. First her own boys, Tim and Keith, who had grumbled loudly at having to go and live with a vicar ('We'll have to go to church every Sunday. Probably *twice*'), and then poor Kathy Simmons's two little girls, after Kathy and their baby brother had been killed in a bombing raid.

A lot of elderly men would have been completely at a loss at having a ready-made family of youngsters foisted upon them. But Mr Beckett, a thin, spidery man who could be seen every day pedalling his old bicycle around the village, had received them with joy, becoming a kind of honorary boy and organising games of cricket in the garden in summer or building snowmen in winter. Church had come into it too, of course it had – you couldn't expect it not to, Jess had told her sons, and it wasn't as if they didn't go regularly when they were at home – but they hadn't minded once they realised it didn't also mean prayers all day and every day at home. Apart from grace at meals, and 'Matthew, Mark, Luke and John' when they went to bed, they would hardly have known he was a vicar.

'But *why* couldn't the girls stay with you?' she asked. 'Even if it's a different authority, surely anyone could see they had a good home with you and Mrs Mudge. It was obvious they were happy – well, as happy as they could be in such terrible circumstances. Taking them away, sending them to a strange place with more strange people – and *separating* them, too – why, it's cruel.'

'I feel that myself,' he said miserably. 'I suppose I shouldn't say so, but ... Apparently it will help them get over their loss more easily. They'll forget, you see. Especially little Muriel – she's barely nine.' He didn't sound as if he believed a word of it, and Jess's heart ached for him as well as for the little girls.

4

'And there's really nothing you can do?' she asked. 'I'd offer to have them back here, but now that Tim's here again after all that muddle with the school, and with Rose back because she never really settled away from home, and baby Maureen who's got to be with me, and us only having two bedrooms ...'

'They wouldn't allow it anyway. The authorities, I mean. If they won't let them stay at Bridge End, where they knew so many people and had so many friends, they're not likely to let them go back to Portsmouth ... Little Sammy Hodges, who thought the world of Muriel, is quite distraught, and I've had a stream of people coming to the door offering to have them, but it's useless. They've gone, and that's all there is to it.'

Jess felt his hopelessness reach out to her across the miles and tears came to her eyes. She brushed them away and said, 'Well, we can at least write to them. We can keep in touch, and perhaps when things have settled down a bit we can—'

'I'm afraid we can't even do that,' the vicar said desolately. 'The billeting officer said it was best to sever all ties. She refused to give me an address or any hint as to where they might be going – she said it was *none of my business*' – his voice rose to a squeak – 'and when I asked if letters might be forwarded, she said most definitely not. A clean break, she said, and then she shut her mouth as if it were a trap and marched the two poor little souls away.' He stopped and sighed. 'I shouldn't have spoken like that. I'm rather upset.'

'I should think you are!' Jess said roundly. 'So am I, and so will everyone else be that knew them. It's absolutely ridiculous. And like I've already said, it's *cruel*.'

'Yes,' he said in a quiet, despairing tone. 'And the worst of it is, there's nothing we can do about it. Nothing at all.'

There was a short silence. Then Mr Beckett spoke again. 'I'm sorry, Mrs Budd. You really rang up to speak to Keith. He's here, waiting for you. And how is Tim getting along? Such a fine little lad – they both are. Sons to be proud of, both of them.'

Jess murmured something, and he said goodbye and handed the receiver to her younger son, who was now, since Tim had come home a few months earlier, the only child left in the vicarage. He must be feeling rather lonely, she thought as she heard his voice saying hello. But not as lonely as those two poor little girls, orphaned and then separated and sent to live with strangers, and allowed no contact at all with those who had loved and looked after them.

What were the authorities, whoever they were, thinking of, to do this to helpless children who had lost so much? And what were the little girls themselves thinking now? Did they believe they had been abandoned?

Nothing we can do about it? she muttered to herself as she finished talking to her son and left the kiosk for the next person in the queue. Surely there's something. There must be *something* we can do ...

'I don't know as there is,' Jess's husband, Frank, said when she'd finished telling him the story. 'We knew it was on the cards, after all. The vicar told us they might be took away when we went out to talk to him about our Tim that time, back before Christmas. You know what the authorities are – what they say goes, especially in wartime. Look how they can take over big houses, never mind who lives there, and just turn the owners out for the duration. And that's people with money, people with a position. What chance have people like us got?' He sighed and shook his head. 'It's not even as if the girls are any relation to us. We don't have any right to a say in what happens to them.'

'We've got a right to say if we think it's wrong, though,' Jess argued. 'Those two poor little mites lived here with us before they went out to Bridge End. We know them better than anyone. And I know they'll hate being separated. Look how Stella looked after her sister – a little mother, she was, just like our Rose here with Maureen.'

Rose made a face. She had been twelve when her own little sister had been born, and at first she had indeed been a little mother, doing everything for her bar change nappies, which she flatly refused to do. But as Maureen grew into an inquisitive toddler, with her nose and fingers into everything, Rose hadn't been so enthusiastic, and she certainly wasn't keen on having to share the front room downstairs with her.

'We're not having them back here,' she said quickly. 'There's not room. Me and Maureen are having to sleep on the bed settee as it is, so that Tim can have the bedroom. Just because he's a boy,' she added sulkily.

'And very pleased I am to have him here,' Jess said sharply. 'You know you missed him when he was out at Bridge End. Now, if only we could have Keith back as well ...'

'Keith's all right where he is,' Frank said. 'And there's no question of us having the Simmons girls here, Rose. If the authorities won't even tell Mr Beckett where they've been taken, they're not likely to tell us. And they certainly won't let the kiddies come back to Pompey. There's still a war on, even if there don't seem to be so much bombing at the moment.'

There was a brief silence. Jess picked up the sailor's square-rig collar she had been sewing as part of her war work. Everyone had to do something; even Rose was knitting socks with thick khaki wool for soldiers. Frank's job, apart from working on ship repairs in Portsmouth Dockyard, was fire watching when there was an air raid. While the rest of the family was down in the Anderson shelter he had dug at the bottom of the garden, he stood in the darkness, his fire extinguisher close at hand, scanning the sky for incendiary bombs falling from the planes high overhead, or watching out for parachutes.

'What about seeing if Dan Hodges can find anything out?' she asked. 'His Sammy's out at Bridge End, and Dan's started to go out to see him now the weather's better, so Tommy Vickers told me. Sammy used to knock about a bit with Keith and our Tim so he'd have known the girls as well. The vicar said he and Muriel were quite thick. In fact, now I come to think of it, they got into some sort of scrape with Sammy's foster mother's parrot – took it out on a picnic or something.'

'Dan told me about that,' Frank said. 'Mrs Purslow was in a right old stew about it, and Dan walked in right in the middle of the row and found young Sam crying into a bowl of bread and milk. He near as a toucher brought the boy home straight away.'

'Well, he wouldn't have been much better off back here,' Jess said wryly. 'You know what a state Dan Hodges has been living in since poor Nora died. And I'm sure Ruth Purslow wasn't ill-treating Sammy. I knew her when I was at Bridge End, at the beginning of the war. She's a nice little soul, and a nurse too. I expect she was just cross over the parrot. Everyone gets cross with boys now and then.' She went on sewing for a few minutes, then asked, 'So you

7

don't think there's anything at all we can do to help them?'

Frank heard the despondency in her voice and looked at her, feeling his heart soften.

'I'm sorry, love, I don't think there is. I know they've had a bad time, but they'll be looked after. And even if they're separated now, they won't forget. Kiddies don't forget that easy. They'll find each other one day, when they're grown up, you'll see.'

Jess laid down her sewing and stared at it. The tears burned her eyes and one dripped on to the navy serge.

'I don't think it'll be that easy, Frank,' she said sadly. 'It'll be years before they're old enough to do that, and who knows what might have happened in the meantime? And even if they do, they'll have missed all those years together. They'll never be little girls again, growing up as sisters should.'

Chapter Two

Bridge End

The two little girls had been even more bewildered than the adults when they were first told, back in November, that they would be leaving the vicarage, where they had been looked after for the past few months. They stood in the drawing room in front of the wood fire and Mr Beckett, the old vicar, drew them both close to his bony knees and held their hands.

'I've got some news for you, my dears, and I want you both to be very brave about it.'

'It's bad news, then,' Stella said instantly, and he sighed in self-reproach. He had tried so hard to find the right words, discarding phrases like *I'm afraid* or *bad* so as not to upset them, and he'd failed with the first sentence. Who would ask children to be brave about good news?

'You may not like it to begin with,' he said carefully, 'but I'm sure as time goes on you'll settle down happily and see that it's all for the best. Mrs Mudge and I will miss you very much, of course, but—'

'We're being sent away!' Stella butted in, and he could have kicked himself. He was going about this in entirely the wrong way. He should have left it to his housekeeper, who would have known how to talk to the two orphaned children. Even Keith Budd or Sammy Hodges would have made a better job of it than he.

'You're sending us away,' Stella repeated, and stared at him accusingly. 'I suppose it's because we're girls and you like boys best.'

'No!' The denial burst from him and he caught himself up.

9

It would do no good to let himself get upset – any more than he already was, anyway. He forced himself to speak more calmly. 'No, indeed it isn't, Stella. You know how welcome you are here. I'd like nothing better than for you to stay for as long as the war lasts. For as long as you want to stay. But it isn't up to me to say.'

'Who is it up to, then?' Stella demanded, looking as if she meant to go straight off and have a word with whoever had made this decision. And she would too, he thought, gazing at the fierce little face. She'd probably even get her way. But who was going to listen to an eleven-year-old girl, even if she was the one most affected?

'It's up to the authorities,' he said, thinking what a vague term that was. 'The ones who decide where children are to be billeted. You've seen Mrs Tupper. Well, when—'

'She's a horrible lady,' Stella said decisively. 'Nobody likes her. Keith says she looks like that old settee in the doctor's waiting room.'

'Yes, she does rather,' the vicar agreed, thinking of the broad-beamed woman in her brown tweed suit, carrying her folder of documents. 'But that isn't the point. The thing is, she billeted you here to begin with when everything was all right, but now things have changed.'

'You mean Daddy's died. I don't see what difference that makes. It was all right for us to be here when Mummy and Thomas were killed, so why not now?'

I'd like the answer to that question myself, Mr Beckett thought, but he knew what the difference was, although he had hoped he might not have to explain it.

'It's because your daddy agreed that you could come here. But now he – he can't agree any more, so the authorities have to decide. And they think you would be better in a children's home.'

'A children's home?' Stella echoed. 'You mean an *orphanage*?'

He nodded unhappily. 'They're perfectly nice places, Stella. They're just like a school that you live in all the time instead of going home each night. They—'

'Like in Enid Blyton?' Muriel piped up. It was the first time she had spoken; she had just stood there, gripping his hand with one of hers, the other holding her doll close to her chest. 'I read a book about girls at a boarding school. They had midnight feasts and—'

'No,' Stella cut in. 'It won't be like that. That's where rich children go. It'll be more like the workhouse in *Oliver Twist*. There won't even be feasts during the day.'

Muriel stared at her and looked as if she were about to cry. Mr Beckett intervened hastily.

'Children's homes aren't quite like either of those places; they're certainly not like the workhouse in *Oliver Twist*.' He thought of the workhouse in Southampton that he had visited occasionally and wondered if there was really that much difference. But it wouldn't do to let the girls know he had doubts. 'They're places for children to go to who have no other homes or people to look after them.'

'But we've got you,' Muriel said. 'You look after us. Well, Mrs Mudge looks after us, but you play with us. So we don't need to be sent away and you can tell Mrs Tupper next time she comes, and everything will be all right.' She gave him a smile of such radiant confidence that he felt his heart come close to breaking.

'I'm sorry, Muriel, my dear,' he said gently. 'It really isn't as easy as that. It's as if I've only been allowed to borrow you, you see, and now I have to give you back—'

'Like a library book,' Stella commented.

'Well, not quite like a library book, perhaps, but—'

'Brian Collins had a library book,' Muriel said. 'It was about boxers and he didn't want to take it back so he told them he'd lost it. But they said he'd have to pay two shillings for it so he took it back and said he'd found it again. They still made him pay a penny for keeping it out too long, though,' she added thoughtfully. 'Would they let you keep us if you said you'd lost us and then found us again? I know we'd cost more than a penny, but I've got one and fourpence I was saving up for Sammy's birthday. I don't think he'd mind if I gave you that. And there's our sugar money too, you could keep that, and—'

'Oh *Muriel*!' her sister exclaimed. 'Be quiet! It's nothing like that at all.' She looked at the vicar again. 'But I still don't understand why we've got to go away when we're all right here.'

Mr Beckett sighed again. 'It's because now that you don't have parents, you come under a different authority. Mrs Tupper looks after children who are evacuated from their own homes and have parents who say what is to happen to them. But now that you – well, as you are on your own now' – oh dear, this was so difficult – 'and don't even have any other relatives to look after you, a different authority has to take you over. And they've decided that you must go to a children's home.'

'I still don't see why we can't stay here,' Stella objected. 'Can't this new authority say we could do that?'

'I've asked them,' he said. 'I'm afraid they just say no. It isn't suitable, you see, for two little girls to stay in a house with just an old man to look after them.'

'Why isn't it?' Before he could think of an answer to that one, she went on, 'Daddy didn't mind, so why should they? Anyway, we haven't just got an old man, we've got Mrs Mudge as well, and she's the one who does all the washing and cooking.'

'But Mrs Mudge is my housekeeper, you see – an employee. She might leave. They don't really count her in law.'

Stella stared at him, and for a moment he thought she was going to refer to *Oliver Twist* again and say that in that case, the law was an ass. He felt inclined to agree, although he knew that there were perfectly valid reasons why two small girls could not be left with an old man. Nevertheless, it was heartbreaking to see his little family broken up like this, and he had not yet told them the worst.

'So this place we're being sent to,' Stella said ungraciously. 'This *orphanage*. Where is it? Will we still be able to come and see you?'

'We could come to tea,' Muriel said. 'Sunday tea, because there are cakes then. Or on Wednesdays, when Mrs Mudge does sausages.'

Mr Beckett gazed at them and shook his head. This was, he thought, the worst task he had ever had to undertake.

'I don't think you will be able to come to see us, I'm afraid. You see, I don't know where you will be taken, and Mrs Tupper said they won't tell me. They won't tell anyone.'

There was a stunned silence. Then Stella echoed incredulously, 'Won't tell *anyone*? Not anyone at all? Not even you and Mrs Mudge?'

'Not Keith or Sammy?' Muriel asked, her voice rising as she named her two heroes. 'Not even our *teacher*?'

He shook his head. 'I'm afraid not.'

'But then how will you ever be able to find us? How will you be able to write to us? How will Sammy be able to tell me about Silver?' The reality seemed to have hit Muriel at last. She turned frantically to her sister. 'And Auntie Jess, in Portsmouth – how will she know where we are? We went there for *Christmas*. She said we could go again.'

'I'm very sorry,' the vicar said. 'I'm afraid nobody will know.'

'We'll write to you,' Muriel said with decision. 'We know your address. We'll write to everybody and tell them. We *won't* be taken away!'

Stella pulled her hand away from the vicar's knee. She turned to her sister and, taking the younger girl by the shoulders, looked at the frantic little face and said in tones of angry desperation, 'It's no good, Muriel. Don't you understand? We're being taken away so nobody knows where we are, and we won't be allowed to go out on our own any more, we won't be able to write to people or even send them Christmas cards. It's going to be like being in a prison. We're orphans now, and nobody can do anything to help us.'

The news struck at everyone in Bridge End just as it had those in April Grove.

Sammy Hodges, who had lived in April Grove before coming to Bridge End, was more upset than Ruth Purslow had ever seen him. He sat beside Silver's stand, his face creased with misery, pouring out his troubles to the parrot as he often did, but it seemed that this time nothing even Silver could say would comfort him.

'They're sending her away,' he said, bewildered by the unfairness of it. 'And Stella, as well. Just because their father died. It wasn't *their* fault, Silver. It wasn't their fault he had to go to sea in his ship and got torpedoed by the Germans. Why should they be sent away because of that?'

'Dip, dip, dip, my little ship,' said Silver, who seemed to have an uncanny knack of finding the appropriate words for any occasion. 'Sails across the water, like a cup and saucer. Time for tea. I'm a little teapot, short and stout ...'

'And Stella was supposed to be going up to the Big School after the summer,' Sammy went on, ignoring the parrot's comments for probably the first time ever. 'Do you think they'll know that, where she's going?' He turned as Ruth came in, carrying two plates of

13

beans on toast. 'Auntie Ruth, do you think they'll know that Stella's supposed to go up to the Big School after the summer? Suppose she gets left behind, like Tim Budd?'

'Well, that was a mistake about his age.' She set the plates on the table. 'I don't think it's likely to happen to Stella. Wherever the girls go, they'll get a proper education.' She looked at the woebegone little face. 'I know it's a shame and we're all upset, but there's really nothing we can do about it. And you'll still have Keith and the other children to play with.'

'But not Muriel,' he said sadly, laying his head against the parrot's grey feathers. 'Muriel was my special friend.'

Ruth sighed. She knew this was true, and she understood how precious a 'special' friend had been to Sammy, who had seemed so friendless when he had first arrived here. This war was very hard on children, she thought. Torn away from their homes, losing their friends and all too often their families as well. Did the people who started these things ever think about that? Did they have any idea at all what they are doing to a whole generation – a generation that was going to inherit the consequences of the havoc they were wreaking now?

'Come and eat your supper, Sammy,' she said quietly. 'It's beans on toast – your favourite.'

He gave the parrot's head a last rub and got up to come to the table. But she could see that even beans on toast wasn't going to compensate for the loss of his special friend, and her heart grieved both for Sammy and for the two homeless girls who soon would not even have each other.

Chapter Three

The vicar had not had the heart to tell the girls that they were to be separated as well as being taken away from Bridge End.

'You'll have to break the news soon,' Mrs Mudge told him, busily knitting khaki socks as they sat beside the open range in the kitchen. 'Didn't that Mrs Tupper say they'd be moved in the next few days?'

He nodded. 'It could be almost any day now. I know I have to tell them, but it seemed cruel when they were so upset already.'

'They need to spend time together before they're taken. They've got to be able to say a proper goodbye.'

'Do you really think so? Such young children ...'

'They've lost enough people already that they couldn't say good-bye to. Their mother and baby brother, killed in their own kitchen, their father lost at sea ... They've got to have time with each other, even if they don't properly understand it.' She concentrated for a moment on turning a heel. 'They can't just be torn apart without knowing what's happening. It's cruel.'

'I know,' he said sadly. 'You're right.' He sat gazing despondently into the flames for a few minutes, then said, almost to himself, 'I was so pleased to have children about the place, you know. Young faces around the table, laughter bringing this rambling old house to life. All the fun of building snowmen and having snowball fights, or playing cricket in the summer. Tim helping me in the garden, and Keith and Muriel going off fishing for tiddlers in the stream. Stella helping you in the kitchen – I remember those first rock cakes she made. "Rock" was the word!' He smiled. 'I've always longed for that sort of family life, you know. But when my dear Charlotte died giving birth to our first child, who died with her ... well, it seemed that the good Lord had other plans for me. I never found anyone to take her place and so there was never any prospect of a family. And then the war came and brought me all these delightful children and I thought I'd been given my family at last.' He shook his head. 'I was wrong, so very wrong, to feel that I could benefit from such terrible events. I suppose this is my punishment for such vanity.'

Mrs Mudge stared at him. He had never spoken to her like this before; she had never even known that he had once been married. It was true that there was a portrait of a young woman hanging on his bedroom wall, but she had always supposed that it was his mother, or perhaps a sister. Now she realised that it was probably his wife.

'You mustn't think that,' she said, laying down her knitting. 'You're not being punished at all. God isn't so cruel. Why, he may even have been rewarding you, for all you went through yourself.' She blushed at her own words, for although she saw the vicar daily and attended church every Sunday, they seldom discussed their faith. 'We can't ever know what his plans are,' she went on. 'But whatever they are, I know you've given these children the best home they could have wished for. You've been as good as a father to them.'

He smiled. 'A grandfather, perhaps. And sometimes a big brother! I've enjoyed our games as much as they have. I must be grateful for that.'

'And you still have Keith,' she pointed out, picking up her knitting again.

'Yes,' he said, but he frowned a little as he gazed into the flames. 'I still have Keith. But he's going to miss the others sorely. With Tim back at home in April Grove and the girls gone, I'm afraid he's going to be a rather lonely little boy in this great rambling vicarage.'

Mr Beckett broke the rest of the bad news to the girls the next day. He had lain awake almost all night, worrying about and dreading the task, and as the three children sat round the kitchen table at breakfast, he could bear it no longer. He glanced at Mrs Mudge, who was pouring a second cup of tea all round, and drew in a deep breath.

'I'm afraid I have something else to tell you, my dears,' he began, and Stella paused with her last piece of toast halfway to her mouth. Her eyes were fixed on his face and he would have given anything in the world not to have to go on. But there it was – it must be said, and he was the one who must say it.

'Are we going today?' she asked, before he could speak again. 'Are they taking us away now? Can't we even say goodbye to our friends?'

Mrs Mudge had been right, he thought. The girls needed to be able to wish farewell to all those they knew in Bridge End. To the places they knew. To himself and Mrs Mudge. But most of all to each other.

'No,' he said.' You're not going today. At least, I hope not. I hope the authorities will give me notice of when you are to go. No, it's something else.' He paused again. This was quite definitely the worst thing he had ever had to do, worse even than breaking the news of a death. Death was, even if unexpected at the time, an inevitable process. This tearing apart of little children, for no good reason that he could fathom, was not.

'Have they decided we can stay here?' Muriel asked hopefully. 'I told the lady when she came before that we didn't want to go. So perhaps ...' She turned to Keith, who was sitting beside her at the big kitchen table. 'We could make that den Sammy was talking about, down by the river. We could—'

'No, my dear,' Mr Beckett cut in before she could embark on a long list of what they could do, 'they haven't decided that. I only wish they had. You are still going away. But ...' He looked again at Mrs Mudge, knowing that she could do this far better than he, but knowing too that it was his responsibility and he could not burden her with it. 'But you're not going to the same place,' he said at last, all in a rush. 'You'll be going to different children's homes.' He stopped abruptly, unable to continue.

The three children stared at him. Muriel's eyes grew so large that he was almost afraid they would pop out of their sockets. He saw her feel for her sister's hand. Stella gripped the questing fingers firmly, without taking her eyes from his face.

'Different homes?' she repeated. 'Like different schools?'

'Well, in a way, I suppose. But—'

'So Muriel will come to the one I'm at when she's eleven? But that won't be for two years. Nearly *three*.' Her brows came together in an angry frown. 'So when will we be able to see each other? Just at weekends?'

'I'm afraid you won't see each other at all,' he said miserably. 'And Muriel won't come to your home when she's older. You'll both stay at the same ones until you're old enough to leave. Unless someone adopts you,' he added, remembering that he had been told this was a possibility.

'I don't want to be adopted,' Muriel said instantly, although he doubted if she understood exactly what that meant. 'I want to stay with Stella.'

'And I want to be with Muriel,' Stella stated firmly. 'She's my sister. She needs me to look after her.'

Mr Beckett knew that both these statements were true. Muriel depended on her sister for all sorts of things, from buttoning the shoe straps that were never long enough for her high instep to brushing the tangles from her curly fair hair. He looked helplessly at Mrs Mudge and saw that now that the news was broken, the housekeeper seemed ready to enter the conversation.

'I won't go without her,' Stella continued before anyone else could speak. 'They can't make me. We're *sisters*.'

Mrs Mudge sat down on her chair beside her. 'I know you are, you little dear, and if it was left to me, you wouldn't even be going away at all. But the vicar's right, you see. It isn't up to us any more and we can't do anything about it. If they say that's what's going to happen, that's what will happen.'

Stella turned a furious face towards her. 'But I promised Daddy I would look after her. It was a *promise*.'

Mrs Mudge sighed. 'I don't think that counts for much with the authorities. It's like the vicar told you the other day – if you don't have any parents, nobody else is allowed to say what happens to you. It's the law, you see.'

'Then the law's *stupid*,' Stella said, reminding Mr Beckett again of Mr Bumble's words in *Oliver Twist*. 'Anyone can see we're quite all right here.' She looked at him with sudden hope. 'Couldn't *you* adopt us? Then we could stay, couldn't we?'

He smiled sadly and shook his head. 'I only wish I could. But it wouldn't be allowed, my dear. I'm a man and I'm not married, so you wouldn't have a mother as well, and I'm far too old. They wouldn't even countenance it.'

'But we didn't have a mother before,' Muriel said. 'And daddies are men. And—' She glanced at Mrs Mudge, and the vicar intervened swiftly before she could suggest he married his housekeeper.

'It wouldn't be allowed,' he repeated. 'Believe me, my dear, nothing would make me happier, but it's out of the question. There really is nothing we can do.'

There was a heavy silence. The two girls looked at each other, and enormous tears welled up in Muriel's eyes. She began to cry.

'I don't want to go to a different home!' she wailed. 'I want to go with Stella.' She turned to Keith, who had been sitting silent and bewildered through all this. 'Your mummy and daddy could adopt us. We've stayed at your house lots of times. We could be your sisters and live with you.'

'But we've only got two bedrooms—' he began, and she cut in scornfully.

'We'd still go on living here, silly. We'd still be evacuated.' She looked back at Mr Beckett. 'Tell them that Auntie Jess and Uncle Frank will be our mummy and daddy. Then they wouldn't take us away and make us go to different homes. You can tell them, can't you?'

He gazed at her helplessly. It was all so simple in her mind, yet so impossible. Jess and Frank Budd might have all the sympathy in the world for these two little mites, but they couldn't take them on as part of their family. The war would be over one day, and what then? He shook his head. It was not even to be thought of.

'I don't think the authorities would agree to that either,' he said gently. 'I'm really very sorry, Muriel, my dear. There's nothing we can do.'

Stella pushed back her chair, scraping it noisily on the stone kitchen floor. She glowered at the two adults and then reached out her hand and pulled Muriel to her feet.

'Come on, Mu. Nobody's going to help us, so we'd better go and say goodbye to all our friends. We're never going to see any of them again once that lady with the brown suit takes us away. They'll forget all about us and nobody will care any more.'

'Stella!' Mrs Mudge cried, her eyes filling with tears. 'Don't say that! Of course we'll care. We all will.'

Stella turned at the door. Her face was set in hard lines and she was gripping Muriel's wrist so hard that the smaller girl whimpered. Her eyes were like stones.

'And what good is that going to do?' she asked in a voice as cold as ice. 'Muriel and me are being sent away. You'll never see us again. We're never even going to see *each other* again. It doesn't really matter whether you care or not. It's not going to make any difference to us. We'll probably end up as *slaves*, and none of you will ever even know.'

She marched out, towing Muriel with her, and slammed the door behind her. Mr Beckett and Mrs Mudge looked at each other. Keith started to snivel, and tears began to roll down the housekeeper's cheeks.

'Oh dear,' she said at last, pulling a handkerchief from her apron pocket. 'The poor, poor little mites.'

'I didn't handle that at all well,' the vicar said miserably, but she shook her head.

'I don't know what else you could have done. They had to be told and anyone could see that they would be upset. It's a terrible thing to do to small children, and terrible to expect you to tell them.'

'Better than that woman telling them.' He sighed heavily and then looked at Keith, who was crying openly now. 'I'm so sorry, Keith, but you had to know too. I couldn't let them be taken away without you understanding why.'

'I won't have to go too, will I?' Keith asked in a small voice. 'They won't take me away and make me a slave?'

'Stella and Muriel aren't going to be slaves. They'll be well and kindly looked after.' He hoped this was true. 'And you certainly won't be going. As long as I am here, Keith, and as long as your parents want you to stay, you will be welcome. You must never, ever worry about that.'

Chapter Four

Christmas had come and gone, January's icy grip had loosened and the days had begun to lengthen, and it was on the last day of February, when the grass beneath the apple trees in the orchard was white with snowdrops, that Mrs Tupper came at last to take the two Simmons sisters away.

'They've been here too long already,' she told Mr Beckett when he made one last plea for them to be left with him. 'If places could have been found for them sooner, they would have gone before Christmas. It's been a most unsuitable arrangement.'

'But why can't they stay here?' he begged, knowing that it was useless but compelled to try. 'You can see they're happy and well looked after. They're *loved* here. Why take them away?'

'*Loved*?' she echoed in a scandalised voice. 'Mr Beckett, you're a *vicar*. Must I remind you that these two little girls are no relation to you? Why, you're not even married!'

'I have a very good housekeeper ...'

'A housekeeper!' she repeated scornfully, and shook her head. 'There's no more to be said. Of course they can't remain here. Now, I'll be grateful if you'd fetch them, together with whatever possessions they have. I don't have all day.'

Mr Beckett sighed and went to the door. The girls were in the kitchen with Mrs Mudge. All three looked at him fearfully, and at the sight of his expression the children pressed closer to the housekeeper, who put both arms around them.

'I'm very sorry,' he said heavily. 'It's time to go now, my dears. Mrs Tupper has come to take you to your new homes. You must say goodbye.'

Mrs Mudge shook her head. Her mouth was working and tears spilled from her eyes. She held the girls against her and they pressed their faces to her plump body. Muriel curled her fingers into the broad cotton apron and began to cry.

'I won't go! You can't make me! I *won't!*'

'Muriel, my dear ...' He turned to the older girl. 'Stella, please ...'

Stella was stony-faced. She stepped away and stood a little apart, shaking her head.

'You know we don't want to go. Why are they making us?'

The vicar lifted his hands and held them palms outwards. 'My dear, I don't know. But there's nothing I can do about it. We all have to do as we are told.'

'Because there's a war on,' she said flatly, and he bowed his head.

It was the phrase used whenever someone had to do something they didn't want to – put up the blackout, go without butter or sweets, not have nice new clothes. *Don't you know there's a war on ...?* And now it was being used to tear small children away from people they knew and loved, even away from each other, and there was nothing anyone could do to stop it.

'I'm so very sorry,' he said miserably, and knew, for the first time, the true meaning of the phrase *his heart smote him* that he had used so often in church. It was such a piercing blow that he staggered, and the housekeeper started towards him in alarm.

'Mr Beckett! Are you all right, sir? You've gone as white as a sheet.'

He lifted one hand to ward her off. 'Thank you, I'm quite well ...' He rested his other hand on the back of the nearest chair. 'Stella – Muriel – my dears, you must say goodbye to Mrs Mudge now. Mrs Tupper is waiting for you.' As if on cue, the kitchen door opened and the billeting officer stood there, broad and implacable in her brown suit. He gestured helplessly towards the housekeeper, and Stella, still glowering, gave her one last hug and turned away.

'Come on, Mu,' she said in a bitter little voice. 'We've got to go.'

Muriel gave a cry of despair and clasped her arms all the more tightly around the housekeeper's waist. Mrs Mudge drew in a shuddering sob and bowed her head towards the little girl, and Mrs Tupper, losing all patience, stepped forward and dragged the clutching fingers away. Muriel began to cry loudly and Stella to shout with anger.

'Really!' Mrs Tupper exclaimed above the noise. 'I can see these two have been left here far too long. Utterly and completely spoilt! Well, *that* will soon be dealt with!'

Mr Beckett started towards her. 'Please! They're upset. They're not used to being treated like this. They—'

'I can see *that*,' she said contemptuously. 'I can't imagine what the authorities have been thinking of, to leave them here for so long. Now, if you'll kindly fetch their things, I'll put them into the car and wait for you there. And please be quick. I've other calls to make today as well as this.'

Subdued and miserable, he went to collect the two small suitcases containing their few clothes and the meagre collection of toys, most of them made by Tim and Keith Budd during long winter evenings in the vicarage kitchen. The little boat Keith had made out of balsa wood; the model of a Spitfire that had been Tim's most prized possession. The doll that Muriel had been given after she had lost her own Princess Marcia in the bombing raid over Portsmouth that had robbed them of their home. And the rather wonky carving of a parrot that Muriel's special friend, Sammy Hodges, had made to remind her of Silver, whom they had taken out on a picnic one day and nearly lost.

'There,' he said, going out to the car that stood before the front door. The two girls were standing beside it, quiet now, although Muriel's face was still streaming with tears and Stella was as stony as ever. 'And remember that we all love you and don't want you to go. Remember, whatever happens, that you were loved at Bridge End.'

'And in Portsmouth,' Muriel said through her sobs. 'Mummy and Daddy and Auntie Jess and Uncle Frank and everybody loved us there too.'

'Yes, of course they did.' He knelt in front of her on his spindly knees and took her face between his knobbly hands. 'Remember to say your prayers every night, Muriel, my dear, and I'll say mine. We'll remember each other then.'

He heard Mrs Tupper draw in a long, impatient sigh and turned to kiss Stella as well. But she turned away, her face set, and climbed into the car, where she sat staring grimly ahead, and he sighed in his turn and straightened up.

Mrs Tupper slammed the car door shut and got into the driving seat. She said a curt goodbye and the car moved forward. In less than half a minute there was nothing to be seen but Muriel's face peering through the back window, and then they were gone.

There was a short silence. Then Mrs Mudge turned to her employer, her face crumpling with distress.

'Oh, Mr Beckett! Those poor little mites! Whatever is going to happen to them?'

He rubbed his knees absently and took a long, quivering breath before he could trust himself to answer.

'They'll be well treated, Mrs Mudge. I'm sure they'll be well treated . . .'

He hoped it was true. But how could people be trusted to treat children well when they had dealt with them so harshly in the first place? What hope was there in a world that could do this, while at the same time fighting what he had always believed to be a war against evil?

He turned and walked heavily back into the vicarage, feeling suddenly ten years older. Then he stopped.

'Keith!' he exclaimed. 'Where's Keith?' And shame overwhelmed him as he realised that he had almost forgotten that he still had one child to take care of.

Part Two

Chapter Five

MADDY

'And this is where you'll sleep tonight.' Matron's voice was firm but not unkind as she opened the door to the biggest bedroom Muriel had ever seen, with a long row of narrow iron-framed beds along each wall, every one neatly made and covered with a dark green bedspread. Beside each one was a small cupboard, and there was a row of larger cupboards near the door. At the far end was a line of washbasins with another door leading out of the room. There were no toys, books or discarded shoes or clothes to be seen, and if it had not been for the white cotton nightdresses folded on each pillow, Muriel would not have known the room was occupied at all. It was very cold and smelled of green soap and floor polish.

'This is your bed.' Matron marched her across to one of the beds, which had a small pile of clothing on it, and indicated the cupboard. 'Put your things in there. Nothing is to be left out except your nightdress. There's one here with the rest of your uniform. Change into what you need to wear today and put the rest away.'

'I've got a nightie,' Muriel said. 'Mrs Mudge made it for me out of Mr Beckett's old surplice.'

Matron gave her a perplexed look but evidently decided not to question this. 'Well, you won't be needing it here. Everyone has the same kind of nightdress. You'll hand them in for washing once

27

a week and be given a clean one of the same size, just as with the rest of your clothes.'

'But won't I have my own things?'

'Of course not. Everything is just the same here, and when you grow out of one size you'll be moved to the next. The nurses don't have time to sort any more than that.'

'But what will I do with my blouse that Mrs Mudge made for me, and the mittens she helped Stella knit?'

'Bring them downstairs when you've changed. They'll be given to less fortunate children. Children who have been bombed out of their homes and have nothing at all. Now, stop asking questions and unpack your case. Do you have any toys or games?'

'I've got Ludo and some tiddlywinks that Keith gave me, and my Princess Marcia doll, only she's not really Princess Marcia because I lost the real one when we were b—'

'You can keep the doll,' Matron said, not waiting to hear how Princess Marcia had been lost. 'All the girls are allowed one doll each, and the boys one toy of their own choice, except for guns and catapults, of course. The others will have to go to the games room.'

'But Mr Beckett gave me the Ludo and Keith—'

'Muriel,' Matron said, and there was a steely edge to her voice that cut through Muriel's protests. 'I've told you once already to stop asking questions. That goes for arguing too. You're going to have to learn very quickly how to behave – you've obviously been an extremely spoilt little girl.' She met Muriel's gaze. 'Do you understand? No questions, and no arguing, or you'll find yourself in serious trouble. Now, unpack whatever you need to keep by your bed, and bring the rest down to my office. I'll send someone to show you the way.'

She turned and strode out of the dormitory. Muriel stood for a moment feeling very small in the long, cold space, then sighed and heaved her suitcase on to the bed beside the pile of clothes she was evidently expected to put on. She studied them for a moment. A skirt that looked as if it might have been made out of one of the green bedspreads, a shapeless grey jumper, a pair of dark green knickers with knee-length legs, a vest and a liberty bodice. There was also a coat of the same dull green, a beret and gloves.

Her own belongings were few and would be even fewer when she had removed the clothes she was apparently not allowed to keep. The white nightdress, the blue cardigan knitted with the unpicked wool from one of Mrs Mudge's jumpers, the two weekday blouses and her other skirt. She looked down at the one she was wearing now. It had been Stella's once and had been handed down to become Muriel's best Sunday skirt. She liked it and didn't want to give it up, even to a child who was less fortunate than herself.

I've been bombed out too, she thought. *Twice.* That was how she'd lost Princess Marcia. She lifted out the rag doll that Jess Budd had made for her, and stared at the face, with its shoe-button eyes and smiling mouth stitched on with darning wool. At least she could keep this one.

She wondered where Stella was now, and why they had been made to go to different children's homes. Why couldn't they have stayed together? Why couldn't they ever see each other again, as if they were prisoners who had committed some terrible crime? Why was it supposed to be better this way?

Who was going to look after her now? There were women here, she'd seen them in nurses' uniforms, but they all seemed to be busy and in a hurry, and none of them had paid her more than passing attention as Matron had led her through the corridors and up the stairs of this huge building. She wondered how she would ever find her way about.

I want Stella, she thought, fully aware for the first time of what had happened. I want my sister. *She'd* look after me and tell me what to do. *She* wouldn't let me get lost and be all by myself.

A great wave of loneliness swept over her, and she sat down on her bed, forgetting the unpacking she was supposed to be doing, and began to cry.

'Blimey, haven't you even unpacked yet?'

Muriel jumped and looked round as the door opened. A girl of about her own age stood there, wearing the green skirt and grey jumper of the home's uniform. She had frizzy ginger hair, a face sprinkled heavily with freckles and blue eyes that stared inquisitively at Muriel. She came over to the bed and looked down at the suitcase with its contents still as Mrs Mudge had packed them that morning.

'Haven't got much, have you?' she remarked dispassionately. 'Coo, is that Ludo? We've lost a lot of the bits from the one we got now. What's your doll called?'

'Marcia,' Muriel said, sensing that it would be better to drop the 'Princess'. 'Auntie Jess made her for me after we were bombed out.'

The other girl nodded, as if being bombed out was barely worth mentioning. 'What's your name? Mine's Eileen.'

'Muriel Simmons.'

'You won't be allowed to be called that,' Eileen stated. 'We've already got a Muriel in our class. They don't let two people have the same name.'

'But it's my *name*. I was born with it.'

'No you weren't. You were given it after you were born. Anyway, they'll change it, see if they don't.' She picked up the suitcase and turned it upside down, scattering its contents on the bed. 'You'd better get changed and put your stuff in the cupboard and then shove the rest back in here and we'll take it downstairs. Matron don't like being kept waiting. Here, I'll help you.'

She sorted the clothes Muriel was to wear now into a small pile and began to separate the rest into those that could be kept and those that must be given up. Muriel felt fresh tears come into her eyes as she saw her favourite cardigan and best blouse packed into the suitcase, along with the nightie made from Mr Beckett's old surplice and the Ludo and tiddlywinks with which she, Stella, Keith and Tim had so often played on the rag rug in front of the vicarage fire.

'Hurry up,' Eileen urged her. 'Here, do you want me to do the liberty bodice?' Her quick fingers took over the rubbery buttons, inserting them into the holes that always seemed a fraction too small. 'Now your jumper. Come on.' She picked up the case and led the way through the door, along the corridor and down a long flight of stairs. The walls were painted a dirty green, not unlike the colour of the bedspreads but a shade or two lighter, with dark brown woodwork. The paint was scuffed and dirty where many bodies had rubbed against it as they passed.

'I'll never find my way round here,' Muriel panted. They were passing school classrooms now and she could hear times tables being chanted behind some of the brown doors. 'What happens if you get lost?'

'You won't. I'll look after you for the first few days and then you'll know your way everywhere. We could be friends. Did you have many friends where you came from?'

'Yes, lots.' More tears threatened. 'There was Tim and Keith and Sammy and Rose and ...' She was prevented from listing every child she had known in both Portsmouth and Bridge End by their arrival at a door with MATRON marked on it in large letters. Eileen stopped and knocked, waited for a voice to bid her enter, and turned the knob. Muriel followed her in.

'Please, Matron, here's Muriel.'

Matron was sitting behind a large desk that reminded Muriel a little of Mr Beckett's desk in his study. But instead of walls lined with books or wood panelling, there were shelves of files and piles of papers against the dull green walls.

There was another woman in the room, wearing a dark blue dress and white apron. She was standing by the window, reading one of the files, and she turned as the two girls came in and gave them a quick, friendly smile.

Matron looked up from her work and scrutinised Muriel through her spectacles. 'You've changed your clothes, I see. Have you brought everything down with you, as I told you to do?'

Muriel nodded and Matron looked displeased.

'Say "Yes, Matron" when I speak to you.'

'Yes, Matron,' Muriel whispered, and felt for Eileen's hand.

'Good. Now, Eileen Baxter here will take you under her wing and show you around for the first day or two, and after that I expect you to know the rules of the home and obey them at all times. We do not tolerate troublemakers here' – she fixed Muriel with a stern glare that seemed to say that she knew a troublemaker when she saw one – 'and as long as we all understand that, we will get along very well.' She paused and looked down at the papers on her desk. 'There's just one thing we have to decide before we introduce you to the rest of the children, and that's your name.'

Muriel felt Eileen's elbow nudge her in the side. She spoke quickly.

'Please, Matron, my name's Muriel. I don't want it to be changed.'

Matron raised her eyebrows. 'Indeed. And why not?'

'Because nobody will be able to find me. My sister won't be able to

31

find me. Auntie Jess and Uncle Frank and Tim and Keith, none of them will ever be able to find me.' She stepped forward and put her hands on the polished wood of the desk. 'Please, Matron, *please* don't make me change it so that nobody will ever be able to find me again.'

The woman in the dark blue dress took a step forward. She reached out as if to touch Matron's shoulder, but her hand was shrugged away. Matron's voice was firm as she addressed Muriel.

'You've already been told that it is felt best that you have a complete break from your previous life and everyone in it. We know what has happened to you and your family, but to keep harking back to it will do you no good at all. It's far better for you to move forward and forget it. From now on, to all intents and purposes, we are your family.' She looked down at the papers again. 'Apart from that, we already have a girl called Muriel and she's the same age as you. It would obviously be very confusing for everyone if you were both to continue with the same name, so we've decided that yours should be changed. It will still be Muriel on your birth certificate, of course – that can't be altered – but otherwise you will be known by the name we choose now. And,' she added with a sudden smile, as if awarding a prize, 'the final choice will be yours.'

Muriel stared at her. Most of what Matron had said had passed completely over her head. She understood only that she was to lose her name, almost the only thing she still possessed apart from her rag doll.

'What am I going to be called?' she asked in a small voice.

'I told you, you can choose that yourself. We think it would be better if you keep your initial, M, and we've made a list of names that nobody else of your age in the home has. Now, which do you like best?' She read from the paper on her desk. 'Millicent, Martha, Mabel, Marjorie, Matilda ... Do you like any of those?'

Muriel shook her head miserably. She couldn't imagine ever answering to the name Millicent, nor to Matilda. Nor to any of them. She looked at the woman in the blue dress. Her eyes were brown and friendly.

'What about something a little different?' the woman suggested. 'Melanie, perhaps. Or Miranda. Or Madeleine.'

'That's too long. And most of our children have sensible, short names.'

'It could be shortened to Maddy.' The brown eyes smiled at her. 'I think that rather suits you, Muriel. Would you like that? Would you like to be called Maddy?'

Muriel hesitated. She turned to Eileen, who nodded. 'I think it's a smashing name.'

'All right,' Muriel said, with a feeling of doom. If she had to lose her name, she might as well have something she liked, something a bit different. She looked back at the brown eyes and then at Matron. 'I'll be Maddy.'

Matron shrugged again, as if it hardly mattered what the child was called so long as it didn't cause confusion. She flicked one hand at the two girls and picked up another piece of paper.

'Very well. Now, run along to your day room. Classes will be over by now, Eileen, so you can spend the time until tea showing Mur— Maddy where everything is. I hope you settle in well, Maddy, and if there is anything you need to know, ask either Eileen or Nurse Powell here. And remember what I said – from now on, we are your family. You'll be safe and well looked after here, until you are grown up and old enough to look after yourself.'

She flicked her hand again and Eileen led Muriel from the office. Outside, she closed the door and then grinned.

'I like "Maddy",' she said. 'We're going to be friends. We're going to have lots of fun!'

Chapter Six

Life in the children's home didn't seem much like fun to Maddy at first. It was like living at school all the time, just like Mr Beckett had said, and never being able to go home in the afternoon. The other children were much like those in any other school – some nice, some not so nice, some spiteful, some bullying. You learned to make friends with those you liked and to avoid the others. But at an ordinary school, you could go home to tea and leave them all behind. Here, you could never get away. There was nobody to go home to, nobody to love you and make you feel safe; no mother or father.

In the past few years Maddy had grown accustomed to living without a mother and father, but the vicarage had become home and Mr Beckett and Mrs Mudge had taken the place of her parents. Now, she had no loving, kind adults to go to, no one for whom she was special. She was nobody's little girl now.

It was a cold, lonely feeling and she cried herself to sleep every night for the first week. Eileen, in the next bed, would reach out a hand to touch her and, reminded of Stella, Maddy would cry all the harder. When she finally did fall asleep, her dreams were a muddle of her home in Portsmouth where the first bomb had fallen on them, the dank and miserable little house in October Street that had been allocated to them afterwards, the Anderson shelter, no more than a hole in the ground covered with corrugated iron, where she and Stella had crouched, terrified, as their mother gave birth to their brother Thomas; and finally, the ear-shattering explosion of the bomb that had killed both him and their mother.

Sometimes she would dream of the day when their father, briefly home from sea, had taken them through the New Forest to the shores of Southampton Water, where they had waved to a ship just setting out. 'We won't be able to wave to you when you go, Daddy,' Stella had said, 'so we'll wave to some other children's daddies for them, and perhaps someone else will wave to you.' And they had stood on the beach, earnestly waving, as the ship steamed out of sight.

They had never seen their father again after that day, and Maddy wondered if the fathers on board the ship they had waved to had come back safely, or if they too had been blown up by a German mine or torpedo and died in the cold, slapping water.

She could not speak of any of this to the other children. They had all suffered their own tragedies, many bombed out of their homes, all orphaned in some way. Her story was no worse than theirs and they were not encouraged to dwell on or even talk about them. Here in the children's home, they were learning to live a different life, and the past was best forgotten. It was not even something that could bind them together.

Some had relatives they could go to occasionally, grandparents or distant aunts who could not take them into their own homes. But most seemed to shrug off their past and the families they had once had, and some seemed never to have had a family at all. In the third week of Maddy's stay, Nurse Powell opened the front door one morning and found a cardboard box outside containing a newborn baby wrapped in an old blanket, with nothing to say who she was or where she had come from. She was taken to the nursery, bathed and fed, and they named her Pearl.

Nurse Powell was Maddy's favourite nurse. From the moment she had heard those soft Welsh tones in Matron's office, she had known that this was someone who could make her feel safe. She tried to be near her whenever they were in the same room and to follow her when she left, but she soon found that a lot of the other children felt the same, and one day Nurse Powell took her aside and explained gently that she could not have favourites amongst the children and Maddy must not always try to be first with her. After that, Maddy knew that she was truly alone and that however many friends she made, she would never again have anybody who would be like a mother to her.

35

She stopped crying herself to sleep. Her tears seemed to collect together and form a hard, dry stone somewhere around her middle, and she carried them within her day and night, never speaking of them. She gradually grew accustomed to the routine of the home and stopped asking about her sister. She even began to smile again. She learned to live like two separate people: the secret Muriel who still yearned silently for her mother, her father, her baby brother and Stella, and the Maddy who was Eileen's friend and fell into the pond fishing for tadpoles, scraped her knees climbing the apple tree and scrambled with the other girls for the best blouse when the clean clothes were handed out.

Matron and the other nurses said she was getting over it, but Maddy knew differently, and when she looked at the other children she wondered if they too carried hard stones of misery deep inside that nobody else could see and nobody would ever be able to soften.

Chapter Seven

Hampshire, March 1943

STELLA

'I know it's hard to understand,' said the matron at Stella's children's home, not far from Winchester, 'but it really is thought to be better this way. Children who have been kept together cling together more. They don't make friends so easily with the other children and it's harder for them to settle down. Your sister will be quite happy where she is, believe me.'

Stella did *not* believe her. Matron seemed kind and even sympathetic, but she didn't know Muriel and she didn't understand how the losses they had suffered made it all the more necessary for Stella to be there to look after her.

'But she's nearly three years younger than me. She's only just nine. She needs me.'

'I know.' Matron looked at her sadly. To tell the truth, she was not at all sure that this splitting up of young children was the right thing to do. She would never let them see her doubts, of course, and she would do her best to help them to settle down and develop their own lives, but she could never rid herself of the feeling that it was wrong to part them. They were family – often, as in this case, the only family left to each other – and families were, in Matron's opinion, the most important thing on earth. 'It's the way it is, I'm afraid,' she said gently. 'There's nothing we can do about it. I'm sure she'll be fine. She'll find friends who will be like sisters to her. And perhaps when you're older, you'll be able to find her again.'

'I don't even know where she is,' Stella said miserably. 'And she doesn't know where I am. How can we ever find each other? It'll be years before we're grown up. Anything could happen in that time. Anything.'

Matron sighed. It was all too true. Cities that nobody had ever expected to be attacked, like Plymouth and Coventry, had been almost flattened, with no warning. Children's homes had been bombed before they could be evacuated. Children like Stella and her sister had been orphaned, and what had happened before could happen again. During this war, no one was safe.

'I'm very sorry, my dear. But there really is nothing we can do about it. All I can say is that she will be well looked after, and as safe as anyone can be. Some homes are still being moved to the countryside, and hers may be one of them. But my job now is to look after you, and yours is to do the best you can for yourself.' She looked at the mutinous face. 'When there's nothing to be done, Stella, the only thing we can do is find something else that we *can* do. We have to make the best of it.'

'Our mother used to say that,' Stella said. 'When our house was bombed and we had to go to October Street and live in a horrible house that smelled of cats and had no electricity, she said we'd just have to make the best of it.'

'And did you?'

'Yes. And Auntie Jess helped. She came over and scrubbed and cleaned, and it looked a lot better. It wasn't like our real home, but Mum said it would do until the war was over. But then that was bombed as well . . .' Her voice quivered a little and she fell silent.

'So now you must do the same again. Remember what your mother said, and make the best of what's happened.' Matron lifted Stella's chin with one finger and looked into her eyes. 'You're an intelligent child, Stella. Your job now is to do the best you can with your own life. There are times when we all have to move forward into the future rather than looking back at the past. You have had a very sad and difficult time, but you're still young and you can overcome all that. You can do something worthwhile. Wouldn't that be better than spending your days being miserable and wishing for what might have been?'

'I suppose so,' Stella said reluctantly. 'But I can't help feeling miserable. I'm not doing it on purpose.' She heaved a huge sigh. 'I don't know how to stop.'

'Work can help,' Matron said. 'Work hard in your schooling. It will occupy your mind and help you to forget—'

'I won't forget Muriel! She's my sister – I'll *never* forget her.'

'No, of course you won't. But it will help you to forget how sad you are about her now. And it will help you in the future. When you leave here, Stella, you'll need to find work, and if you do your lessons and pass your examinations, you could get a good job – as a civil servant, perhaps, or a nurse or a teacher. And then you will be able to look for your sister again.'

'A civil servant?' Stella said. 'What's that? A maid in a big house?'

'No, it's quite different. Civil servants work in offices. They help the government to run the country.'

Stella gazed at her. 'I could do that? Be a civil servant, or a teacher?'

'I think you could, if you work hard now. You'll need to pass the examination to go to the grammar school. Do you think you could do that?'

'I don't know,' Stella said slowly. 'I suppose I could try.'

'Then try, my dear. It will help you now and in years to come. And if you are ever worried about anything or need advice, you can come to me. I am here all the time. Now, go and join the other children before lessons begin.'

Stella went slowly from the room. She knew now that she was not going to find Muriel until they were both grown up. She might never find her. But that would not stop her from going on living, and since she had to live, she might as well be useful. The idea of working in an office or a school had never entered her head, but now that it had been put there, she found herself feeling a small tremor of excitement.

Perhaps Matron was right. If she became a teacher or a civil servant, she would have a better chance of finding her lost sister.

Part Three

Chapter Eight

Burracombe, July 1943

'I tell you what it is, Dottie,' Jacob Prout said, resting on his long-handled shovel. 'It's war – and, like they say, all's fair in love and war. The Germans started it, and 'tis no use them carrying on now about us bombing places like Dresden and Cologne and such. Look what they done to us here. Look at London and Coventry. Look at Plymouth. The whole city centre gone in a night. Hardly one brick left standing on another. They got *nothing* to complain about.'

'I know.' Dottie Friend was on her way back from the general store and had stopped to show him the newspaper. 'But it's the people who live there that I worry about. The old people and the little children who haven't hurt anyone. It says here there was a firestorm – what's that, Jacob?'

'It's when there's so many fires that they create their own wind – you know how a fire at home can make the room draughty – and that sets off a whole lot of others and they all just come together in a mass and blow theirselves along.' He frowned and stuffed his pipe with tobacco. 'As for the old people, don't forget that a lot of them were in the Great War, trying to kill us then, same as the younger ones are doing now. But the children – no, I got to say that don't seem right. Even if they *are* going to grow up to be Germans.'

'It's to be hoped things will be better by then,' she said, folding the paper. 'Maybe the world will have seen a bit of sense. But it don't seem to be getting any better to me. I know we're not being bombed here in England like we were, but the rest of it's going on

43

just the same everywhere else. Africa ... Japan ... India ... Where's the sense in it all, Jacob? How did we come to this?'

'I dunno, maid.' He drew in a deep breath of smoke. 'I dunno at all. And I can't see no way out of it, neither. Hitler don't seem ready to give in, and I'm bothered if I can see that Mr Churchill will. He'll keep on to the bitter end, like a bulldog in a fight. What was it he said? "Blood, toil, sweat and tears"? Well, there's been plenty of them, but I can't see as we're any nearer winning.'

They stood in silence for a moment or two. Jacob was busy sweeping the roads and lanes around the village, as he always did. He had fought in the First World War – the Great War as it had been called, as if there could be anything great about any war – and now worked as a general handyman, as well as serving in the local Home Guard. Dottie, who had several jobs, including working behind the bar at the Bell Inn and cooking at Burracombe Barton, as well as making scones and cakes for George Sweet's baker's shop when he could get the rations, had been shopping and needed to hurry home, but would never have dreamed of passing Jacob without a word or two. They had grown up together here in Burracombe and knew each other almost as well as brother and sister.

'Oh, here's a bit of better news,' she said, putting the newspaper into her basket. 'Miss Hilary's coming home for a bit of leave, and Miss Forsyth – that actress I used to work for – is coming to stay at the Barton as well. You know she's Mrs Napier's friend; they used to be at school together.'

'So I've heard. Well, Mrs Napier'll enjoy that, having her friend and her daughter home at the same time. It'll be more work for you too, I dare say.'

'Yes, I'll have to put my thinking cap on to make some special meals. It's a pity the squire can't be here too. Stephen will be home from school in a week or so, and that would mean the whole family being together for a while. Well – almost the whole family.' Her smile faded. 'Poor souls, I don't know if they'll ever get over losing their elder boy.'

Jacob nodded solemnly 'Another day or two and Mr Baden would have been at Dunkirk and rescued, like as not. Cruel, that's what that was, and him the apple of his parents' eyes. If it hadn't been for this dratted war, he'd have been working with his father today, learning to manage the estate, and now what'll happen to it? Young Stephen don't seem to have the same interest at all.'

'Give him a chance,' Dottie said. 'He's only thirteen. He'll probably come to it when he's older.'

'It's to be hoped so.' Jacob bent and began to scrape at some mud lying along the edge of the ditch. 'Because Burracombe's a big estate and takes a deal of managing, and if the squire's son don't take it on in years to come, we could all be in trouble. Mark my words.'

Dottie walked on to her cottage. The sun was hot and she could smell the scent of the roses that scrambled along the cottage walls and fences bordering the lane. Apart from the fact that most of the other flowers, even in the front gardens, had been replaced by vegetables and soft fruits, you would scarcely have known there was a war on. Yet it was only two years since Plymouth had been bombed and, as Jacob said, almost flattened. You could see the glow of the flames right out here in Burracombe, on the edge of Dartmoor. The sky had been lit an angry, scorching red and the roar of German aircraft and the explosion of the bombs had gone on almost all night. There must have been firestorms there too, she thought, remembering that she had been told that the glass in some of the windows had turned to liquid and that gold from the jewellers' shops had melted and run down the gutters like water from drainpipes.

And so many people had been killed or injured. Just as in London, Coventry, Portsmouth and the other cities and towns that had suffered a similar fate; just as in Germany and France. So many children and old people, so many women trying to keep their homes together, so many soldiers and sailors and airmen with nothing in their minds but to kill.

Why? What was it all for?

It was because of Poland, she thought as she opened her back door. All we wanted to do was save a little country from being invaded, and it led to all this. There were so many countries involved now, each with their own particular quarrel, each with a different hatred. How could anyone bring an end to this madness that had spread over all the world?

She dumped her shopping basket on the kitchen table and gazed at the vase of roses she had picked and brought in yesterday afternoon, wondering yet again when the men who had brought about these terrible wars would realise that all most people wanted to do was to live peacefully, with their families and their homes and their gardens.

Chapter Nine

Hilary Napier and Fenella Forsyth came down from London to Tavistock together on the train. They had known each other since Hilary was a baby, although Fenella's career had kept her in London most of the time. Now she was travelling abroad to entertain the troops and had just come home from a tour in India.

'And you've been in Egypt, I hear?' she said to Hilary as they settled themselves into a ladies' compartment. 'I think I'll be going there next, after I've had a little time off for a rest. I suppose it's every bit as hot as India.'

'Probably,' Hilary said with a smile. 'It's nice to be here in our cooler summers. But I'll be going back again after my leave.'

'And how will your mother like that?'

'Not at all, probably, but she knows I have to do war work of some sort, and with Father being an army colonel she understands what service life means. It's just that she never expected a daughter of hers to go into the army!'

Fenella laughed. 'Well, it's not something that's ever happened before, is it! Not until the last war, anyway, and that was only for the duration. Still, it changed a lot of things for women.' She gave Hilary a thoughtful look. 'I suppose you would have been preparing for your first Season – being presented at court and all that sort of thing.'

'In another year or so,' Hilary agreed. 'Until then, once I left school I would have just stayed at home, helping to arrange flowers and entertain and all that sort of thing. At least the war saved me from that. I was dreading it – all those parties and balls, and dress fittings and so on. And the worst thing of all would have been the feeling of being paraded in front of the young men as a possible wife – like a heifer at a cattle market. You know what it was like. If you didn't find a suitable husband, you were considered a failure and your mother was humiliated before all her friends. Never mind that you might be miserable for the rest of your life.'

Fenella shuddered. 'It sounds appalling. Thank goodness it never happened to me. My father said he couldn't afford it, and anyway I was determined to go on the stage. Where it is all too easy to find an *un*suitable husband!' She gave Hilary a wicked sideways glance. 'Not that it's necessary to marry at all – unless you want children, anyway.' She fell silent for a few moments, gazing out of the window at the countryside they were passing through. Then she turned with a smile and said, 'But you're engaged, aren't you? So you didn't need a Season after all.'

'Oh yes.' Hilary felt at her uniform shirt collar and drew out a thin gold chain with a ring dangling from it. 'We're not allowed to wear jewellery in ATS uniform, so I have to hide it.'

Fenella examined the ring. 'A half-hoop, with five lovely diamonds. It's very pretty. You must be longing to wear it on your finger.'

'I will, once we get home and I can change into civvies. Mother would like us to get married as soon as possible, so that I can leave the ATS, but we shan't until the war's over. Henry's abroad at present, and even if he did get leave we probably wouldn't have enough notice to arrange a wedding. Not the sort of wedding Mother would want me to have, anyway. And Father probably wouldn't be at home to give me away, so it's all rather impossible.'

Fenella eyed her. 'You don't sound all that disappointed.'

'I'm not, really.' Hilary tucked the ring back under her collar. 'To tell the truth, I'm rather enjoying life. Being abroad, driving brigadiers and colonels about in a nice car, mixing with all kinds of other people. We have a lot of fun, when we can find the time. We get famous people like you come to entertain us, for a start!'

Fenella laughed. 'So you're enjoying the independence of a single young woman away from home. Well, my advice is that you make the most of it. Once you're married, it will all be very different.'

'I know. "Love, honour and obey" and all that.' Hilary made a face. 'I don't mind so much about the "love and honour" bit – you wouldn't marry anyone you didn't feel that for – but I'm not so sure about *obeying*. I mean, I obey the army rules and so on, and if I'm told to do something by my superior officer, I do it – but obey *Henry* for the rest of my life? I'm not so sure about that.'

Fenella gave her another thoughtful look and seemed about to reply, but hesitated and then said, 'Marriage does have its compensations, though. You'll probably have a family of your own and have too much to do to worry about being obedient.'

'Oh, yes, I'll be expected to produce a quiverful of heirs and spares. Henry's an elder son, you see, and their estate's even bigger than Burracombe. At least three villages and goodness knows how many farms. He'll be out all the time managing it all. We'll probably barely see each other.'

They were both silent for a few minutes. The train drew in at Exeter and stood for a while as the engine was given more water ('Like a dog,' Hilary remarked), then set off again towards Okehampton and then Tavistock. The heather-clad hills and rocky tors of Dartmoor came into view and both women gazed out at the familiar scene.

'Even war hasn't made much difference to this,' Fenella said thankfully. 'I love it when we start to see the moors. It must be even better for you, to come home and know you'll be meeting so many people you've known all your life.'

'Not that all of them are there now,' Hilary said, a little sadly. 'Most of the young men are away fighting and some have been killed, and quite a few of the women are in the services too. Oh, but this is a funny thing – who do you think I met when I was in Egypt? Val Tozer – you know, from Tozers' farm. Alice and Ted's elder daughter. We couldn't believe it when we ran into each other in the camp. We see quite a lot of each other now. She's a VAD.'

'I think I remember her,' Fenella said, frowning. 'I know her parents, of course. Theirs is the farm whose boundaries meet yours, isn't it? But they're not tenants.'

'No, they bought their farm years ago. I can't remember how it came about – Father doesn't like selling off his properties. It may not even have been him who did it. It might have been Grandfather. Anyway, they've always been good neighbours, and Ted's a good farmer, so it works very well.'

'They've got sons, haven't they?'

'Yes, Brian and Tom. Both away now, of course. They've got two or three Land Girls to do the farm work.'

Fenella nodded. 'The person I'm most looking forward to seeing – apart from your mother, of course – is Dottie Friend. I miss her so much – she was the best dresser I've ever had. She could sew anything. But she had to leave me before the war to look after her father, and she never came back.'

'Old Mr Friend died four or five years ago, but Dottie had settled back into village life by then. I think you'd have another war on if you tried to take her away again!'

'She works for your mother now, doesn't she?'

'Some of the time. She cooks when there are visitors, and she also works in the village inn, and I think she does a bit for the local baker as well. She's the busiest person you could imagine, yet she always has time for a chat, and she's so good-hearted.'

'It always surprised me that she never married,' Fenella said. 'She would have made a lovely wife. Not for anyone in London, but down here in Devon ... A lovely mother, too. How was it she was never snapped up as a young woman?'

'I don't know. She's always been just Dottie to me. But it is odd, now I come to think about it. She must have been really pretty as a girl, with all those blonde curls and lovely brown eyes.'

'The young men of Burracombe must have had poor eyesight back in those days!' Fenella said with a laugh. 'Oh, look at the moors. They're so beautiful. I'm looking forward to some long walks with your mother and the dogs while I'm here.'

'And I,' Hilary said, stretching out her arms, 'am looking forward to some long, lazy lie-ins and plenty of Dottie's home cooking!'

Chapter Ten

The Tozers heard all about the visitors from Dottie, who called in at the farm on her way up to the Barton to prepare a special dinner for their first evening.

'It's two years since I saw Miss Fenella,' she said, accepting a cup of tea and a scone from Minnie Tozer, Ted's mother. 'Been all over the place, she has, entertaining the troops. It's wonderful work. They go to real dangerous places, you know.'

'She's a lovely lady,' Alice Tozer commented as she rolled pastry for a pie. 'I saw her once on stage in Plymouth, before the war. That theatre down Union Street, it was. She's got a beautiful singing voice.'

'She's a wonderful actress too,' Dottie added, stirring a saccharin tablet into her tea. 'She was in a lot of those big musicals they did in London. A real star. I'm looking forward to seeing her again.'

'And Miss Hilary's coming home too, for a bit of leave,' Alice said. 'Mrs Napier will like that. It's a shame the colonel's not here as well.' She paused in her rolling out, frowning a little at the pastry. 'I'm hoping she'll call round to give us a bit of news about our Val. I'm not happy about her all that way away in Egypt. There's something in her letters home lately – something I can't quite put my finger on ...'

'They see a bit of each other out there, do they?' Dottie enquired, and Alice nodded.

'Got quite pally, it seems. It's funny when you think they grew up practically next door to each other, but then us didn't mix all that much with the Napiers before the war started. 'Tis all different now. Lords and ladies rubbing shoulders with farm workers, and all those Americans coming over. Not to mention the Poles and Czechoslovakians at Harrowbeer airfield, by Yelverton. They say some of them are princes!'

'Nearly every chap in Poland is a prince,' Ted Tozer said, coming into the kitchen and stopping at the door to take off his boots. 'And if you want an introduction to one, Ivy Sweet's the woman to ask, so I've heard.'

'Ted!' Minnie scolded him. 'That's nothing but gossip, and you didn't ought to demean yourself by repeating it.'

'I never said nothing that isn't true,' he defended himself. 'All I meant was, with her working in the pub over in Horrabridge, she's bound to know a few of them. I don't know what else you could have thought I meant, Mother. Are those scones for now?'

Minnie gave him a stern look. 'You can have one with your cup of tea, after you've washed your hands. They're covered in muck. Where's young Joanna?'

'Just finishing sweeping down the milking parlour. She'll be here in a minute or two.' He turned to their visitor. 'I haven't said hello to you yet, Dottie. How are you keeping?'

'Well enough, Ted, thanks for asking. I'm just on my way to the Barton with a few bits and pieces for their dinner tonight.'

'Ah, I heard Miss Hilary was getting back for some leave. Her mother'll be pleased about that. She never liked the girl going off to join the ATS as it was. And that actress lady, she's going to be there too, I hear.'

'For a man who spends most of his time on the farm with a lot of cattle and sheep,' Minnie remarked to no one in particular, 'our Ted do seem to pick up a lot of information. What else have you heard that us might be interested in, Ted?'

'Nothing, and if I had, I wouldn't be repeating it,' he retorted with a grin. 'Gossip, that's what it would be, and you wouldn't want me demeaning myself.' He went over to the sink and pumped up some water to wash his hands.

'Got you there, Mother!' Alice chuckled. She finished rolling the pastry and spread it over the pie dish, cutting round the rim and knocking it back with her knife to make a crusty edge. 'I'll just put this into the larder to rest for half an hour, then I'll butter some more of those scones – not that you can call it buttering when we has to spread it so thin you can see through it. Will you have another, Dottie?'

'Thank you, Alice, but I'd better be getting on my way. I'll tell Miss Hilary you'd like to see her, if you want me to. She'd probably come over anyway, seeing as she and your Val are thick now, but you know what Mrs Napier's like. She'll have half the county coming over to say hello to the girl and Miss Hilary'll have a job to get a minute to herself.'

'That's kind, Dottie. And come in again yourself anyway and tell us how they all are. You know you're always welcome here.'

Dottie smiled and picked up her basket. As she went out towards the back door, it opened and a tall young woman came in wearing the check shirt and olive-green breeches of the Land Army. She stood back for Dottie to pass and then came through to take Ted's place at the sink.

'There's some nice warm scones here, Joanna, fresh from the oven,' Minnie said, pouring her a cup of tea. 'Have you seen our Jackie anywhere? She went over to play with the Crocker children, but I'd have thought she'd be back by now.'

'I'll walk over there to meet her if you like,' Joanna offered. She sat down at the big kitchen table and picked up her cup. 'Oh, that's good. I've had a real tussle with one or two of the cows; they seemed determined to hang on to their milk. I tried everything before they finally let me have it.'

'Well, if you couldn't get them to let it down, no one could,' Ted remarked, taking a scone. 'You're a marvel with the cows, and when I think what you were like when you first came here, straight from Basingstoke ... Is there any jam for this, Alice?'

'No, there's not. I've put butter on them now, and you know full well the rule is butter on its own, or jam with margarine. I know we're better off out in the country for that sort of thing than folk in the towns, but that don't mean we should indulge ourselves.'

Minnie poured Ted a second cup of tea and then turned to her daughter-in-law. 'What did you mean about Val, Alice? You said there was something in her letters you didn't like. You don't think she's in any sort of trouble, do you?'

'No, of course not!' Alice said quickly, and then hesitated. 'Well, not *trouble* exactly. And it's nothing she's said. It's just a sort of

53

feeling I've got. As if she's holding something back.'

The others gazed at her. Then Joanna said, 'I expect she's missing her fiancé – Eddie, isn't it? It must be getting on for two years since she saw him.'

'You don't think she's fallen for someone else?' Ted said, helping himself to another scone, and Alice turned on him angrily.

'No, I don't! What a thing to suggest, Ted Tozer. You ought to be ashamed of yourself for even thinking it. Our Val's a decent young woman, been brought up respectable and knows right from wrong as well as anyone sitting round this table. She's promised herself to Eddie and she's not the sort to back out of a promise.'

'All the same,' Minnie said, 'Joanna's right, it's a long while since she saw him and a lot can change in that time. And in wartime, and away from her family – out there in the desert ...' Her voice faded as she caught Alice's eye. 'I'm only *saying*, maid. People have had second thoughts before now, without having a war to make them change their minds.'

'Well, our Val hasn't changed hers,' Alice stated firmly. 'If she had, she'd say so straight out. Anyway, it's nothing she's said at all, just a feeling I got, and I wish I'd never mentioned it. Ted, do you want a bit of this jam on that last scone or not, because if you don't, I'll put it back in the cupboard.'

Ted looked at her in surprise and opened his mouth to speak, then thought better of it. Meekly he accepted the pot of home-made strawberry jam and spread some thinly on his scone. Joanna kept her eyes on her plate and Minnie sighed.

'It's no good getting aeriated, Alice. We all worry about our children and it's even worse these days. You've got three abroad; it's not surprising you get upset thinking about them. And even though I know my Joe's a grown man and safe enough over in America, it don't stop me worrying about him. Nothing ever will.'

Alice took a moment or two before she replied, and then she nodded. 'I know, Mother. It's just all so different from how I thought it would be. I remember how we used to sit round this very table when they were all young, and I'd look at their rosy faces and feel so blessed to have been given such a fine family. And now they're all over the world – Brian in the army, Tom goodness knows where, and Val in Egypt seeing things no young girl should ever see, and nothing is how I expected it to be. I know we mustn't grumble and we've got to keep smiling through and all the rest of it, but it seems so hard at times. And there's Miss Hilary, getting leave and coming home for two or three weeks, too. Why couldn't our Val have got leave? It just don't seem fair.'

'You must think it isn't fair that I'm here and she isn't,' Joanna said quietly. 'Why couldn't she have been your Land Girl? She'd have been far more use to you in the early days, when I hardly knew one end of a cow from the other.'

Alice shook her head and reached out a hand towards her. 'No, my dear, us'd never think that. It was a good day for Tozers' Farm when you walked through the door, with your smile and your willingness to do whatever us asked you. And that's the only thing that'll made us sad when the war's over at last – that you'll have to leave us. We shan't want to say goodbye to you, Joanna, and that's a fact.'

Chapter Eleven

I sobel Napier was at the door of the Barton to meet them when Hilary and Fenella arrived. Fenella had insisted on paying for a taxi from Tavistock railway station, saying her days of waiting for country buses to trundle their way round the lanes were long past, and Hilary had been grateful not to have to carry their luggage up from the end of the drive. She helped the taxi driver get the cases from the boot while Fenella, having paid him, surged up the steps to greet her old friend.

'Isobel! What a treat to see you, and looking so well, too. It must be true what they say about country air and all that cream and butter and lovely rich milk. Doesn't she look wonderful, Hilary?'

Hilary came up the steps more slowly, a suitcase in each hand, and dumped them at the top before turning to kiss her mother. 'Hello, Mummy. How are you?'

'Very well, thank you, darling.' Isobel held her daughter a little away from her for inspection. 'And how are you? You're very brown.'

'There's a lot of sun in Egypt. I'll just get my kitbag.' Hilary ducked away and ran down the steps to retrieve her own luggage. When she returned, it was to find her brother Stephen emerging through the big front door. 'Oh, hello, Steve. Heavens, you've grown!'

'I don't know why everyone seems so surprised,' he observed, lifting one of Fenella's cases in each hand. 'It would be more surprising if I *hadn't* grown. Have you seen the Sphinx? Have you been up the Pyramids?'

'Yes, and no,' she laughed, following him into the house. 'But

I've done a lot of driving around the desert and I hope to get a chance to go up them one day. One of them, anyway. They really are a magnificent sight.'

'Stephen, take Aunt Fenella's cases up to her room,' Isobel said. 'You might as well take your bag up as well, Hilary. We'll be in the drawing room having tea. Fenella, darling, you must need to wash your hands. You know the way, don't you?'

'I ought to, after all the times I've been here.' The actress swished away along the corridor and Stephen led Hilary up the wide stairs.

'We've been doing Egypt at school,' he informed her. 'I've got some stuff to do as my holiday task, so you can help me with it.'

'Thanks, I'll look forward to that,' she said wryly. 'But we haven't had a lot of time to look into the local history, you know.'

'You've *been* there. That's all that matters. Have you been bombed much? Mother won't tell me a thing. How long do you think the war will go on? I'm hoping it will be years yet, so that I can be a pilot. I can get a flying licence when I'm seventeen, so it's not too long.'

'Too long for a lot of people.' Hilary opened the door to her bedroom and carried her kitbag inside. 'Oh, it *is* good to be home!'

'I feel like that when I get home from school. Did you know I'll be going to Kelly College after the holidays? Mother says I've still got to board, even though it's only a few miles away. I don't see the point of that, do you, Hil? I mean, boarding school's for boys who live too far away to go home every evening. She says it's because we can't get petrol for the car to take me every day, but that's silly. I could easily go on my bike.'

'Perhaps she thinks you'll miss a lot if you don't board.' Hilary was at the window, gazing out over the gardens. Most of the flower beds had been dug up now and were filled with vegetables, and the lawn was a vast potato patch. 'School isn't just about lessons.'

'We'll have games too, every afternoon. I needn't come home until after them.'

'And what about prep? At my school, we used to do our prep after tea, until supper time. You'd have to stay for that.'

'Ye-es. But—'

'And by the time you came home it would be supper time here and you'd have to go to bed soon after. And in the winter, you'd be

57

cycling in the blackout. I don't think anyone would want you doing that – neither Mother and Father nor the school. And you'd be left out of so much, Steve. You know what it's like when there are boarders and day boys. You just wouldn't belong properly.'

He sighed. 'Oh, well. It was worth trying. I'd better take these cases to Auntie Fenella's room. Why do I have to call her Auntie, Hil, when she's not really any relation?'

'It's because she's Mummy's friend and she didn't want us calling her Miss Forsyth. A lot of people call their parents' friends Auntie and Uncle.'

'*You* don't.'

'No, because I'm grown up. I suppose I still could, but it seems different now. Which room is she in?'

'The same one as she always used to have – the pink room. Ma said she'd feel at home there.' He opened a door further along the passage and they went in. Hilary glanced round approvingly.

'It looks lovely. Isn't that a new bedspread? Wherever did Mummy get the coupons for the material? And matching cushions, too. I love the colour. It's not really raspberry – it's almost as dark as a loganberry.' She took another look, frowning a little. 'Actually the pattern looks a bit familiar.'

'Dottie Friend made them from the old library curtains. Ma said we didn't need curtains there as well as the blackout.' He put down the cases. 'Should we unpack for her?'

'Good heavens, no! She'll do that for herself.'

Stephen looked disapproving. 'We always used to have a maid to unpack for visitors, but they've all gone to do war work now.'

'I know. People have to do a lot more for themselves than they used to, and a good thing too. Anyway, we'd better go down now and have tea. Has Dottie made any of her cakes?'

He brightened. 'Yes, a fruit cake – she's been saving the dried fruit for weeks – and a Victoria sponge. And some scones, with strawberry jam she made only last week and some cream from the Tozers' farm.'

'Strawberry jam and cream! It sounds scrumptious.' Hilary followed him out and along the passage. 'I must go and see the Tozers and thank them. They'll be wanting to hear about Val, as well.' A slight shadow crossed her face. She wasn't quite sure how much she should tell the Tozers about their elder daughter. 'At least I can tell them she's well,' she murmured as she followed her brother down the stairs. 'That's really all they want to hear.'

Chapter Twelve

Isobel and Fenella were in the big drawing room with the French windows wide open to the terrace. If it hadn't been for the cool breeze, Isobel remarked as she sat Fenella down on the sofa, they could have had tea outside. 'Although it's not quite the same, looking out at potatoes and cabbages, as it used to be when we had sweeping lawns and rose beds. But nothing is the same these days.' She sighed and took the armchair by the fireplace, glancing up at the portrait on the wall above the mantelpiece as she did so.

Fenella followed her glance. 'You must miss him so dreadfully.'

'I always shall. A mother never gets over the loss of a child, you know, and when it's her firstborn ... the elder son ... We had such hopes for him, Fenella. He was his father's pride and joy – mine too, of course, but perhaps in a slightly different way. For Gilbert, to have his elder son follow him into the army and rise so quickly as an officer was all he had ever dreamed of. And the estate, too – it was always clear that he'd take over the reins when the time came and be as good a squire as the estate and village could ever wish for.' She paused, her voice saddening. 'And all gone – gone in a matter of days. The retreat to Dunkirk ... it was the most appalling time of our lives. We had no idea what was happening. Even Gilbert couldn't find out to begin with. And then, when Mr Churchill asked for all the small boats that had only been registered a fortnight or so earlier to cross the Channel and help bring the men back – well, it was unbelievable. Defeat on such a scale, so early in the war! They never expected to rescue so many, you know, but even so there were still thousands lost. And our dear Baden was one of them.'

Fenella leaned over and took her friend's hand. 'My dear ...'

'I try not to think about it too much,' Isobel said. 'There are many other mothers in just the same situation, with sons they thought would outlive them, taken away too soon. And as an army wife, of course I know that there is always a risk. But you *hope*, Fenella. You always hope. And pray, too.' She was silent for a moment or two, then said, very quietly, 'It's just over three years ago now, yet it seems like yesterday.' And then, more briskly as she leaned towards the little table, 'But this is no way to welcome my dearest friend. Let me pour you a cup of tea. Do you use saccharin? And please help yourself to one of Dottie's scones – she made them this morning, and the cream comes from Tozers' farm. They're not allowed to make very much now, so it was kind of them to let us have it.'

Fenella took a scone and spread it with jam and cream. Before the war, the scones would have been spread in the kitchen, and any uneaten ones would have been thrown away. Nobody wasted food now. She accepted the tea and shook her head to the saccharin tablets.

'Horrid things. I decided simply to give up sugar, and do you know, I really think the tea tastes better like that, once you get used to it.' She sipped. 'And how is Stephen getting along? He's so tall now! I can't believe he's barely thirteen. Will he go into the army too, do you think?'

'Oh, very likely, although his head's full of aeroplanes and becoming a pilot at present. You know what young boys are like. But I'm sure he'll want to follow in his brother's footsteps. Gilbert will certainly expect him to. But there are five years at least before we need worry about that, and the war will be over by that time.'

The door opened and Stephen and Hilary came in. Stephen made immediately for the tea things. 'Cream! And strawberry jam with real strawberries in! We never get that kind of thing at school.'

'I should hope not,' his mother said with some asperity. 'You're not there to be indulged, and the food is perfectly good for growing boys. And remember your manners, please. Sit down properly before you take anything, and don't pile your plate. And offer your Aunt Fenella and your sister something first.'

Stephen grinned and picked up a plate of cakes, holding it out as Fenella finished her scone and Hilary sat down beside her. They each took a slice of Victoria sponge.

'So you'll be going to Kelly College after the summer holidays?' Fenella said to Stephen. 'Are you looking forward to it?'

Stephen made a face, then caught his mother's eye. 'I don't suppose it's any worse than anywhere else, and at least it's near home.'

'Stephen would like to be a day boy,' Isobel observed. 'But his father won't hear of it. He says you only do well if you board, and of course Baden did very well. He was head boy in his last year.'

'I don't suppose I'll ever be head boy,' Stephen said carelessly. 'Anyway, I don't want to be.'

'Don't be silly, Stephen. You want to make your father proud of you, don't you?' Isobel's eyes went briefly to the portrait of her elder son, smart and imposing in his army uniform.

Stephen said nothing, and Hilary quickly filled the slight pause with a question about the village.

'Oh, everything's much as usual,' her mother replied. 'The Women's Institute meets regularly – I'm president, of course, and Mrs Warren is secretary and does a lot of the organisation. She seems to enjoy having her finger in a lot of pies, and I must say she's a very useful sort of person. Her husband is a solicitor in Tavistock,' she explained to Fenella. 'They came to live here just before the war. Oh, and the new vicar, Basil Harvey, has settled in very well, although he always reminds me of Alice in Wonderland's White Rabbit, perpetually worrying about being late. His wife, Grace, is quite an asset too.'

'Surely they've been here for a while,' Hilary said. 'A year or two, at least.'

'Two years, but he's new to Fenella. Most of the young men are away at the war, and we've lost several. I suppose when it's all over their names will be on the war memorial by the church gate that was put up after the Great War.' Her eyes drifted again to the portrait, but she went on determinedly, 'What else, now? The headmaster of the school, Mr Wilson, has retired, and Miss Kemp, his assistant, has been promoted to his position and moved into the school house.'

'That's good,' Hilary said. 'She's a really nice woman and a good teacher. It's lovely that she can have her own house after living in lodgings all this time.'

Fenella finished her tea and brushed crumbs from her skirt.

'Would you mind if I go and have a chat with Dottie now, Isobel? I expect she'll be going home soon, and I must at least say hello.'

She got up and left the room. Stephen spread a scone as thickly as he dared with jam and cream and Hilary lay back against the sofa cushions.

'It really is lovely to be home. I'm going to enjoy every moment of my leave and just revel in luxury.'

Her mother glanced at her. 'Do you have to go back, my dear? I know you want to do your bit and all that – we all do – but does it have to be in Egypt? I'm sure there are just as valuable jobs you could do here.'

'Mother, I'm in the ATS. I don't have a choice.'

'Oh, but surely your father could—'

Hilary sat up. 'No! Please, Mummy, don't ask him to pull strings for me. I won't have it, and I don't suppose he'd agree anyway. You ought to know what army life is like, and this is wartime. We simply can't do that sort of thing.'

Isobel sighed. 'I suppose not. I know you're right really, but ... It's just that I feel so alone, with all of you away, and Baden gone. I almost feel inclined to agree to Stephen's being a day boy at Kelly, just for the company.' She raised one hand as Stephen looked up eagerly. 'I won't, of course. But if you could just be back in England, Hilary, and able to come home every now and then. Able to *telephone* even ... Egypt is so very far away.'

'I know, Mummy.' Hilary reached out a hand. 'You're all by yourself in this great house, which for some reason I don't understand has never been requisitioned for war use, and I'm thousands of miles away in the Egyptian desert, and half the time you don't have any idea at all where Dad is. It's horrible. But there's nothing we can do about it. It's war, and we all have to take whatever comes.'

'I know,' Isobel said sadly. 'It's war.'

Chapter Thirteen

Dottie was making the preparations for supper when Fenella came into the kitchen. She looked round and her face broke into a beaming smile.

'There you are, maid! I was hoping you'd pop in for a word. Let me have a look at you.' She came over and Fenella kissed her cheek and stood back while they regarded each other. 'You'm looking well enough, though a mite too thin for my liking. Still, us'll soon fatten you up while you're here in Burracombe. And where is it you've been now?'

'India. It was very hot – they eat a tremendous amount of rice and curry. I'll have to show you how they make it.'

Dottie wrinkled her nose. 'Never been much of a one for fancy spiced foods myself. I'd rather have good, honest meat and two veg any day. Not that there's been much meat about for the past few years. Bert Foster does his best, but nobody can make a few ounces a week into a decent meal for a working man. It's a good thing offal isn't rationed or we'd all be skin and bone.'

Fenella shuddered. 'Offal! I hate liver and kidney, unless it's in a pie with plenty of steak. But I didn't come to talk about meat, Dottie. How are you? I miss you so much – nobody can make or repair a stage costume like you can.'

'Well, you know my dear old mother died and I had to come home and look after Father. And now he's gone too, I seem to find plenty to do around the village. I was thinking I would be asked to take an evacuee, and I wouldn't have minded that at all – nice to have a bit of young life about the place – but a lot of them have gone back home now the bombing seems to have stopped. There's still a few around – those whose parents think they're better off in the country, and some whose homes have been bombed – but it doesn't look as if there'll be many more coming. Not that we want them to, if it means those terrible blitzes starting again. I never thought to see anything like what happened to Plymouth.'

'The blitzes were dreadful everywhere,' Fenella agreed. 'But would you really have liked an evacuee, Dottie? I've heard that some of them could be a real handful, and they had no idea of country life. Someone told me they had a little girl who refused to drink milk or eat eggs once she'd seen where they came from! She said that in London, where she lived, they had *clean* food!'

'The poor little dears didn't know any better. If you ask me, it was good for them to learn about where their food came from. Yes, I'd have liked having a kiddie around. It's something I've always missed, not having had any of my own.'

'I know.' Fenella's face grew sober. 'I've felt that too. But to have children, you have to be married, and somehow that's never come my way.'

Dottie stared at her. 'Miss Fenella! There must be a hundred men who would have married you!'

'But would I have married them? No, Dottie, there's never been anyone I wanted to share my life with. Not permanently.' She paused, then added pensively, 'No one who was available to share it with, anyway.'

Dottie said nothing. As Fenella's dresser, she had been very close to the actress and seen a good many men – actors, stage-door johnnies, even titled and well-born men-about-town – squiring her to theatres and parties. There were even one or two she had thought might be coming close to marriage. But when Fenella's face took on that wistful, almost yearning look, she could not help thinking of one man in particular who had seemed to have caught at her heart. He had been a regular visitor and their outings had been simpler events – walks in Hyde Park, or occasionally further afield to Windsor Great Park; visits to the zoo, boat trips on the Thames. He had never taken her anywhere where they might be photographed, and Dottie suspected that he was already married.

And then, one day, he had just disappeared from Fenella's life. Fenella had said nothing but had looked pale and drawn for some time, her smiles less dazzling, her zest diminished. Clearly, they had parted – perhaps Fenella had sent him away, perhaps he had chosen to stay with his wife, perhaps neither of them had wanted a scandal. Perhaps something even worse had happened and Fenella couldn't even grieve openly. Dottie never knew and never asked. But now, she thought he was the man in Fenella's mind.

'It was much the same with me,' she said, thinking back to the days of her youth, when she could have had the only man she had ever really wanted, but had lost her chance. Thrown it away, really, she told herself. 'And at the time, it's not children you're thinking of. It's only later, seeing the little ones around other people's feet, that you realise what you've missed.'

Fenella smiled at her. 'It's not too late, though! Oh, it probably is too late to have our own children, but you might still get an evacuee, and I ... well, Dottie, I've been thinking of adopting.'

Dottie stared at her. 'Adopt a child? You?'

Fenella laughed. 'Why not? I can afford it. I could give a child a good home, an education ... Wouldn't that be a lovely thing to do?'

'Well, yes, of course it would, and any kiddie would be lucky to be taken up by you. But how could you look after it? You're away so much. You couldn't take a little one on tour to India and Africa and all those dangerous places.'

'No, of course not. I couldn't do it until after the war. But *then* ... And I could send it to you for holidays in the country, Dottie, so you'd share it with me. Wouldn't that be fun? We'd both get what we wanted, and the child would have a better life.'

Dottie shook her head in wonder. 'It's something I'd never have thought of. Adopt a kiddie! Well, I dare say there'll be plenty needing homes when all this is over. You'll be able to take your pick.'

Fenella nodded. 'Yes, I probably could, although it seems wrong somehow to look at it like choosing a puppy or a kitten from a litter. I think I should wait to see what – or who – comes along. And since this war looks like going on for some time, sadly, it's not likely to happen for a few years yet and I shall be that much older by then. I might not even be allowed to adopt. Now, tell me all about yourself and what you're doing these days. Mrs Napier says you're the mainstay of the village.'

Dottie laughed. 'I wouldn't say that! I just help out wherever I can, but I must say I do enjoy the WI meetings. Mrs Napier and Mrs Warren between them really get things going. There's one on Wednesday afternoon – you could come as a visitor, if you'd like to.'

'Could I? Would that be all right with the members? I wouldn't want to intrude.'

'Intrude? You?' Dottie laughed again. 'Why, they'll be thrilled to bits to have a famous actress visit them. You'll be as welcome as the flowers in May!'

Chapter Fourteen

Alice used the very same words the next afternoon, when she welcomed Hilary into the farmhouse kitchen. Minnie was out in the garden picking broad beans and Alice called out to her that they had a visitor and she would bring tea outside. Hilary followed her indoors and sat at the big table while Alice bustled about, filling the kettle at the sink and putting it on the range, which was kept burning even in summer.

'I was hoping you'd look in, my dear. We were all pleased when we heard you were coming home for a spell. I expect your mother hardly knows herself, with both you and Miss Forsyth visiting together.'

'I've left them having a good old chinwag,' Hilary said with a smile. 'I know my mother gets lonely, with me and Father both away, and it's especially hard since we lost Baden.'

'I know. Terrible sad that were. Too many mothers have lost their sons in this awful war, and even those that haven't lost them live in dread.' Alice shook her head and went to the dresser for cups and saucers.

Hilary gave her a sympathetic look. 'It's bad for you, I know. Do you hear much from Brian and Tom?'

'Only when they can manage to send a line or two, but they're not allowed to tell us much. We know Brian's in Africa somewhere, and Tom was in Italy last time we heard. All we can do is hope and pray. Same as everyone else, I suppose.'

'I'm surprised they weren't allowed to stay at home. Isn't farming a reserved occupation?'

'Only for some that they reckon are too old, like my Ted, or can't be spared. They brought in all these Land Girls, you see. Reckoned if they couldn't fight, they could do farm work. Useless bits of girls some of them were, too! You should hear old Abel Pettifer go on about the ones they sent him! Frightened to go near the cows, said their feet were cold in wellington boots and half screamed the place down when they came across a nest of rats in the barn. More interested in doing their hair and painting their nails bright red, they were. He sent 'em packing and took on a couple of old chaps who used to look after the sheep up over Wedlake and weren't afraid of a bit of hard work.'

Hilary laughed. 'But you've got some good ones, haven't you?'

'Oh yes, we were lucky. Joanna's like one of the family now and don't mind turning her hand to anything. She lives here with us and the other two lodge in the village with Aggie Madge. Aggie lost her husband so she's glad of the money. I was saying only yesterday, we'll be sorry when Joanna goes.'

'Perhaps she'll marry Brian or Tom,' Hilary suggested wickedly, and Alice chuckled.

'That'd be a happy ending all right, but life don't often work out that way. Now, I'll just put these rock cakes on a plate and we'll take it all outside. It's time Mother had a bit of a rest.'

'She's looking really well,' Hilary commented, picking up the tray despite Alice's protestations. 'She must be nearly eighty now, surely.'

'Seventy-eight,' Alice said proudly. 'And looks like she'll go on till she's a hundred. Always busy. She says that's what keeps her healthy. Don't you, Mother?' she added as the old woman came up the path towards them carrying a trug filled with beans.

'Don't I what? Oh yes.' She nodded as Alice repeated her words. 'That's the secret of a long life – keep yourself busy. Don't do no good sitting around and getting rusty.' She dumped her trug on the ground and sat down on the wooden bench Ted had put by the back door. Her face, as wrinkled as an old apple, creased with smiles as she turned to Hilary. ''Tis a pleasure to see you, maid, and very good of you to come by. I dare say you've brought news of our Val.'

'Well, not news, exactly,' Hilary replied. 'But I thought you'd like to know how she's getting along.'

'We certainly would. Put the tray down on that little table, my dear. It's an old one Ted cut the legs off, so it's the right size when we're sitting on this bench. I'll bring a chair from the kitchen.' Alice disappeared and came out a minute later with a kitchen chair. 'You have this, Mother, you'll be more comfortable with a back, and I've brought a cushion too.' She took Minnie's place next to Hilary on the bench and passed them both a cup of tea. 'Now, you help yourselves to a rock cake and let's hear all about life in the desert.'

Hilary took a cake and bit into it. 'Mm, that's good. There's nothing like home cooking. Not that we aren't fed very well in the mess, but it's never quite the same.' She looked at the two expectant faces. 'There's really not that much to tell. I'm sure Val has told you in her letters all about what she does – her work and so on. I don't know much about that, I'm afraid, because she's a nurse while I just drive cars. But we see each other when we're off duty.'

'And what do you get up to then?' Alice enquired. 'Val's mentioned dances once or twice.'

'Yes, mess dances and things like that. It's all above board,' she added, understanding that the idea of girls like herself and Val, already engaged, going to dances with other men might be a difficult one for the two countrywomen to take in. 'It's just for relaxation after work. People like Val, who have such a hard job to do, really need that.'

'I was never in favour of her going as a VAD,' Alice said. 'She could have stayed as a nurse in Tavistock. There's plenty of sick people here.'

'No, she couldn't,' Minnie argued. 'She was of an age to be called up for war work of some sort, and if it weren't that it could have been the ATS, like Miss Hilary here, or the Wrens or WAAFs. She'd have had to go away from home come what might.'

'She could have stopped here on the farm, then. Joanna herself said that, only yesterday. Said it seemed daft for Val to go away, having been brought up on a farm and knowing how to do most of the work, and girls like her brought in from towns. You got to agree with that.'

'Well, she's a nurse anyway,' Minnie said. 'There's nothing to be done about it now.'

'Yes, and out in Egypt, away from her mother's eye, where us don't know what she's doing.'

'And won't know, if we don't let Miss Hilary tell us. Just be quiet for a minute or two, Alice, and let the maid speak. She's walked over from the Barton specially.'

Alice turned to their visitor. 'I'm sorry, Miss Hilary. I've been forgetting my manners. Tell us some more about these dances, and what else you and Val do in your spare time.'

'Well, we don't get much of that. Val gets less than I do and works shift hours, so we're not often off duty together. But we have to socialise when we can. The men need it – the officers, you know, and sometimes the patients as they start to recover. It really doesn't mean anything more than that.'

She thought of those desert nights. For herself, the life was easier – ferrying high-ranking army officers about in one of the camouflage-painted army vehicles, sometimes helping with office work, lending a hand wherever she could. But for Val, nursing casualties who had come in from the 'blue', as the desert was called, horribly injured or burned, often with only hours or days to live, the work was hard and exhausting. Hilary knew that the nurses were not supposed to allow their emotions to get the better of them, but many was the morning when she had encountered Val on her way back to the long wooden hut that was her ward, red-eyed and worn out before she even began her shift.

She wondered if she should tell Alice and Minnie about such things. Or about the nights when they let their hair down with the young men who had barely recovered from their wounds before being sent back to the front line. It might be their last chance to hold a girl in their arms, to feel that they were loved. Not many of the girls could be so hard-hearted as to refuse a few kisses, and sometimes more, to a young subaltern or pilot who might meet his death before the next sunset.

And then, she thought, there were those who did come back. Those who were a little more special. And sometimes there might be one who came to be very special indeed ...

No. She could not tell Alice and Minnie of these things. If they were ever to know, it must be Val herself who told them.

'We always have a party at Christmas,' she said. 'Someone made a tree last year, out of green sluice aprons and crêpe paper. It looked quite realistic. And we all gave each other presents and sang carols and played games like Charades and Hunt the Thimble.' The thimble had been found in some very odd places, but she wouldn't mention that. 'Oh, and a group of us went camel-riding in the desert. That was fun.'

'And is it all really sand?' Minnie asked. 'Like on Bigbury beach?'

'Well, not quite like that, but yes, it is all sand. It gets everywhere. Val says the men who come in from the desert seem to wear it like a second skin – no matter how often they bathe them, there always seems to be more. But the flies are even worse. They're everywhere, masses of them, and do they bite! They can cause really nasty sores. They're about all day, and then at night they disappear and the mosquitoes start instead. And the bedbugs. Val says they have a lot of trouble with those on the wards.'

The women stared at her. 'It sounds like living in a slum,' Alice said at last. 'Our Val's never said anything about all that.'

Hilary wondered whether she should have said anything either. But the disapproval on Alice's face and in her voice when she had talked about Val's volunteering as a VAD, and about the mess parties, had upset her, and she thought maybe Val's mother ought to realise what her daughter was enduring.

'I don't suppose she wanted to worry you,' she said. 'It's the same for all of them, you know, and a lot are girls like me, from families who never expected them to do any kind of work. I know several who were debutantes and presented at court and never thought they'd have such a thing as a job. But they all turn to, and bathe and shave injured soldiers, and help surgeons at operations, and dress horrible wounds and burns, with never a murmur of complaint.'

'Is it just flies and mosquitoes?' Minnie asked after a short silence. 'I've heard there are a lot of creepy-crawlies in the desert. Scorpions and such.'

'Yes, there are. And huge spiders – tarantulas. But you get used to looking out for them. And some of the creatures are rather lovely, like the chameleons that can change the colour of their skin and catch flies with their long tongues. I thought of bringing one home for Stephen, but I wasn't sure he'd be allowed to take it to school and I knew my mother wouldn't want to look after it!'

Minnie laughed and then looked at Alice. 'Sounds to me like our Val earns her bit of fun after all that. We can't begrudge her a party or two, or even a dance, as long as it's all above board. They're young folk, after all, and this war's taking enough away from them as it is.'

Alice nodded. 'You'm right, Mother.' She turned to Hilary. 'I'm glad you've told us this, Miss Hilary. Like you say, she never said anything because she didn't want to worry us, and our Val never was one to complain anyway. It sounds like she's doing good war work out there.'

'She is,' Hilary said with relief. 'You really mustn't worry about her, Mrs Tozer. She's a good nurse and there are a lot of men who have reason to be grateful to her.'

Alice stood up. 'I'll make a fresh pot of tea. This one's gone cold. You'll stay a few minutes longer, won't you, Miss Hilary? I'd like you to meet Joanna when she comes in from milking. And we can give you a bit more village news, if you haven't been given it already.'

Hilary smiled. Alice's village news was likely to be different from her mother's, but Hilary had always felt more in tune with village life than had her parents, who tended to remain aloof. This was something else the war was changing, she thought. Villagers and those from the big house were mixing more, in organisations such as the WI, which had been started during the Great War, and other war efforts, ranging from raising money for Spitfires to collecting old clothes to send to people bombed out from their homes. Rationing, too, affected everyone in the same way and gave them all a sense of bonding. And in the services, courage and ability had begun to matter more than background, and medals could be won by the private who had been a plumber or a carpenter at home just as well as by the officer who had never worked at any civilian job.

When Alice came out with a fresh pot of tea and a plate of home-made biscuits to replenish the cakes, their talk turned to village affairs and Hilary heard how Bert Foster's 'Coker' sausages (named after the thick fingers of the village blacksmith) had become stick-thin, and how a fish and chip van came round every Friday dinner time. Fish from a fish and chip shop was not rationed, so the van did good business and was well patronised during its half-hour stay before going on to the next village. She heard how Edie Pettifer was getting friendly with Bert Foster, and how the two Friend sisters – cousins of Dottie – had taken over the post office after their father had died. Their brother Billy, who was rather tubby and slow but always seemed to be happy and smiling, still lived at home with them and helped Mr Foster in the room behind the shop where Bert prepared what meat he could get, although Billy was never allowed to handle the knives.

'Poor Billy,' Hilary said. 'He's never been quite right, has he? I wonder why it is that some babies are born like that.'

'That's a mystery nobody will ever solve,' Minnie said. 'Mind you, Sarah Friend was over forty when he was born, and they do say that has something to do with it, though I can't see how.' She looked down at the trug of beans. 'If you two don't mind, I'll start shelling these for our supper. Ted always likes a good helping of broad beans, fresh from the garden with a nice sprig of mint.'

'I must go anyway,' Hilary said, getting up. 'I've taken up too much of your time already. The tea and cakes were lovely, Mrs Tozer, thank you. And I mustn't forget to thank you for the cream you sent over yesterday, either. It was a real treat.'

'Bless you, you're welcome. It's been a pleasure to see you, and thank you for coming to talk to us about Val. You'll come again before you go back, won't you?'

'I will.' Hilary smiled at the two women and then, on impulse, bent to kiss each one on the cheek. 'It's been lovely sitting here in the sun with you – and not being bitten to death by flies! I'll see you again soon.'

She swung down the garden and through the gate. From the farmyard there was a gate that would take her to the boundary of Tozer fields with estate land. She walked through it and strolled home, revelling in the feel of being under a gentle English sun rather than the searing heat of the Egyptian one.

She felt pleased with her afternoon. She had satisfied Val's mother's curiosity and given her cause to be proud of her daughter, rather than disapproving. What Val did while she was in Egypt was her own business, and nobody else's.

Chapter Fifteen

Minnie and Alice looked at each other.

'It do sound like our Val's doing good work out there,' Alice said at last, taking a pod from the trug and extracting half a dozen fat broad beans.

'Well, of course she is,' Minnie said a little sharply. 'Stands to reason she would be. They don't have nurses out there for nothing, and you know she's a good worker and did well in her training.'

'Yes, but I also know what it's like when girls are a long way away from home with no mother's hand to guide them. Look at what the Land Girls get up to here – not our Joanna, I know, but some of them are proper little hussies. And out there, where it's hot at night, and there's all those parties and dances, and you can get away from everyone else into the desert ...'

'Sounds like you know all about it!' Minnie said, raising her eyebrows. 'When did you ever go out to Egypt without telling us, Alice? Or perhaps you've just been reading too many of those silly books they've got in the penny library.'

'I'm just saying, there's a lot of temptation for a young girl, that's all. They can get up to all sorts, knowing their mothers and fathers will never hear about it – until they find themselves in trouble.' Alice closed her lips firmly and tore at a bean pod as if it had done her an injury.

'I don't think you should worry about your Val,' Minnie said quietly, watching her. 'You should trust her instead. You brought her up to know right from wrong, and she's never been a flighty girl. Miss Hilary says she's doing good work, and to my mind, a young woman who's spent her day looking after soldiers and airmen who have been badly hurt fighting for our country deserves a bit of fun in the evening. Val won't let it go too far. She's got a nice young man and a ring on her finger, and that counts for a lot.'

'I know, Mother.' Alice stopped mutilating the beans and laid her hands in her lap. 'I heard what Miss Hilary said, and I do trust my girl. I just worry about her, that's all. It's easy to get carried away and no real blame to either party, that's all I'm saying, and I wouldn't want Val to get into any difficulties.' She paused, then added, 'I think the world of her for what she's doing. Don't think I don't. But you know yourself, you never stop worrying about your children, and maybe we worry more about the girls than the boys.'

'That's probably true,' Minnie agreed. 'It was always a sorrow to me that I never had girls, and only the two boys. We didn't have the care in those days that young women get now when they're expecting. There were a lot of miscarriages and stillbirths, and babies that only lived a little while. There's not many families didn't suffer that way.'

Alice nodded. 'Me and Ted were lucky, having four healthy youngsters. But now look – three of them away at war. That's not what us had in mind when us started a family. With the Great War behind us, we thought we were building a land fit for heroes, like we were told. They didn't tell us the heroes were going to have to go and fight another war.'

The garden gate opened and Alice's younger daughter, Jackie, burst through it. Almost ten years old, she was the tomboy of the family, with her dark hair flying behind her in pigtails and her shirt hanging loose over a pair of her brother Tom's khaki Boy Scout shorts, cut down to fit her. Neither Alice and Ted nor Minnie approved of her wearing boys' clothes, but the cotton frocks Alice made her didn't last five minutes once she was off playing with the rest of the village children. Jackie was always first up a tree, or balancing on a log across the Burra Brook, or fishing for minnows and falling into the water, and with clothes on ration they just couldn't afford to let her go out wearing anything decent.

'Jackie, just look at you!' Alice scolded, more out of habit than anything else. 'You look as if you've been pulled through a hedge backwards. Whatever have you been doing?'

'Helping with the harvest, of course. I took the cider over for the men and some lemonade for the girls and Dad said I could stop and give a hand. I've been stooking.'

'Well, at least you've been making yourself useful,' Alice said, looking at her daughter's sunburned face. 'You'd better shake the dust out of those clothes and have a good wash at the kitchen sink, and then put on something tidy. I suppose you'll be wanting to go again tomorrow.'

'Dad says I can. He said I'd been really handy. I led Barley as well.'

'I'm surprised you didn't ride him home,' Minnie observed. 'Or have they decided to carry on for a while? I dare say they'll be working till sunset in this weather.'

'Yes, they sent me home for some sandwiches and more cider and lemonade. I can go back, can't I, Mum? I don't have to stay here and wash yet? They're waiting for their tea.'

'And that's what they'll get,' Alice declared, standing up with the bowl of podded beans in her hands. 'It's all ready on the kitchen table – a big box of sandwiches and a cake. I'll make a pot of tea, that'll be better than cider at this time of day, and we'll take it out together. We'll have a picnic. You can walk over with us too, Mother.'

'I will,' the old lady said, picking up the trug of empty pods. 'I've always liked taking food out to the men at harvest time. Though it's more women now, with all the Land Girls.'

'Oh, there's men too,' Jackie said, as she turned to scamper into the kitchen. 'American airmen. They came over in a truck and said they'd help. They told me they'd have brought chocolate, only it would have melted.'

'American airmen!' Minnie echoed, and looked at Alice. 'Seems to me young women don't have to go all the way to Egypt to find temptation. It's coming here, right to our doorsteps!'

Chapter Sixteen

'I've had some lovely news,' Isobel said when Hilary came in from a morning ride a few days later. Once of the things she missed most about being away from home was her bay gelding Beau, who had been given to her on her eighteenth birthday. A visit to him in his stable was a priority whenever she returned home, and she looked forward to her first ride with as much excitement as a child looking forward to its birthday.

'What's that, then?' She sat down at the breakfast table. Isobel breakfasted late and there were still a few slices of toast in the rack. Hilary took one and spread it with margarine and some of Jacob Prout's honey.

'Your father's coming home! He's managed to get a few days' leave and he'll be here by the weekend. You'll have some time together before you go back.'

'Oh, that *is* good. I haven't seen him since he left Egypt. It must be eight or nine months. I expect he'll want to see everything that's been going on around the estate – we can ride round together.'

'I'll have to organise a dinner party,' Isobel said. 'I hope Dottie will be able to cook for us. She's so busy these days, with her work for the pub as well as helping Dr Latimer's wife some of the time. I must ask her at once.'

'I can help,' Hilary offered. 'I did quite well with my cookery at finishing school. It'll be nice to have the chance to put it into practice.'

'And I'm a champion potato peeler,' Fenella declared. 'I was famous for it all over India.'

The other two laughed. 'Go on, you wouldn't know a potato

78

peeler if it hit you on the nose,' Hilary mocked. 'But you can come into the kitchen if you like and do some training. You never know when you might need to help out in the officers' mess when you're on tour.'

'You speak more truly than you think,' Fenella told her severely. 'And I *have* peeled potatoes, in my youth. I didn't grow up in a big house like this, with servants to attend to my every whim.'

'You didn't grow up in a workman's cottage either,' Isobel said. 'Or you wouldn't have been at school with me. Now, let's think about menus, and who we should ask. The Latimers, of course ...'

'That should prevent the risk of Dottie working for them that night,' Hilary observed.

'... and Miss Bellamy, naturally. You remember her, Fenella – she lives in the Grey House at the other end of the village. Busy little woman, always on the go. Minnie Tozer was her nursemaid as a little girl. And the Shebbears, we must ask them.' She sighed. 'This petrol rationing is such a nuisance. So many people have had to garage their cars for the duration and can't get around as they used to. There are friends twenty miles from here who I've hardly seen since war was declared, and others we have to meet in Tavistock because it's the only place we can all get to by bus.'

'Shall I go and talk to Dottie?' Fenella suggested. 'She'll be off soon, won't she? It might be a good thing to put a few ideas together before she leaves, since she won't be here this evening.'

'Would you, darling?' Isobel pushed her plate aside and went to the little desk in the corner for a pencil. She took an envelope from the pile of post on the table and began to write on the back of it. 'Hilary, you can help me with the guest list. Now, how about the Boultings? Stephen plays with their boys when they're all at home. And ...'

Fenella left them to it and walked down the corridor to the kitchen, where Dottie was beginning on the washing-up. Before the war, there would have been at least two maids as well as the cook-housekeeper, but now Isobel was reliant on Dottie, who only worked part-time, and Mrs Purdy, who also cleaned at the school and came in to do the 'rough'. A dinner party would be quite demanding, Fenella thought, and she and Hilary would be called upon to help.

'Squire coming home?' Dottie said when she was told the news. 'Oh, that's lovely. Mrs Napier gets very low sometimes, here all by herself. I do wonder now and then why the government never took over this big house like they did so many others, but I suppose they've got enough in Plymouth. Why, the squire has let the old gamekeeper's cottage, down in the woods, to a couple from Plymouth because their house was taken over. Optician, he is, and has to go in by train every day. I wonder if Mrs Napier will invite them to the dinner party.'

Fenella thought it unlikely, but you never knew these days. However, there were still enough of the Napiers' friends living within reasonable reach, so there would probably be a full table.

'Mrs Napier wants a few ideas for a menu,' she said, picking up a tea cloth. 'I don't know what's available at the moment, but I'm sure you do.'

Dottie thought for a moment. 'Well, there's plenty of salad stuff, but that's never satisfying enough for the gentlemen. And they do like their meat, but what with rationing and everything ... You can't really ask them to hand over their own coupons, can you! I could ask around for a few rabbits and make a terrine. Pity Arthur Culliford's not here; he'd have had no trouble getting whatever we wanted!'

'Arthur Culliford? Who's he?'

'Oh, he's a bit of a ne'er-do-well. Goes by the name of Jim sometimes, but whichever he is, he's a varmint. Lives in that cottage down the other end of the village that always looks such a mess. His wife Maggie's not much better, neither, always got a fag hanging out of her mouth, and the children look as if they've never seen a bar of soap.' She sighed. 'Still, I mustn't criticise – he did join up, soon as war was declared, and then got caught at Dunkirk. Been in a prisoner-of-war camp ever since.'

'Oh dear. That must be very hard on his wife.'

Dottie nodded. 'She's not a bad young woman, when all's said and done, just got no idea how to look after a home and cook a decent meal, and it's not easy for her to manage, with no man. But she gets his army pay same as if he was active, so they don't starve.'

Fenella finished drying the cereal bowls and started on the plates. 'What work did he do before the war?'

Dottie snorted. 'As little as possible! Rather be out half the night poaching than do an honest day's toil. But the squire turns a blind eye most of the time, and we've even bought a rabbit or two at the kitchen door – the squire's own rabbits, mind – to help them along. That's one of the funny things about the war – it's taken the poachers as well as the gamekeepers, in a manner of speaking.'

Fenella laughed. 'There are still a good many of that sort in the towns and cities. Spivs, who will get you anything on the black market for a price.' She cupped her mouth with one hand and lowered her voice to a whisper. 'Even nylon stockings – or so I've heard!'

'Get away!' Dottie said. 'Not that you'd ever lower yourself to buy off the black market, Miss Fenella!'

'Of course not! What an idea!' They both laughed. 'Anyway, we're supposed to be discussing menus, not nylon stockings. What else could you do for meat, if you can't get rabbit?'

Dottie paused with her hands in the hot water and considered. 'Well, there's fish. We might be able to come by a salmon or a few trout. Jacob Prout could help us there, perhaps. He's a good fisherman and knows all the best places. That, with some new potatoes from the grounds and a good hearty salad, might be enough, and I could make some cold beetroot soup to start and a nice crumble for afters, to fill them up. I dare say Alice Tozer might be able to let us have a bowl of cream. It won't be up to what we used to do, but there you are.'

'It sounds delicious,' Fenella said. 'Nobody expects pre-war standards these days. And salmon is always a treat. A whole one looks so luxurious.'

'When is this party going to be?' Dottie asked, drying her hands on the roller towel behind the door.

'I don't know. The colonel's coming at the end of the week, so perhaps Saturday or Sunday. Hilary and I will help with all the preparations. We'll rope Stephen in as chief spud-basher. He'll have to learn how to do that if he ever goes into the services. They all do.'

'What, even the officers?' Dottie asked, scandalised. 'That don't seem right.'

'Well, perhaps not. I'm not sure, to be truthful. Anyway, he's probably learned how to do it already. I expect he's in the Boy Scouts, and they do all that kind of thing.'

Dottie emptied the washing-up bowl and gazed meditatively at the water swirling down the sink. 'It'll be like old times. The colonel and Miss Hilary both at home, and you here as well, and a dinner party with everyone dressed up. It's just what Mrs Napier needs. It's what we all need – a bit of pleasure to stop us worrying about the war.'

'Yes,' Fenella said, hanging up the tea cloth. 'It's exactly what we need. It's what I try to give the troops when I go abroad to entertain them. A bit of pleasure and a touch of glamour, to stop them thinking for just a few hours how grim their lives really are.'

Chapter Seventeen

Dottie set out down the drive, her basket over her arm, her mind busy with ideas for the dinner party. It was seldom that anyone held such an event these days and she knew that Mrs Napier would want a good table. For that matter, Dottie's own pride and pleasure in her work demanded it too, and she was already wondering whether plain salmon – supposing one could be procured in the time – would be sufficiently grand. Perhaps someone might have a couple of fowls they wanted killed, but that seemed unlikely. Any hen that wasn't laying well would have been dealt with already. There was no room for passengers these days, even if they were only chickens.

No. Even if the whole family contributed, there would certainly not be enough meat coupons to make a good show. It would have to be game, and with the shooting season for most birds still weeks away, that meant rabbit or fish. She would have to speak to Jacob Prout.

As it happened, Jacob was the first person she saw as she reached the road. He was clipping the hedge that ran along the Barton boundary and looked round as she approached.

'Morning, Dottie. How are things up at the house?'

'Very well indeed, Jacob. They've just heard that the squire's coming home for a few days. Just when Miss Hilary's here too. Isn't that nice for them?'

'Dare say that's why he arranged it,' Jacob said, pushing back his old cap to reveal his bald head. 'Not much good being a colonel if you can't give yourself a spot of leave when your only daughter comes home.'

'Well, maybe,' Dottie agreed. 'Anyway, the thing is, Mrs Napier wants to give a dinner party and I'm to cook for it, so I've got to think of something to do.'

'A dinner party! That's a bit of a tall order, isn't it, what with all the rationing? How many is she inviting?'

'I don't know yet, but there's five of them in the house if you count young Stephen, which I expect they will, and he'll need to eat anyway, even if it's only in the kitchen. So I should think she'll ask at least another five. I heard something about Miss Bellamy, so that would be two couples as well. Maybe even three.'

'Ten or twelve,' Jacob ruminated. He fixed her with a bright blue eye. 'And why be you telling me this, then, Dottie?'

She flicked a smile at him. 'Partly because you asked, Jacob! And partly because I hoped you might help me out a bit – *what with all the rationing.*'

'Ah,' he said, returning her grin. 'I walked into that one, didn't I? Not that I didn't know what you were getting at all along. So you'll be after a few rabbits, I reckon.'

'I don't know what else I can do,' Dottie confessed. 'I'll never be able to make the family's meat ration go round that many, and we can't ask folk to bring their own. You could find me something, couldn't you, Jacob?'

''Tis no use you putting your head on one side and acting all coy and winsome, Dottie Friend,' he said sternly. 'I've knowed you since you were a little maid, remember. Well, I dare say I might be able to stumble across a rabbit or two, but grand folk like the Napiers aren't going to be content with that, so I suppose you'll want me to look for a salmon as well.'

'If you would. The rabbits would make a nice terrine to start with, but a whole salmon always looks special. I'd better go into Tavi to do a bit of shopping. I wonder if Creber's have got any aspic on their shelves. They've got so much hidden away in that shop, you never know what they might find.'

'Can't say as I know what that is,' Jacob observed, 'but if it's to go on a salmon for a dinner party, they might have a bit left over from before the war. When do you want all this, Dottie?'

'I'm not sure. I don't think they've decided on a date yet but it will be sometime next week. I'll let you know as soon as Mrs Napier tells me. And now I'd better get on. I've my own work to do before I go to the pub for the dinner-time customers, and I want to call in at the bakery to see if George Sweet wants me to make anything for the shop.'

'Blimey,' Jacob said. 'Is that all? Couldn't you fit in a bit of spring cleaning up at Mrs Warren's, and do the milking for Ted Tozer? I dunno how you manage it all, Dottie. I reckon there must be two of you. You were twins all these years and nobody ever knew.'

'Don't talk so foolish, Jacob. As if you weren't just as busy yourself! If you're not hedging and ditching, you're digging graves or looking after someone's vegetable patch. It's the same for us all these days – more than enough to be done and not enough hours in the day to do it in.'

'And nothing wrong with that, neither. A busy life's a good life, that's what my old dad used to say. Better than sitting about twiddling your thumbs. That's what makes folk miserable, and miserable folk are neither use nor ornament. And talking of ornaments, I reckon if the squire's coming home I'd better make a good job of this here hedge. He do like to see it looking smart and tidy along the roadside.' He raised his shears. 'You let me know when you wants your fish and rabbits, Dottie, and I'll see what I can do. I know a pool down the Burra Brook where there's one or two big chaps lie up, and there's plenty of fat little bunnies over in the warren these fine evenings. Shouldn't be too much trouble.'

Dottie thanked him and went on her way. She came to the village green with its great spreading oak tree and the Bell Inn set near the church path, and crossed to George Sweet's bakery. There were fresh cottage loaves in the window, and buns and doughnuts, and a few Cornish pasties filling the air with the enticing smell of meat and potato. She opened the door and went inside, and the ping of the bell brought George's wife Ivy through from the back.

'Oh, it's you, Dottie.' As usual, she sounded as if she'd rather it had been anyone else, Hitler included, and her mouth turned down at the corners. The two women had more or less grown up together, along with Jacob, Ted Tozer and many of the others who, being just too old to be called up for war service, were still around the village, but they had never been real friends. 'George said you might be in.'

'Just looked in to see if he wants any baking done,' Dottie said cheerfully. 'I'll have time to make a few sausage rolls and scones before I go to the Bell, if he wants them. They'll be fresh for the men's dinner crib and the kiddies' tea time then.'

'He's upstairs, getting some sleep,' Ivy said ungraciously. 'But he left a note ...' She pulled out a drawer under the counter and fished about for a minute or so, then held up a scrap of paper with writing on both sides. 'This must be it. Three dozen sausage rolls and the same of scones. He put the sausage meat by. I suppose you've got fat and flour.'

'Still some left from the last batch I did,' Dottie said. 'But I'd be glad of a couple of your wooden trays to bring them back in.' She waited while the baker's wife turned to take the trays from the shelf behind her. 'So how are things going over at the Horrabridge pub, Ivy? I hear you're getting all sorts of foreign airmen in from Harrowbeer these days. Polish and whatnot, as well as Americans.'

Ivy stared at her and turned a dull red. 'I don't know what you mean by that, Dottie Friend.'

'I don't mean anything. It was just a civil question.'

Ivy snorted. 'The sort of civil question some folk ask when they want to cast aspersions.'

'Aspersions?' Dottie asked, astonished. 'Whatever aspersions could there be in that? I'll take a loaf as well, if you don't mind.'

'You know very well what aspersions. Asking about foreign airmen in that sort of tone. Making hints. As if ... well, as if there's something going on as shouldn't be.'

Dottie rolled her eyes. 'Don't be silly, Ivy. I wasn't casting aspersions and I never meant to hint there was anything going on. After all, if anyone knows what it's like working behind a bar, it's me. You've got to be polite and friendly to all the customers and that's all there is to it.'

'Yes,' Ivy said sullenly. 'That *is* all there is to it, and don't let me hear anyone imply anything else.' She dumped the trays on the counter and put a loaf in one.

'You needn't worry about me,' Dottie said with a smile. 'I've got plenty more to talk about than foreign airmen. I've got a dinner party up at the Barton to cook for.' She put a couple of coins on the counter. 'That's for the bread. I'll square up with George for the sausage rolls and scones when I bring them in later. Goodbye, Ivy.'

'What dinner—' Ivy began, but Dottie was already through the door. Ivy stared after her, arms akimbo in annoyance and frustration. Dottie Friend does it on purpose, she thought in exasperation. She'd always been the same, ever since she was a girl, always teasing and laughing at you, as if she knew something you didn't, and always popular with the boys. Well, *that* was a turnaround, anyway – of all the girls who had grown up together in Burracombe in the early years of the century, only Dottie had never married. And Ivy herself, while not managing to capture Ted Tozer, the boy she'd really wanted, had still got the village baker, a man with his own business who worshipped the ground she walked on.

So put that in your pipe and smoke it, Dottie Friend, she thought, peering through the shop window to watch the little woman trot away along the village street, her yellow curls bouncing as she walked. Laugh and joke all you like, but I bet you wish you had a man to keep you warm of a winter's night, instead of just a cat!

Chapter Eighteen

Hilary escaped from her mother at last and went to the kitchen to prepare lunch. Dottie had left most of it ready – some salt cod, soaking in a basin of water, a bowl of fresh peas and a mound of new potatoes, with a large shallow dish of junket and a few raspberries to follow. The cod would, she knew, be rather tasteless, but the rest was fresh from their own kitchen garden and they were lucky to have it.

Fenella came in and closed the door behind her.

'Isobel is knee deep in menu cards and dinner party notebooks,' she said. 'I think she must have a record of every meal ever served here, and who ate it. Nobody must be given something they've eaten before!'

'Even if they absolutely adored it,' Hilary said with a laugh. 'Well, I doubt if we'll be able to match those menus anyway. It's more likely to be Lord Woolton pie followed by parsnips masquerading as bananas.'

'I'm sure Dottie will be able to do better than that. She was talking about rabbit terrine and salmon in aspic. But nobody expects anything grand these days, surely. We all know how difficult catering is.'

'Mother seems reluctant to accept it, somehow. She knows that day to day we have to be careful, but she still seems to think she can entertain for a dinner party in the same way as she could five years ago.'

'Nothing is the same as it was five years ago,' Fenella said with a sigh. 'But better times are round the corner, or so the songs would have us believe. And we have to be optimistic. After all, if the

Germans were going to win, they would have done so in the first year. We weren't ready then, but we soon pulled our socks up and showed them we weren't to be trifled with.' Her dark eyes flashed and she lifted her chin.

'I can see why the troops love you.' Hilary smiled. 'When you look like that, you'd make anyone think they could win the war.'

'That's what I'm for, I suppose,' Fenella said. 'That, and to show that there's another side to life other than fighting and killing. It's easy for them to forget that, you know, when they're so far from home, for such a long time. Some have been away for two or three years, and see no hope of getting home. Some have got children they've never even seen, and some have lost their families in the bombing and never had a chance to mourn. It's all so cruel.'

'I know,' Hilary said quietly. 'I've seen it too, and so has my friend Val – the Tozers' daughter. She nurses fresh casualties every day, and some of them she knows won't survive, but she still keeps a smile on her face and tries to give them a little of the comfort they need.'

'You mentioned her the other day,' Fenella said. 'I do remember her – I used to see her around the village when I was here before. I remember thinking what an attractive girl she was. Long brown hair and beautiful eyes, and looked as if she'd be quite tall. So she became a nurse, did she?'

'A VAD. She had begun her training already, but you know VADs don't get paid and she had to persuade her parents to let her volunteer. I don't think either of them was happy about it, especially when she was sent abroad, but they knew she'd have to do war work of some kind.'

'How did you become friends? I don't recall her ever coming to the Barton.'

'No, she wouldn't have then,' Hilary said wryly. 'The Tozers aren't our tenants, but they still wouldn't have been on Mother's invitation list. More's the pity, because they're fine people, and Ted has a good brain. No, Val and I ran into each other in Egypt, soon after we'd both gone out there, and of course we recognised each other and got together, as you do when you're on your own in a strange place and bump into someone you know – even if it's only slightly. And we got on so well that we became real friends, and I hope always will be.'

'So she'll be on *your* invitation list when you're both back at home,' Fenella suggested, and Hilary nodded.

'She certainly will. I just hope I managed to persuade her mother that what she's doing is the right thing for her.'

'Why shouldn't she think so?' Fenella asked in surprise. 'Surely she must be proud of her.'

'As far as the nursing goes, yes, I'm sure she is. But you know – it's different for girls who have never left home before, and difficult for their parents, too. I mean, I was sent to boarding school at the age of eight and never really lived at home again, except during the holidays. I was accustomed to being away from home and my parents, and they were used to my being, to a certain extent, independent of them. I know Mother didn't want me to join up and leave home again – she'd been looking forward to my staying here, doing the Season and then getting married – but she wouldn't have missed me as Alice Tozer misses Val. Val had never been away, and it's hard for Alice and Ted to get used to the fact that she's living a life they know nothing about, making her own friendships and her own decisions.'

'They just have to trust her.'

'Yes, and in a way they do, but in another way they're afraid to. They can't quite believe she can manage without them, and they're dreadfully afraid that she'll be swept off her feet by some unsuitable man and they'll never get their Val back in one piece.'

'I suppose that could quite easily happen. I've seen it myself.' Fenella was silent for a moment. 'But doesn't she have a sweetheart to keep her on the straight and narrow? Or is she footloose and fancy-free?'

'Yes, she's engaged to a nice boy called Eddie who lives a few miles away. But ... well ...' Hilary drew a pattern on the kitchen table with her forefinger, 'being engaged doesn't always stop people falling in love with someone else.'

Fenella gave her a sharp look. After a moment, she said carefully, 'Do you think that's what's happened? To Val, I mean.'

Hilary seemed to have drifted into abstracted thought, but she looked up quickly and smiled. 'No, I'm sure it hasn't! There are lots of what you might call desert romances, of course, but most of them don't mean anything. Most of them mean nothing at all.'

Again her thoughts seemed to have drifted away and her face had saddened. Fenella decided it was time to end the conversation.

'So what do you think your mother is going to offer her guests for dinner?' she asked. 'And are we all going to have to give up our meat ration to provide it?'

Jacob had been as good as his word and came to the back door with two fat rabbits, freshly skinned, and a salmon that although not quite as handsome as Dottie would have liked was still a respectable size. She had also managed to coax Mr Creber to search amongst his stock in his grocery shop in Tavistock until he found some aspic, and there were plenty of new potatoes, vegetables and salad available, together with a basket of gooseberries from the kitchen garden, which Isobel tended herself with help from Billy Friend, who enjoyed looking after the plants when Bert Foster didn't have much work for him in the butcher's shop.

'I'll make a gooseberry crumble. Gentlemen always like a crumble, and they'll want a hot pudding after a cold main course. And a light chocolate mousse for the ladies. Alice Tozer gave me a recipe from her magazine for one with cocoa and only a couple of eggs. I'll make some of my ginger snaps to go with their coffee.'

'Camp, of course,' said Hilary, who was in the kitchen helping Fenella to wash the lunch dishes.

Fenella rolled her eyes. 'I hope not! It's loathsome stuff. It's never seen a coffee bean in its life. Whoever came up with the idea of making coffee from chicory, of all things?'

'We should think ourselves lucky,' Hilary said. 'The Germans are making it from acorns, so I've heard. I'm not even sure it's *safe* to eat acorns.'

'Let's hope they'm deadly poison, then,' said Jacob, who was sitting at the kitchen table with a cup of tea. 'It would save us making all those bombs and risking our chaps' lives flying over to Germany. We could just drop packets of acorn coffee on them instead.'

'Very Christian, I'm sure,' Dottie said. 'Not that I'm not half inclined to agree with you, Jacob.' She turned to Hilary. 'Anyway, what do you think of my menu? Will it satisfy your mother?'

'She'll be thrilled to bits. It'll be a meal fit for a king – every bit as good as the King and Queen themselves sit down to at Buckingham

Palace. And you must let me help you with it, Dottie. We don't expect you to do it all yourself. You'd have had two or three maids to help prepare it, before the war.'

'I wasn't working here then, but I dare say you're right, and I'll be grateful. Cooking for ten or twelve needs more than one pair of hands.'

'And I'll see to laying the table,' Fenella offered. 'There are lots of flowers in the garden still, and I can make some pretty decorations and put out the cutlery and everything. What about wine, Hilary?'

'Oh, Father will see to that. He won't let anyone into his wine cellar.' She glanced at her watch. 'Heavens, is that the time? I'd better go and get ready – I'm meeting him at Tavistock railway station at three. Thank you for the rabbit and salmon, Jacob.'

'You'm welcome, maid.' He finished his tea and got up. 'I must be getting back too. I've the top corner of the churchyard to clear. Don't want the squire to think the place is being neglected while he's away.'

'He'll never think that while you're in Burracombe, Jacob!' Hilary whisked out of the kitchen and Jacob disappeared more ponderously through the back door. Left alone, Dottie and Fenella looked at each other.

'You know what I think?' Dottie asked after a moment. 'This dinner party is brightening us all up. It's time there was a bit of enjoyment at the Barton. Mrs Napier's on her own too much these days, and to have all her family around her – except poor Mr Baden, of course – is doing her a lot of good. And I'm including you in that, Miss Fenella.'

'Thank you, Dottie. I think you're right. We all need some pleasure from time to time during this terrible war. We need to come together and enjoy each other's company, and a good dinner makes it all the better. If we don't remember that, we might forget just what it is we're fighting for.'

Chapter Nineteen

Colonel Napier stepped off the train as if he expected a welcoming committee to be awaiting him. Resplendent in his army uniform, he stood upright, his head held high, scanning the faces of those meeting the train until he caught sight of his daughter hurrying towards him.

'Hilary. Good to see you, my dear.' He scrutinised her and then enveloped her in a hug. 'You're looking well.'

'It's all the Egyptian sunshine, Dad.' She stepped out of his embrace and smiled at him. Tall and heavily built, with his mane of iron-grey hair swept back beneath his cap, he seemed to dwarf all those around him with his presence. She caught sight of a few interested glances from other passengers, but Gilbert Napier, Squire of Burracombe, was a well-known figure in the area and the glances were respectful. The stationmaster himself came forward, touching his cap, and beckoned to the youth, not yet old enough for military service, who was working as porter.

'Take the colonel's bags, Fred, and look sharp about it. Do you have a vehicle outside, Miss Hilary, or should I call a taxi?'

'No thank you, Mr Martin, I've got the estate truck. Your kitbag will have to share space with some bags of chicken feed,' she told her father. 'I took the chance of collecting some to make the journey worthwhile. We're not supposed to use estate vehicles for private business!'

'Quite right too.' He allowed Fred to hoist the kitbag on to his shoulder and follow them out of the station. 'Thank you, my boy. Got your papers yet?'

Fred shook his head. 'I'm not sixteen until December, sir. I can't wait to go, though. Do you think the war will last long enough?'

Gilbert Napier looked at him. 'What I know, I can't talk about, and what I think doesn't matter. Here ...' He handed the boy a threepenny bit. 'Give that to your mother and tell her to be thankful she's got her son at home for a year or two yet.' He watched the boy depart and shook his head slightly before turning to Hilary. 'Doesn't look old enough to be out of short trousers, but there's boys not much older firing machine guns. Strange sort of world.'

'I'd have thought you'd be pleased to see a boy keen to go and fight,' Hilary said as they got into the truck.

'A boy who was cut out for an army career, yes. A boy who wanted to join up, war or no war. But youngsters like that one?' He shook his head again. 'It's all glamour to them, Hilary, but you and I know the truth. You must have seen plenty of it, out in Egypt. The wounded coming back from the desert to that hospital. It's not a pretty game of soldiers played round the garden.'

'I know, Dad.' She let in the clutch and the truck gave a grunt, bucked a little and stopped again. 'Oh, drat. It's always doing this.' She got out and took the starting handle from under the front seat. Napier watched disbelievingly as she put it in position and gave it a determined swing. The engine emitted a startled yelp and began to run, and she pulled out the handle and jumped back into the driving seat before it could die again. 'You have to take it by surprise. It's as temperamental as a cat.'

'I can't get used to the idea that you spend your life driving army personnel about in trucks and lorries,' he said in a grumbling voice. 'Never thought to see a daughter of mine working as a chauffeur, and not even in a decent vehicle.'

'I drive big cars too, Dad, you know that. I've even driven you once.'

'You don't have to remind me. Never been more embarrassed in my life. Driven by my own daughter, with two generals and a brigadier in the car!'

Hilary laughed. 'It's war work, Father. We all have to do it.'

'Hm.' He was silent for a minute or two, then asked abruptly, 'How's your mother?'

'All right, I think. She's very lonely, of course, but she keeps busy with the WI and various war efforts, and she's so happy we're all going to be at home together for a few days.' She glanced sideways at him and added quietly, 'All that can be, I mean.'

'It's all right, Hilary, I'm not a child. I know we can't have Baden back. And how about young Stephen? Shaping up well, is he?'

Hilary wondered just what he meant by that. Shaping up for what? An army career like his elder brother? To be fit to take on the name of Napier and the Burracombe estate? Or just for adulthood? She said, 'He's only thirteen, Father. He's got plenty of time.'

'I knew exactly what I wanted when I was thirteen,' Napier stated. 'And so did Baden. I remember him coming to me the day before he went to Kelly College for the first time and telling me he wanted to join the army, like me. At that age, any boy should be starting to look to his future.'

'I think things are a bit different now, Dad. The world's so unsettled, nobody can look ahead more than a few weeks. If that. We have no idea how long the war is going to last, or even who will win—'

'Hilary! That's defeatist talk. I'm surprised at you.'

'Well, we don't. Not really. Oh, we *hope* we will win, we even *believe* we will win, but we can't *know*. Not for certain. This secret weapon Hitler's supposed to be developing . . .'

'All talk. Propaganda to frighten us.'

'I hope you're right,' she said soberly. 'But what I'm saying is that the world is too unsettled for a boy like Stephen to be sure what he wants to do with his life. And not everyone wants to join the army, you know.'

Her father turned in his seat and stared at her. 'Are you saying that Stephen – *my son* – is one of these so-called conscientious objectors? A *coward*?'

'No, of course not.' How had they got into this, she wondered, almost before they were out of Tavistock? 'He's as brave as anyone and I'm sure that if the war is still going on in five years' time – heaven forbid – he will fight as willingly as . . . as young Fred back there. All I'm saying is that if there isn't a war, he might want to do something different. That's all.'

'Hm.' Her father was silent again, glowering out of the window. They were driving across the moor now, away from the town and towards Burracombe. After a few minutes he took a breath, squared his shoulders and turned back. 'Very well, Hilary. We'll leave it there. Don't want to arrive at the door like a pair of fighting cocks. Tell me what's happening at home. Is Fenella still with us?'

'Yes, she is,' Hilary said, thankful that the awkward moment had passed. 'She and Mother and Dottie Friend are planning a wonderful dinner party to celebrate our all being together. I won't tell you what Jacob Prout has brought for us to eat, but I can promise you will enjoy it.'

He nodded approvingly. 'That sounds better. Jacob Prout – salt of the earth, that man. He was in the last show, you know. Mentioned in dispatches. The sort any village would be proud of.'

'Yes, and so is Dottie Friend. We're lucky to have people like that around us.'

'You're right, and we should take care of them. That's what a squire's job is. Pity I can't be here to attend to it myself, but Bellamy seems to be doing a good enough job for the time being. Seen much of him since you've been home?'

'Yes, and I've been out with him two or three times, visiting tenants and looking at the land. He's a good manager, Father. He's like all the Bellamys – as much a part of Burracombe as the moors themselves. You can see the resemblance to Miss Constance, even though they're only distantly related.'

'Getting on a bit, that's the only trouble. He'll be wanting to retire again before we know it. Willing enough to come out of retirement and take over when I had to go away, but how long is that going to last? He must be nearly seventy.'

'Sixty-seven. He told me the other day he's good for a few years yet. I'm not sure he ever wanted to retire in the first place, and he jumped at the chance of coming back as manager. He says he didn't think you'd ever be willing to hand over the reins!'

'Case of having to, wasn't it?' They were passing the turning to Little Burracombe, and his glance roved over the swelling hills of the moor, each with the craggy granite rocks of a tor at its summit. 'He'll have to hand them back, mind, when all this is over. I'll be wanting to send in my own papers then and settle back into country life. An army career's a fine thing, Hilary, but it's a young man's game and they won't want old stagers like me when peace is declared at last. You'll be able to start your life then too, my girl.

Marry Henry and settle down with a few children round you. Make your mother and me grandparents.' He paused as they came at last into view of the church tower. 'That's what it's all for in the end, you know. Families, living as they should. Peace on earth, goodwill to all men.'

Hilary glanced at him, surprised. Her father seldom spoke in this manner. He seemed lost in thought for a minute or two, then added in a quiet tone, 'Not that there's much goodwill about at present, nor ever will be, if you want my opinion. Not to *all* men, anyway. Human nature doesn't allow it.'

Hilary swung the truck between the big gateposts and they trundled up the drive and came to a halt by the front steps. The door opened immediately and Stephen came flying out, leaving his mother and Fenella standing, all smiles, at the top.

'There you are, Dad,' Hilary said, turning to him. 'Home again.'

'Yes,' he said, and pushed open the door to clamber down and shake his son's outstretched hand. 'Home.'

Chapter Twenty

Gilbert had only a few days at home, and there was so much he wanted to do that they quickly filled up. Hilary went with him on a tour of the estate, where he talked with the tenant farmers, gamekeepers and woodsmen, listening gravely to the problems the war had brought them and offering advice and help wherever he could. As squire, he took his responsibilities seriously, and Hilary, watching and listening, remembered his words and decided that he was right. Managing the land, taking care of those who worked his inheritance, watching their families grow in the old traditions was a far better way to spend time than killing strangers, who almost certainly had their own families and gardens and even farms to tend. How had the world got into this state? she wondered. And how would they ever get out of it?

'It's a sad situation,' her father commented as they drove home. 'Land worked by old men and young girls barely out of school, while the able-bodied sons are learning to use machine guns and bayonets instead of ploughs and pitchforks. Upside down, the whole world.'

'But you're a soldier,' she said. 'I thought you'd expect all young men to want to join up and fight.'

'In times like these, yes, of course,' he answered with a touch of impatience. 'It's their duty, always has been. But in normal peace-time, we don't need 'em in the military, and we *do* need 'em on the land, and in the factories, places where hard work and loyalty are called for just as much. That's what keeps the country going. Makes Britain great.'

Hilary was silent for a moment. Then she said carefully, 'So you're happy for people to follow their own calling? Do what they believe they'll be best at?'

'Well, of course. Why shouldn't I be?'

'And Stephen? You'll let him follow his own path? You won't expect him to go into the army, like you and ... Baden?'

Her father turned and stared at her. 'Stephen? What does Stephen have to do with it? He's a Napier. Of *course* he will go into the army.'

The dinner party was to be held the next evening, and Hilary spent the day helping prepare for it. She was relieved to have Fenella there to assist Isobel in the house, arranging furniture, bringing cushions for the drawing room, laying the table and creating flower displays. Hilary could do all these things, of course, but she preferred to escape to the kitchen and join Dottie. Together they went out to the garden to pick fresh peas and pull up young carrots, and came back indoors to scrub new potatoes and wash lettuces. The tomatoes had just begun and Dottie had been ripening a few on the sunniest windowsill, and there were radishes, spring onions and cress.

'I remember growing this on a flannel at school,' Hilary said. 'We were so proud of our efforts and made everyone eat it in egg sandwiches.'

''Tis good for you,' Dottie said. 'I grow it myself, just like that. Adds a good peppery flavour, cress does.' She turned to Stephen, who was sitting at the kitchen table whittling a piece of wood with his penknife. 'If you'm going to be here in my kitchen, young man, you'd better make yourself useful. You can top and tail these gooseberries, and don't eat too many.' She slid the bowl across the table towards him.

'No, don't,' Hilary said. 'You'll be up half the night with stomach ache. Here's a pair of scissors.'

Stephen made a face but started willingly enough. Dottie had turned on the wireless and they listened to *Music While You Work*. She was also preparing lunch – a fairly scratch affair, by her standards, of toad in the hole and steamed jam pudding. There were a lot of eggs involved, but as she said, getting out the packet, dried egg was just as good for some recipes.

'It's all we get at school,' Stephen observed. 'Half of us have forgotten what a real egg looks like.'

'It's the nutrition that matters,' Hilary told him. 'Growing boys never stop eating; they can't expect fresh eggs all the time.'

'And a lot of the best food goes to the serving men,' Dottie added. 'They're the ones need it most. An army marches on its stomach, that's what they say, and a man spending the day fighting needs a good breakfast inside him.'

'So do men who don't fight. Anyway, I'm not going into the army. I want to be a pilot and fly Spitfires.'

Hilary looked at him. He had said this before but she hadn't taken him too seriously. Now, looking at his face, she began to wonder if he really meant it.

'You know Dad will want you to go into the army,' she said.

Stephen's face flushed. 'And what about what *I* want?'

Hilary sighed. He was wearing the set, mutinous expression that indicated that he didn't intend to give way. 'There's plenty of time anyway,' she said placatingly. 'You're only just about to start at Kelly College. You don't have to decide anything for at least five years.'

'I've decided now. And if the war's finished by the time I leave school, I want to go to Oxford. Or Cambridge, I don't mind which.'

'Well, yes, of course, but—'

'I want to do mathematics,' he said, and added, 'It'll be useful for when I'm a pilot.'

'Will it?' Hilary was momentarily diverted. 'I don't see ...' She brought herself back to the matter in hand. 'Look, Steve, don't you think it's best if you don't say anything to Dad about all this at present? You've got years at school, and by the time you leave, a lot of things might have changed. We're in the middle of a war and Dad's got an important job to do. There's no point in upsetting him now. Nothing can be decided until you're older, anyway.'

'Your sister's right,' Dottie said. She had been crumbling margarine, flour and sugar together in a big mixing bowl. 'No sense in meeting troubles halfway. You just get on with your school work and don't worry about what might or might not happen in five years' time.' She glanced at the bowl in front of him. 'What *I'm* worried about is what's to happen to all them gooseberries if they don't get topped and tailed in time for me to make this crumble. You've been holding those scissors up in the air for the past five minutes and not so much as crossed their blades.'

Stephen grinned and went back to his work. Hilary carried on scrubbing potatoes. 'It's a godsend having you here,' she said to Dottie. 'I don't know how my mother would manage without you.'

'Well, I'm not here that much when she's on her own,' Dottie said. 'She don't need much help then. Quite able to cook her meals, she is, and I just come up two or three times a week and do a bit of work about the place, washing and ironing mostly. And us makes jam together when the fruit's ripe, and do a bit of bottling, that kind of thing. We rub along together well enough.'

'I'm sure you do a lot, and with your work at the pub and making extras for George Sweet, it doesn't leave you much time to yourself. What always surprises me is that you didn't have an evacuee when they all came here early on.'

'Miss Forsyth said just the same thing. But it was tricky then. My old dad was poorly and we didn't really have room. After he passed on, they were starting to drift back to London. Some came back later, but they all had places to go to and I wasn't needed. So I just filled up my time working at whatever folk wanted me to do, and being in the WI. They could always find me a job.'

'I suppose so.' Hilary took down the big fish kettle, which had been waiting on a shelf. It had taken some time to find it, nobody having used it for some time, but it had finally been unearthed at the back of a cupboard, and Jacob's salmon would just fit inside. 'I'd better give this a good wash; it hasn't been used for years.' She took it over to the sink.

'So who be coming to this party then?' Dottie enquired. 'I know there's to be twelve at table, but Miss Fenella didn't know who'd been invited in the end.'

'It was quite a struggle to find people who could come,' Hilary admitted. 'So many are away, either in the services or in different parts of the country doing war work. And those who are at home can't afford to use their petrol ration. In the end, it came down mostly to local people. The Boultings are the furthest away, but they said they'd cycle over and change when they get here, so of course Mother said they must stay the night. They can use the yellow room, as it's near the bathroom. The others can walk. That's Dr Latimer and his wife, the vicar and Mrs Harvey and Miss Bellamy. It's a good job the weather's quite settled at the moment.'

Dottie finished making the crumble and took the bowl of gooseberries from Stephen. 'It'll be like old times, having a dinner party here. Just like old times.'

By lunchtime, the house was looking like a new pin, with bowls of fresh flowers to greet arrivals in the hall and posies placed along the centre of the big dining table. All the best porcelain plates and crystal glasses, seldom used in the past three years, had been brought out of sideboards and cupboards, and washed and polished until they gleamed, and the table itself had been rubbed with a chunk of Jacob Prout's own beeswax to a shine that looked like clear water. Hilary had had some difficulty in convincing her mother that it didn't matter that the candles were plain white wartime ones, but eventually she had accepted that smarter ones just weren't to be had, and that it was the food and the guests that mattered most.

'Everyone has to make sacrifices,' Hilary told her. 'Nobody's going to question a few candles.'

'You're right, of course. And they're really a very small sacrifice to make.' Isobel regarded the table she and Fenella had set. 'It all looks lovely. Thank you both very much for all your help.'

'It's been a pleasure,' Fenella said. 'I haven't been to a dinner party like this for years. I'm not sure I still know how to behave. You may laugh, Isobel darling, but remember how long I've spent pigging it with soldiers in the desert. Half the time we don't even have plates, just mess tins to eat from.'

Hilary laughed. 'I'm sure they find you a plate, Fenella. Anyway, you're entertained by the officers, not the men.'

'Don't be too sure. I like to meet those who are doing the real fighting. Not that the officers don't fight as well, of course, but ...' She sighed. 'It really is a different world out there. I'm glad we make sacrifices at home too. It wouldn't be at all right, to live like this all the time while they're giving up so much.'

'Where's Father now?' Hilary asked. 'I haven't seen him all morning.'

'He had to go into Plymouth,' her mother answered vaguely. 'He caught the train soon after breakfast. Some business or other – he didn't say much about it. He's having lunch there, which is convenient because we can just scratch something together for ourselves. Now, are you sure the yellow room is ready for the Boultings? It's intrepid of them to cycle over; we must make them comfortable.'

'They'll be so comfortable they won't want to go home,' Hilary said. 'Dottie has surpassed herself – flowers on the dressing table, the best sheets and eiderdown, and suspiciously new-looking feather pillows. I can't think where she got those from.'

'They *are* new,' Isobel said. 'At least they were before the war, and they've never been used. I bought them in Dingle's when we were refurbishing Baden's room, but then ...' Her voice trailed away and Hilary reached out to touch her arm.

'I'm sure he'd be pleased to know they were being used now. Julian Boulting was one of his best friends and he stayed with them quite a few times.'

'Yes, that's what I thought. Not that they'll know, of course! Anyway, they should be here soon after three – they said they'd arrive in time for tea so that they could settle in and relax before the others come. It will give us time for a chat on our own, too. Although I'll have to be in the kitchen some of the time, of course.' She sighed. 'Everything is so different these days.'

'No you won't,' Hilary said. 'Fenella and I will help Dottie, and you know what they say about too many cooks. You and Father enjoy the time with your friends, and just treat us like servants!'

'Hilary, really!' Isobel laughed and shook her head. 'As if I would. But if you're both sure ... It does seem to be rather taking advantage, when Fenella is a guest too.'

'We're quite sure,' Fenella said firmly. 'And haven't you always said I'm to think of myself as one of the family? I can't be a guest as well! Anyway, I'm here for much longer than your dinner guests, so I will fade gracefully into the background and leave you to enjoy them.'

'As if you could ever fade into the background,' Hilary commented. 'But we mustn't stand here gassing. We'd better have our lunch or people will be arriving before we've had a chance to get ourselves ready. Dottie's made us toad in the hole and I suggest we have it on the terrace, since the kitchen table's full of things being prepared for dinner, not to mention fresh scones being made for tea. You two go on out and I'll round up Steve to help me bring out a couple of trays.'

They all agreed later that the dinner party was as successful as any that had been held pre-war. The rabbit terrine was tasty and substantial enough to contrast with the creamy flesh of the freshly caught salmon, and the gooseberry crumble added a tartness that was offset by the rich clotted cream Alice Tozer had provided. Although it was intended mostly for the gentlemen, the ladies all had a small portion as well, and professed themselves delighted to share their chocolate mousse in return. (Stephen had two helpings of everything, explaining that his sister had told him that growing boys needed to eat a lot.) The meal was accompanied by bottles of Gilbert Napier's finest wines, laid down before the war began, and there was to be port for the men afterwards, when the ladies had returned to the drawing room.

Just as this moment had been reached, however, and after several toasts had been drunk, Gilbert held up his hand for attention. The chatter fell silent as they all turned towards him.

'I have something to tell you,' he said. 'It's a family thing really, but since the details were only finalised today and no one else knows about it – apart, of course, from Isobel – I thought I might as well announce it now.' He waited a moment as they all stared at him, wondering what he was about to say, and Hilary felt a knot half of anxiety and half of excitement clench her stomach. Was it something to do with the war? Another promotion, perhaps? She glanced at her mother, wondering how she had remained so calm throughout the meal with such knowledge – whatever it might be – hanging over her.

'I know,' Gilbert continued, 'that a number of people have had to move out of their homes for the duration – people with large houses such as this one that have been requisitioned for war use as military headquarters or hospitals. Some are now highly secret establishments and very few people know what goes on there. We all understand that this is essential for the conduct of the war, but none of us really enjoys having to give up our home, not knowing how or when it will be returned to us.'

Hilary glanced again at her mother. Isobel's face was still calm, although a little paler. Hilary felt a spurt of annoyance that nothing had been mentioned to her before this. As their only daughter, couldn't she have been told before people who were, after all, no more than friends and neighbours?

'You can probably all guess what I am about to say,' Gilbert went on. 'It looked for some time as if Burracombe Barton would for some reason – and not because of any influence I myself might have had, which of course I would not have used even if it had been possible – escape this fate. I have no idea why. Perhaps it was just thought to be in the wrong place, with so many large houses available in Plymouth – although since the Blitz flattened the city, they must clearly be seen as less suitable. But now ...' Thank goodness, Hilary thought, he's getting to the point at last. '... now it seems that the powers that be have noticed us and decided that the Barton does, after all, have a purpose to fulfil.' He paused – he'd always been one to delight in making announcements, Hilary thought resignedly – and took a deep breath.

'From the beginning of next month,' he said, 'Burracombe Barton will become a children's home. Children from families that have been torn apart by the war – most of them orphans whose parents have been killed either by bombing or in the service of their country – will find new lives in the countryside. Isobel and I hope that they will be welcomed warmly and given the peace and tranquillity they need to grow up in the way that our own children' – his voice wavered a little, and Hilary knew he was thinking of Baden – 'have grown up here. Strong, healthy and happy, and ready to serve in their turn, in whatever capacity they are called upon to fulfil.'

He sat down and there was a moment's silence before the babble of talk, questions and comments burst out. And Hilary, meeting her mother's eye, felt her irritation ebb away. She knew that Isobel would face this disruption – for she would surely have to move to one of the estate cottages – with equanimity and treat it as just another part of her own war work. And how could Hilary herself, who was not even here most of the time, begrudge such children time in the home and the village where she had known a happy and secure childhood?

Poor little scraps, she thought, trying to imagine what they had suffered – their homes bombed, their parents killed, everything they knew and loved torn away from them – and visualising their bewildered and unhappy faces. How could little ones who had endured all this ever forget, ever learn to laugh and play again as children should? How could they ever live normal, happy lives again when their childhood had been so horribly disrupted?

Yes, she thought. Yes, indeed. They can come to Burracombe and live at the Barton and be children again. And welcome.

Part Four

Chapter Twenty-One

Winchester, July 1943

STELLA

'Come in, Stella, and sit down. It's all right – you're not in any trouble.' Dorothy Marsh smiled kindly at the child she had grown especially fond of during the past few months. As matron of the children's home, she was not supposed to have favourites, and tried her best not to, but you couldn't help taking more to some children than others, and in Stella Simmons she had found a spark of spirit that appealed to her. With the right sort of opportunity, this child could turn into a very special young woman, she thought. And the chance that was being offered her now might well prove to be just the one she needed.

Stella did as she was told. She liked Matron, and under her care she had begun to learn acceptance of her present life. The rebellious anger she had felt at first had quietened, but she was still determined to find her sister Muriel one day, even though she understood that nothing could be done until they were both much older and able to decide their own lives. The years that lay between still stretched ahead like an empty wasteland – they would never regain their lost childhood sisterhood – but one day, she knew, they would be together again.

Dorothy Marsh, however, had helped her to see that the years need not be wasted. Quietly but firmly, she had encouraged Stella to use her intelligence, to do well in her school work, and to develop the gentler side of her character, bringing out the patience and nurturing nature that was evident in Stella's love and anxiety for her younger sister. Here in the making was a fine teacher, or perhaps a nurse, and Dorothy did not intend to let such good material be lost in resentment and anger.

Now, looking at the child who had already, in the few months she had been in the children's home, begun to develop the coltish, long-legged look of a child on the edge of her teens, she felt a sadness that she was not to be able to offer guidance for much longer.

'I have some news for you, my dear,' she began. 'I hope you will think it good news – I certainly do. I believe it to be an excellent opportunity for you and one that you should take eagerly.'

She paused. Already Stella's eyes had taken on a wary look, and it was not surprising, for not many excellent opportunities had come the child's way so far. She went on.

'I know how much all the children here would like to belong to a family again. I'm sure you feel that too. However hard we try to make the home a family, it can't ever be the same. I understand that.' She paused again. Stella's eyes remained expressionless and she plunged on. 'But sometimes the chance does arise for a child to have a family again. To be part of one, with a mother and father who care as a mother and father should. And I'm very happy to tell you, Stella, my dear—'

Stella broke in, rather more rudely than Dorothy liked, but she let it pass without reproof. 'My mother and father are dead. I can't ever have a family again, not like that.'

'I know, my dear. Not exactly like that, it's true. But you can have two people who want to be as a father and mother to you, who want a child to live with them and love them and to be looked after by them. It's the next best thing, Stella, and it's a chance not many children ever have.'

There was a brief pause. Then Stella said, 'Do you mean there is someone who wants *me*?'

'Yes,' Dorothy said with relief. 'That's exactly what I mean.'

The pause was longer this time. Eventually Stella said slowly, 'But they haven't even seen me. How do they know it's me they want?'

'They have seen you, my dear. They've been here three times, walking in the grounds, watching you and other children playing games, talking to the staff and to me. It really is you they want.'

'They've been watching me? *Spying* on me?'

'No, not at all!' But Dorothy found it difficult to explain the difference – if indeed there really was any difference – to the bewildered child in front of her. 'They just came to see the children and they looked at everyone and picked out you. They want you for their little girl, Stella. They really do.'

Stella was silent for a moment. Then she said, 'Would they have Muriel as well?'

Dorothy Marsh sighed. However hard she tried – however hard anyone could try – Stella was never going to understand why it was thought best for her and her sister to be parted, not even to know where the other was. And it was harder for Dorothy than for most people in her position, because she did not, in her heart of hearts, believe that it was the right thing to do. She felt pity well up in her for the two sisters, wrenched apart for no better reason than that they were now orphans, and wondered yet again who had decided that this was right, and what possible grounds they had for such a decision.

But as a matron, she had no say in the matter. Stella had been brought to her care and she knew no more about what had happened to Muriel than did Stella herself.

'I'm afraid not, my dear,' she said gently. 'We don't know where Muriel is, do we? And she may well have been adopted herself by now.'

Stella stared at her. 'You mean she might have a new mother and father – not real ones, but people who wanted her like these people want me? She might not be in a children's home any more? She might have gone to live somewhere else? She might even have a different name?'

'Well – yes. It's quite possible. And wouldn't you be pleased to think that had happened, Stella? To think of her happy and safe, in a family, with people who love her and want to look after her? Just as you could be, with Mr and Mrs—'

Stella burst into tears. Her face turned scarlet and she brought clenched fists up to her mouth. For a few moments she sobbed as if the woes of the world lay on her shoulders, and then she raised her streaming eyes to look directly at the woman behind the desk.

'But if they change our names, we shall never find each other. I promised to look after my sister and now I'll never see her again!'

'I think she's coming round to the idea now,' Dorothy Marsh said to the couple who sat opposite her. 'She was very distressed at first to think that it was another step further away from finding her sister again, but I've explained to her that it would be very unlikely anyway. It's so difficult to trace children who have been parted in this way, and in wartime the difficulties are even greater. She's an intelligent child and I think she understands, although there's still a small part of her that hopes they will come together again one day. And I'm sure she would be happier in a family environment. Any child would be. Whatever care we give the children here, we can never give them what people like yourselves can offer.'

Mr and Mrs Lacock looked at each other. Dorothy knew little about them, other than that they were from a village near Winchester, and that he was a chief cashier in a bank. He looked almost like a pin man, tall and thin with a round head and black hair that fitted his head like a skullcap. He must, she thought, be in his forties to have escaped military service, although his wife looked younger and was, in contrast, small and pretty, with curling brown hair and a plump, smiling face. They had never had children of their own and seemed to have given up hope of ever having any.

'It might be better to look for another child,' Mr Lacock said doubtfully. 'If Stella's not going to settle with us ... We don't want to find ourselves with a child who might be troublesome.'

'No guarantees can be given with any child,' Dorothy said a little stiffly. 'You have to remember that every child here has its own particular tragedy. They've all been orphaned one way or another, and in wartime it's likely to have been especially violent. And Stella is by no means the only child to have lost a brother or sister – indeed, some have lost more than one, either by separation or by death.'

'But children get over these things, don't they?' Mrs Lacock said hopefully. 'People always say how resilient they are. And Stella's looked happy enough when we've seen her playing. She seems so good with the younger ones, too.'

'Yes, she has shown a very caring and responsible side, which I had hoped to nurture if she had been staying with us. I believe she could make a very fine teacher.'

Mrs Lacock looked at her husband again. 'We'd like that, wouldn't we? A daughter to be proud of. Or she might even decide to work in the bank.'

'She certainly has the intelligence,' Dorothy Marsh said. 'Her education has been rather disrupted and held up, but she's catching up fast, and once she settles down, I think you would find her an easy child to bring up. She's never shown any signs of being troublesome here.' She hesitated. 'Would you be considering taking on another child, at a later date, or do you prefer to have just the one?'

'Just the one,' Mr Lacock said firmly, before his wife could speak. 'If we take a child on at all, we would want to do the best we can for it.'

'Yes,' Mrs Lacock added, a little less positively. 'Although a second child doesn't cost so much as the first, does it – not so many clothes or toys, you know. Not that there are any toys available at present,' she added with a sigh. 'But I have some of my own dolls and books and so on that I've kept, so—'

'We can provide perfectly well,' her husband broke in. 'Stella will not want for anything if she comes to us.'

'That's very kind of you,' Dorothy said, thinking that the only thing Stella would ever really want was her own sister. But there was nothing to be done about that. 'So can I take it that you've made your decision?'

Again husband and wife looked at each other. Celia Lacock's hands were clasped and her eyes full of eager pleading, while the expression on her husband's thin face was less easy to read. But he must be as willing as she, Dorothy thought, to have come this far in the process.

'You don't have to take the final step just yet,' she said. 'As you know, we prefer that you foster the child for some time before legally adopting her. The process takes a little while anyway, and it's in Stella's interests that we make sure she will be happy with you. As I'm sure she will be,' she added hastily as Mrs Lacock's mouth opened in protest. 'But if you are willing to take her on those terms, she can come to you almost immediately. You'll need to meet her, of course, so that you can get to know her a little first. After all, you've only seen her from afar, so to speak, and Stella has never seen you at all.'

'Could we do that this afternoon?' William Lacock asked, and Celia chimed in eagerly. 'Oh yes! Could we meet her now? Just to ... to say hello?'

'You can indeed.' Dorothy Marsh smiled in relief. For a few moments she had felt doubtful about the strength of William Lacock's wish to adopt any child at all, but perhaps it was simply that he was a man who didn't easily display his feelings. There was certainly no doubt about his wife's desire.

'The children will be coming in for tea about now,' she said as a bell rang somewhere in the building. 'Those of school age go to the village school, but as you probably know, most of the children only go for half the day with so many evacuees to accommodate as well as the village children themselves. Ours go in the mornings, so they have games in the afternoon and then some extra lessons after tea with our older girls. Stella can have tea here in my office with you, and then she can be excused afternoon lessons so that you can have more time together. Perhaps you could go for a walk.'

She left the office and the Lacocks looked at each other again.

'I hope we're doing the right thing,' William said slowly. 'A child with problems that we can never hope to solve ... It's a lot to take on, Celia. We'll never be able to give her back her sister.'

'I know. But we can give her so much else. A settled, happy home. You know how much I've always longed for a child, William. We both have. And to be given a daughter we can be proud of – it's such a wonderful opportunity.'

'Yes,' he said. 'Yes, I think it may be. But only to foster for a start. We'll take it a step at a time. We'll make no irrevocable decisions until we can be absolutely sure. For the child's sake as much as for our own.'

She clasped her hands again and looked at him with shining eyes.

'I quite understand, William. But it will all turn out splendidly, I know it will. And – I think I hear her coming now.' She stood up and took a step forward. 'Oh, *William* ...'

Footsteps sounded along the corridor and the door opened. Dorothy Marsh walked in smiling, and behind her came the girl the Lacocks had picked out from all the other children as they'd watched them playing. She stood in the doorway, uncertain, cautious and a little suspicious.

Celia Lacock moved quickly towards her, both hands held out.

'Stella! My dear, I'm so very pleased to meet you. I'm Mrs Lacock and this is my husband, and we both want you – we want you *very* much – to come and live with us. Do you think you'd like that? Do you think you could be our little girl?'

Chapter Twenty-Two

'I know it may seem very strange at first,' Dorothy Marsh told Stella before she went to stay with them for the first weekend. 'It won't be easy to think of them as your mother and father, but if – *when* – the adoption process goes through, that's what they will be, in law. And I'm sure they'd like you to call them Mummy and Daddy.'

Stella looked at her. 'I can't call them that. I had a proper mummy and daddy. Can't I call them something else?'

'Well, I suppose there are other names you could use. Mum and Dad, perhaps, or Mama and Papa, though that sounds a little old-fashioned. Or you could call them Mother and Father, but that sounds rather too formal, don't you think? Perhaps you can settle on a name between you, when you get to know each other better.'

The idea of anyone having to get to know their mother and father seemed very peculiar to Stella. You knew them as soon as you were born, didn't you? You didn't have to get to know them, as if they were strangers. But then, Mr and Mrs Lacock *were* strangers.

She said goodbye to the other children after school on the Friday and went off with Mrs Lacock, carrying the small suitcase Matron had lent her. She would be back on Sunday evening so didn't need much, and if this weekend went well there would be two or three more before she finally moved in as their foster daughter, while the adoption process began. In a few months, she would legally be their daughter.

And I won't be Stella Simmons any more, she thought as Celia led her along the quiet street towards the house. I'll be Stella Lacock. How is Muriel ever going to find me? And suppose she's adopted and has a new name too? Hopelessness descended upon her and she walked in silent misery beside her foster mother.

It had been a long way on the bus and Celia said that her husband would be home soon, so they must hurry as he liked to have a cup of tea as soon as he came in, and before that she wanted to show Stella her new bedroom.

'It will be lovely for you to have a room to yourself again, after sleeping in a dormitory,' she said, fitting her key into the lock. 'I expect you're looking forward to that.'

'I've never had a room to myself,' Stella said. 'I've always shared with my sister.'

Celia looked at her doubtfully. Miss Marsh had told her that it was best not to let Stella dwell on thoughts of her sister, but Celia, who had a sister of her own, could not imagine ever being able to forget such a person. She said, 'Well, come in, dear, and let's take your case straight upstairs. Your— Mr Lacock will be in soon and he'll want to see you settled in.'

It seemed that she felt as awkward as Stella did about their new relationship. She turned and led the way upstairs, Stella following.

The stairs went up from the front door, with a passage running beside them to other rooms whose doors were closed. At the top was a landing with four doors leading off it. Celia opened the first.

'This is your bedroom, Stella. I hope you like it. It's not been redecorated, I'm afraid, because we can't get wallpaper or paint just now, but I've made some new curtains from our old sitting-room ones, and I made the rag rug last winter to cheer it up. There's a little wardrobe, see, where you can hang your frocks, and a chest of drawers for your other clothes.' She was speaking rather quickly, almost as if she were nervous. 'Now, the bathroom is that door there, so you can wash your face and hands, and then you can un-pack. Come downstairs as soon as you're ready.' She put the little case on a chair, closed the door behind her and left Stella alone.

Stella stood beside the narrow bed and looked around. It was a small room and the bed was pushed against one wall to give space for a little cupboard beside the head. There was a table lamp on the cupboard and a pile of half a dozen books, mostly school stories by Enid Blyton and Angela Brazil, and one called *Swallows and Amazons* that looked more interesting because it seemed to be about children on holiday doing things without adults, rather than being cooped up in a boarding school, which wasn't very different from a children's home. Stella looked through its pages and put it back down.

On top of the chest of drawers she saw a pile of boxes containing jigsaw puzzles and a game of Ludo, with a cluster of dolls sitting beside them. Stella wasn't much interested in dolls, but she took one down and looked at it. It reminded her of her sister Muriel's doll, Princess Marcia, lost in the bombing, and as she stared at it, she was swept by a wave of memories: of that terrible night; of all the anxious days that had followed it while she and her sister and mother shared a small corner of a crowded church hall, waiting to be rehoused; of the small, dingy house they had been allocated in October Street and the kindness of neighbours like Jess Budd who had come to help clean it and make it fit to live in; and most of all, of the mother and baby brother killed in another raid a few months later, and the father who had been lost at sea.

And of course she was reminded yet again of Muriel, never far from her thoughts – the little sister taken away from her and sent to live with strangers, the little sister who might be thinking of her, crying for her, at this very moment.

Stella sat down on the bed. She cradled the doll against her and the tears poured down her cheeks as she rocked back and forth, lost in the grief she had never until now allowed to overwhelm her; lost in the memories that only one person in all the world could share with her, and that person as lost to her as the family that had been taken from them both.

'I couldn't pacify her at all,' Celia told her husband later that evening when Stella had finally been persuaded to go to bed. 'She didn't stop crying for hours and she didn't seem to be able to tell me what the matter was. It broke my heart to see her so upset and not be able to comfort her. And she didn't eat a bite of supper.'

William Lacock shook his head. 'I don't understand it. You'd think a child in her position would be grateful for a nice home like ours with a room of her own. Don't you have any idea what set her off?'

'None at all,' Celia said with a sigh. Her round face was puckered with distress, and she looked as if she were about to burst into tears herself. 'She was just sitting on the bed, clutching one of my dolls and sobbing her little heart out. I did everything I could to find out – sat beside her, put my arms around her, tried to talk to her – but it was almost as if she didn't know I was there. I've never seen anything like it. I just hope she's better in the morning. And I'd got so many nice plans for the weekend, too. It's such a shame.'

He looked solemn. 'It looks as though Miss Marsh wasn't entirely honest with us. She should have told us the child was unstable. I made it quite clear that we couldn't take on a child who might be troublesome, and she assured us that Stella was a sensible, intelligent girl who would be no bother.'

'She's not being *troublesome*,' Celia said defensively. 'Just very upset about something. Once we've found out what it is, we'll be able to put it right, I'm sure. It may be something that happened in the home, before we left. Miss Marsh may not even know about it – you know what children are like between themselves. Nobody can keep an eye on them all the time.'

'I hope you're right,' he said, picking up the evening paper. 'I can't have this kind of disruption every night when I come home from work. I need some peace and quiet. And don't forget I have Home Guard twice a week – it's going to put a lot more work on your shoulders if Stella turns out to be a difficult child.'

'That's all right. I don't mind the work. I just want Stella to be happy.' She looked at him earnestly. 'I've always wanted us to have a child, William – to be a proper family. And now, at last, we have the opportunity. Stella's a lovely girl, just the sort I've always wanted, and I'm going to do my best to be a second mother to her, and give her the childhood she deserves. And I know you feel the same in your heart of hearts – don't you?'

William's thin face softened. He reached out and patted her hand.

'Of course I do, my dear. And if anyone can be a mother to her, you can. I just wish I could be as good a father – but I must admit I feel somewhat out of my depth at present.'

Celia laughed. 'That's because you're a man, William! You'll be a good father once you've got used to having her about. I know you will. You've a kind heart, and that's all that's needed.'

Nobody, not even little girls who have lost all their family, can cry for ever, and Stella woke next morning with puffy eyes and a headache but no more tears. She lay for a while in her bed, letting her gaze move slowly round the room with its wallpaper of brown flowers on a cream background, its blackout curtains and the dolls sitting on the chest of drawers. She was quite able to recognise the effort that Celia had put into making the room welcoming, and felt ashamed of her behaviour last night. Matron – Miss Marsh – had impressed upon her that the Lacocks were kind people who wanted to treat her as their own daughter, and that she was very lucky to be given such a chance. 'I know that you still think about your sister and want her back,' she had said. 'But you really do have to understand that that isn't likely to happen. All you can hope for is that she is happy – perhaps being adopted as someone else's daughter and looked after as your own mother would have looked after you both. And I'm sure that's what is happening. Wish her happiness, Stella, my dear, and try to let her go.'

Stella had tried, but it wasn't easy. It was like climbing an endless flight of very steep stairs, and she felt that last night had pushed her back almost to the bottom. But – and as she thought of this, the surprising thought came – she wasn't quite at the bottom. She was still a little bit higher – just a few steps – than she had been on that terrible day when she and Muriel had been separated. So perhaps she could start to climb once more, and perhaps if she fell again she would still be a little nearer the top, wherever and whatever that was.

She heard a light tap on the door and turned her head to see it open and Celia's face peer anxiously into the room.

'Oh, you're awake!' The plump little woman came in and looked down at her with a face full of concern. 'How are you now, my dear? Did you have a good sleep? Are you feeling better?'

'Yes, thank you,' Stella said politely, struggling to sit up. Celia went to open the dark curtains, letting in a flood of sunlight, and turned to smile at her, and Stella felt ashamed again. 'I'm sorry I cried.'

'My dear, you mustn't be sorry!' Celia came quickly back to the bedside and took Stella's hand. She sat down on the edge of the bed. 'Something upset you, and when you feel ready to tell me what it was, I'll see if I can help you with it. But for now, I'm just worried that you must be very hungry. You didn't touch the supper I brought for you. Now, why don't you get up and have a nice wash, and then come downstairs. I've got an egg for you! You do like eggs, don't you?'

'Yes, thank you.' Stella hesitated. 'Will – will Mr Lacock be there?'

Celia shook her head. 'No, he goes to the bank on Saturday mornings, but they close at lunchtime and he says if we go to meet him, he'll take us out to lunch. Won't that be nice! There's a Lyons in town and we're to be there at one, so we can have the morning to ourselves and you can tell me all the things you like to do. Sewing, perhaps – do you like that? Or we might make a cake together. Anyway, we'll talk about it over breakfast. There's Weetabix as well. Do you like it with hot milk or cold?'

She got up, paused for a moment, then bent and kissed Stella's cheek. Stella could smell her face powder and the faint scent of roses. She tried to remember when anyone had last kissed her, and felt tears threaten again but pushed them away.

Celia opened the door and paused, looking back at Stella's face.

'It's so lovely to have you here, Stella,' she said quietly. 'I've wanted a daughter for such a long time. Be happy with us. That's all we want – for you to be happy.'

It was just a few weeks later when Stella went to live with Mr and Mrs Lacock.

She was still being fostered, rather than adopted. It took several months for that to happen, Miss Marsh had told her, and everyone had to be quite sure. Celia Lacock was quite sure already – had been right from the start, she told Stella, enveloping her in a rose-scented hug as soon as she was inside the front door – and William Lacock also seemed sure, in his more reserved way, as he took Stella's hand and bent his long, thin body to give her a kiss. She went upstairs to the now familiar bedroom and unpacked her small case for what was expected to be the last time. There was little in it: a few school exercise books, which she could take to her new school for the teachers to see her work; some of her sewing and other bits and pieces made in handcraft classes; and two or three books that she had brought from the Bridge End vicarage. One had been given her by Mr Beckett himself, as a parting gift – a copy of one of the Romany books, which she had always enjoyed reading. He'd written a short note in it, encouraging her love of nature, and she put it on the shelf with Celia's collection.

Over the weekend visits, Celia had put together a small wardrobe of clothes for Stella to wear when she was staying, and now they were hers to wear all the time. She was wearing one of the frocks now, since she had had to leave behind the blue dress that all the girls wore at the home. It was a warm woollen dress, dark green, and although it had been made for a bigger girl, Celia had altered it so that it fitted quite well. Celia was a good needlewoman, although not up to Jess Budd's standards, and had managed to acquire several garments to adapt for Stella.

'And now that we'll have your clothing coupons, we'll be able to buy you some more,' she told Stella as the three of them sat at the tea table later. 'You'll enjoy having some nice things of your own, after having to wear uniform all this time.'

Stella had to admit that this was true. It was nice to have a different frock to wear, or the plaid skirt Celia had made from one of her own, with a jersey she had been knitting all these weeks from wool Stella had unravelled herself from an old cardigan. They had spent several evenings over the past few weekends working on these together, and although Stella wasn't especially interested in sewing, she had come to enjoy the hours after tea, with the curtains drawn over the ugly blackout, the fire alight and the wireless on. Mr Lacock – she still couldn't bring herself to call him Dad, or even Father – would be sitting in his big armchair, smoking a pipe and reading the newspaper, and Algy, the black and white cat, would be curled up on the rug, fast asleep.

Sometimes the whole evening would be spent like this, until Celia made a cup of cocoa and Stella went to bed, though at other times Mr Lacock would put his paper aside and get out a pack of cards and they would play rummy or sevens. Once or twice Stella brought down one of the jigsaw puzzles and she and Celia would work on it on a tray on the dining table.

It was just as a family should be, Stella thought, and knew that she was lucky to have been found and accepted as the Lacocks' foster daughter. And, quite soon now, their adopted daughter, which was as near to being a real family as it was possible to get.

She still didn't quite know if this was what she wanted. Nobody had asked her opinion, and if they did, she would be expected to say yes, and be grateful. And I *am* grateful, she thought as Celia put a bowl of jelly with pink blancmange in front of her – a Sunday tea-time treat usually, but made specially because this was her first evening actually living with them. She knew how lucky she was. She could be living in the children's home until she was nearly grown up, and then have to leave and make her own way in the world. Mr and Mrs Lacock – Mum and Dad? – would be here for years and years, and she could stay with them for ever if she wanted to.

She knew she was fortunate to have found such a kind home. But it didn't stop her longing for her lost sister when she went to bed. It didn't stop her adding, when she knelt to say her prayers, a heartfelt plea to find Muriel again one day. It didn't stop her believing that, one day, she would do just that.

Chapter Twenty-Three

'It will be Christmas in a month,' Celia said as she and Stella did the shopping one Saturday morning. 'I thought we would make our cake this afternoon. Your father has some brandy in his cupboard, so we can put some of that in, and it will keep well. You like Christmas cake, don't you?'

Stella nodded. The last time she had eaten Christmas cake was at the vicarage. Mrs Mudge had made it, and two Christmas puddings, with the extra allowance of fruit that the government had announced. Stella and Muriel had helped her by washing the fruit and piling it into a bowl to be soaked in the brandy that Mr Beckett had produced. He must have had it for just that purpose, she thought, since none of the children had ever seen him drink it. There was no icing, of course, because that wasn't allowed these days, but Mrs Mudge had ground some ordinary sugar as fine as she could and made butter icing to go on top. It was a bit crunchy but none the worse for that – in fact Keith Budd, who had gone home for Christmas but had a slice kept back for him, had said he liked it better.

She stood in the queue with Celia, waiting for their turn to be served by the grocer. It took a long time because he had to get every item on each customer's list in turn, add up the prices and cut out all the coupons from the ration books with his scissors. You could easily be there for an hour before you even reached the counter, and when you finally had everything on the list – or everything the grocer had in stock, for there were nearly always a few items he couldn't supply – you still had to go to the greengrocer, the butcher, the baker, the dairy and often two or three other shops as well. It was no good getting impatient, Celia said. It was the same for everyone, and you couldn't even shop with another grocer because you had to be registered with one and buy all your wants from him.

This morning the queue was even longer than usual and Stella offered to go to some of the other shops. Celia looked at her gratefully and gave her a second list – she had one for each of the shops she needed to visit – and some money.

'A cottage loaf if you can get one, and a Coburg if you can't. Then go to the greengrocer's for vegetables. I'll probably catch you up there and we can go to the butcher's together.' As Stella passed the rest of the queue on her way out, she heard Celia telling the other customers what a good girl she was, and how nice to have about the house.

She ran off along the road. Standing on the corner before the rest of the shops was a small group of boys she recognised from school. They were in their last year at the junior school, bigger and older than Stella but in a C class, which meant they would probably go to the secondary modern school rather than the grammar where Stella was expected to go. As she drew nearer, they stepped out and formed a line across the pavement.

'You're that orphanage kid the posh people in Oak Tree Crescent have took in,' one of them announced.

'Went straight into 4A,' added another. 'My dad says it's because the old man's a bank manager and got money. My dad says it's not fair.'

'Mine does too,' the first said. He was a big boy with straggly ginger hair and a pale face smothered with freckles. 'So what are you doing out on your own, then? Don't they want you round the house no more?'

Stella made to step off the pavement to pass them, but they moved out to bar her way. She tried to slip through the gap nearer the wall, but they moved back. Unable to pass, she stopped and faced them. They drew nearer.

'Get out of the way,' she said angrily. 'I've got shopping to do.'

'Shopping, eh?' A third boy lunged forward and grabbed the shopping bag Celia had given Stella. 'Empty. So that means you still got the money, yeah?'

Stella stared at them. The money was in her own purse now, a bag crocheted by Celia on a long strap, which was slung from one shoulder. Automatically she put her hand on the bag and gripped the strap, and the boys laughed.

'See? It's in that stupid knitted bag.' The ginger boy came nearer and pushed his face close to Stella's. 'Give it me.'

'No!' Stella backed away, but the other boys were crowding round her. 'Let me go!'

'We'll let you go when you've give us the money.' He was even closer now, and the others were jostling her.

She felt her heart thump and panic began to rise inside. 'Stop doing that! Let me go!'

Hands were grabbing at her bag, pulling at the strap. Furious as well as frightened, Stella twisted away and lashed out with one foot. She felt it connect with a shin and heard a howl of pain and rage. One of the boys grasped her shoulder and pulled her roughly, and the bag was torn away.

'Give that back! *Give it back!*' she yelled, temper overcoming her panic. She kicked out again and lashed wildly with her fists. One landed somewhere, she had no idea where, but again there was a cry of outrage. All the boys were shouting now, with Ginger bawling orders and Stella being pulled in all directions and punched by rough fists. Her screams were more of fury than of fear, but she knew that the boys were too much for her and she would inevitably be beaten. But not without a fight, she told herself, and kicked out again.

'Stella! *Stella!* Is that you? For heaven's sake, what's going on?' The voice cut through the hubbub and at the same time two hands grasped the two nearest boys by the shoulders and wrenched them apart. The others dropped their fists and stepped back, then glanced at each other and scuttled away.

There was a sudden silence. Ginger and his one remaining accomplice, still in the grip of their captor, tried to twist out of his grasp but found themselves held too firmly. They began to change tack.

'We never meant no harm,' Ginger whined. 'It was only a bit of fun. We knows her from school, see, and she told us to meet her here and if her old woman give her any money for shopping she'd give us half. Honest, that's what she said. Only when it come to it she wouldn't hand it over so we—'

'All right.' William Lacock glared at them. 'You needn't bother to say any more. I can see you're lying. I'll be coming to your school to see your headmaster on Monday, and I dare say he'll know how to deal with you. You can tell your friends the same thing. And think yourselves lucky – if anything like this happens again, you'll find yourselves at the police station. Is that understood?'

The bullies nodded and slunk away, and Stella and her rescuer looked at each other.

'Are you all right, Stella?' he asked. 'Did they hurt you at all?'

Stella shook her head. 'A bit, but not much.' Her voice was shaky. 'Anyway, I think I hurt them too. But ... but they took my bag that Mum made me, with the shopping money in!' Suddenly overcome by shock and misery, she burst into tears and flung herself into his arms. 'Oh, *Daddy* – they took my bag!'

The Lacocks took Stella home together. Celia had come round the corner just in time to see her foster daughter crying in her husband's arms, and after a moment of shock, she hurried forward.

'What's happened? Stella, are you all right? William ...?'

'It's all right, my dear. Stella's not hurt.' He drew back a little so that Celia could take Stella in her own arms. 'But she's very upset. I found some boys bullying her – I've sent them packing and told them I'll be going to the school first thing on Monday morning to see their headmaster. They won't touch her again.'

'Your frock's torn,' Celia exclaimed. 'And that's a bruise coming on your cheek – and look, your leg's all grazed. Oh, you poor little dear. What did they do to you?'

'They took my bag,' Stella said, beginning to cry again. 'The bag you made me. And it had the shopping money in it. Oh, Mum, I'm sorry. I tried to stop them, but—'

'There were too many for her,' William interrupted. 'Bigger boys, rough ones.' He drew his dark brows together and added angrily, 'I told them that if it happened again I'd take them to the police station. I wish I'd done that today. Well, the headmaster will be in no doubt about my feelings, I can tell you that. If I have my way, those boys will be thrashed within an inch of their lives.'

'Come along, my dear,' Celia said to Stella. 'Let's get you home. Once you've had a nice wash – a bath, if you like – and put on a clean frock, you'll feel better. I'll put some Germolene on that bruise and those grazes. We'll light the fire early and you can sit by it with your new library book.'

'But my bag – and the money. And I never did the shopping. There's the bread to get, and the vegetables, and you were going to the butcher, and all the nicest things will be gone, and—'

'It doesn't matter. I can come out again after dinner and finish it.' Stella was quite right, the best meat and vegetables would have been sold by then, and there would be no chance of a cottage loaf, and probably no Coburgs either, but none of that mattered. 'The main thing is to get you home and in the warm. Why, you're shivering.' The three of them began to walk. 'And don't worry about the money, Stella. It's a shame about your bag but I can make you a new one. You can help me; we'll start this afternoon. Making the cake can wait until tomorrow.' She gave Stella an anxious glance. 'You're sure you're not hurt any more than the bruise and grazes? I wonder if we should take you to the doctor.'

'Let's see how she is when she's had a bath and a rest,' William said. 'I'm sure she'll feel better then, won't you, Stella?'

Stella, walking between them with a hand held by each, looked up at him and nodded. For the first time, she noticed how kind his brown eyes were. She was hardly aware that she had at last called him Daddy, but she knew that something had changed between them and she felt warmed by it. He had come to her rescue, and she knew she was safe in his presence.

Celia looked across Stella's head at her husband. 'It's lucky you happened to arrive at just that moment, William. But how did you come to be there at this time of the morning? You don't normally leave the bank until one o'clock on Saturdays.'

'I know, my dear, but one of the clerks was talking about a film he had taken his family to see and it sounded just the kind of thing you and Stella might enjoy, so I left early so that we could go this afternoon. I've worked long hours lately, so the manager was quite agreeable. But after this ...' He looked down at Stella's dishevelled hair. 'Perhaps it would be better to stay quietly at home instead.'

'What's the film?' Celia asked, but before he could answer, Stella looked up in excitement. 'Is it *Lassie Come Home*? Some of the girls at school have been to see it. Oh, please can we go? I'm all right now, really.' She turned to Celia. 'It's about a collie dog who gets lost and has to go miles and miles to find her way home, all by herself. Oh *please* let's go!'

Celia and William looked at each other and smiled.

'It sounds as if you're quite all right now, Stella. But you must have a bath and get those grazes attended to, and we'll need to have something to eat first. And—'

'The shopping!' Stella stopped dead. 'We still need to do the shopping, or we won't have any dinner tomorrow.'

Celia hesitated and William said, 'She's right. You need the vegetables and bread, and there won't be any meat left at the butcher's if you don't go soon. You go on and do that, Celia, and Stella and I will go home.' He looked down into the eager face, streaked with dirt and with the bruise now dark on her cheek. 'You won't mind that, will you, my dear?'

He took Stella's hand and they walked away together, towards Oak Tree Crescent.

Christmas at the Lacocks' house was quiet compared with most of the Christmases Stella could remember. Apart from the one at the vicarage last year, she had spent the last two with the Budds, in Portsmouth, and before that with her own family. Her father, who had been in the Merchant Navy, hadn't always been able to be there, but with her mother and sister, Stella had found Christmas to be a warm, happy time full of games and laughter. And with the four Budd children there had always been plenty going on, finishing with singing round the piano as Jess Budd played carols and songs that they all seemed to know, from old traditionals like 'The Minstrel Boy' to new favourites like 'Run Rabbit Run'.

Celia and William Lacock had a piano, which both could play, but apart from a few carols, their choice was classical music. William often played on a Sunday evening and Stella grew to love the Tchaikovsky ballet music that was his particular favourite – tunes from *Swan Lake* and *Nutcracker* in particular. When the war was over, he told her, he would take her to see the ballets themselves.

Celia had trained as a music teacher long ago, and during the long winter evenings she began to give Stella lessons. There was little bombing now, and although they had an air-raid shelter, there had seldom been any need to go to it, since the area was not often under threat. Apart from the blackout and the rationing, the war seemed like a bad dream, a nightmare that had happened in the past. Until Stella remembered those she had lost in that nightmare, when the horror would flood over her again and she would withdraw into the darkness of misery, and Celia would be at her wits' end in her efforts to console her.

However, those times grew fewer as she settled more securely into life at Oak Tree Crescent. She made friends at school, and the bullies, who had been left in no doubt by their headmaster that such behaviour would not be tolerated, and had been unable to sit comfortably on the hard school benches for several days afterwards, left her alone. She enjoyed her school work, and William helped her with her arithmetic homework. He was still reserved in his manner towards her, and she seldom threw herself into his arms as she had done on that Saturday morning, but a friendship had begun to grow between them, and she knew without being told that he was at least fond of her, and would always do his best for her.

Celia, on the other hand, made no secret of her feelings and showered Stella with love. They did everything together. They sewed, baked, cooked meals and sat together at the piano. Stella learned quickly and could soon read the music, pick out a tune and play simple duets. She told her school teacher that she was learning, and was allowed to play the school piano at the end-of-term carol service. Celia came to hear her and said afterwards that she felt as if she had floated all the way home.

On Christmas Day, they went for dinner with Celia's older brother Bertram and his wife Maisie, who had two sons in the army. Celia's younger brother was in the army as well, serving in Africa, so Stella was the only person there under forty. They made her welcome, but nobody seemed to know quite what to do with her, apart from putting a jigsaw puzzle on a side table. Later on, though, after they had all been for an afternoon walk in their new gloves and scarves, they got out a pack of cards and suddenly everything changed as they played several very noisy games of Chase the Ace,

Speed and Sevens. By the time Celia called a halt and said it was nearly time to go home, even William was flushed and laughing.

'You must have something to eat first,' said Maisie, as if they had not had an enormous Christmas dinner and then a tea of sandwiches, rock buns, jelly and blancmange with a tin of fruit salad, not to mention slices of Celia's Christmas cake. 'I've made some sausage rolls. I'll heat them up in the oven. And I'm sure the men would like a glass of beer. Bertie went to the Bottle and Jug specially.'

When they finally walked home, it was fully dark. Street lights were no more than a memory and torches were forbidden, but once you were outside, your eyes became adjusted and you could generally find your way, especially now that the trees that lined some of the roads had been painted with white bands round their trunks. Stella walked as usual between the two people she was slowly coming to regard as her parents, and thought about her real mother and father, her baby brother and, of course, Muriel. I hope she's having a happy Christmas, wherever she is, she thought wistfully. I hope she's with nice people who are giving her a good time. I hope we find each other again one day.

Celia stopped suddenly. 'William ... I feel a bit queer ...'

Her husband turned in concern. 'What is it, dear? Has the day been too much for you? Maybe the sausage rolls ...'

'No ... no, it's not that. I've felt it a few times before just lately. I thought perhaps it was the excitement of our first Christmas with Stella, but ...' She rested her hand against one of the white-painted tree trunks. 'Give me your arm, William. Take me home.'

Celia went to bed as soon as they got home and didn't want to get up next morning. She was still feeling ill, William said as he clumsily prepared breakfast and took it up to her on a tray. Stella, anxious and frightened, did her best to help. She went up to collect the tray and found the food almost untouched. Her foster mother looked pale and weary, but she struggled to sit up and gave Stella a wan smile.

'You're a good girl, Stella. Help your father as much as you can, won't you, until I can get up. He's not used to doing things round the house.'

'I can do it,' Stella offered. 'You've shown me how to cook, and

I can darn his socks and do the washing and ironing ... You will be better soon, won't you?'

'Yes, of course I will. It's probably just flu or something.' But there was pain in her eyes. 'You mustn't think you have to do everything, my dear. You're not here as a servant.'

Stella took the tray downstairs and put the uneaten Weetabix and toast into the bin. She felt guilty doing it, for you weren't supposed to waste food, but she and William had both had their breakfast and the cereal was now an unappetising brown stodge. She washed up and put away all the crockery and wondered what to do next.

William came into the kitchen, looking as if he felt as lost as Stella. He said, 'It's Boxing Day. Everyone is supposed to be coming to us for tea today, but now ...'

'I can get it ready,' Stella said. 'We brought the rest of the Christmas cake home last night, and there are the mince pies Mum and I made, and some fairy cakes. I can make a jelly and blancmange. It'll be all right.'

He gazed at her. 'I suppose I could help.'

Stella had never seen William do anything around the house. She saw nothing surprising in this. Men didn't. They went out to work to earn a living for the family and their wives stayed at home and did the cooking and housework and looked after the children. The war had changed this, because many of the women now went out to work – the younger ones without a family to take care of were conscripted or did war work in munitions plants or factories, and even the older ones were expected to do something. Jess Budd sewed sailors' collars and Celia knitted gloves, socks and balaclavas for the army. But even though the women had these extra duties, the men still didn't help at home. As often as not they were working overtime and had their own war work to do when they came home, training in the Home Guard or fire watching in air raids.

William Lacock was in the Home Guard and went to training twice a week as well as on frequent weekend exercises. He needed his rest when he was at home, Celia said. You couldn't expect a man to turn round and start sweeping the floors or washing clothes when he'd been busy all day and then had to go to extra training in the evenings.

'Could you set the table?' Stella asked him. 'I ought to make the jelly now, or it won't set in time, and I'll need to make sandwiches as well. And we'll want some dinner, too. I know we brought home some cold meat yesterday, to have with baked potatoes, so we'd better have that with some pickles.'

William nodded and went into the dining room, where Stella heard him opening and closing cupboard doors as he searched for the plates. It seemed strange to her that a man could live in his own home as long as William Lacock had and not even know where the best crockery was kept, but she supposed he had always looked on the house as his wife's domain and left her to organise it as she thought fit. After a few minutes, he reappeared in the kitchen.

'Do you know which tablecloth we should use?'

'The best one, I should think,' Stella said a little doubtfully. She had only seen the best tablecloth once, on the day when she had finally come to live here, and had no idea where it was kept. 'I expect it's in a drawer somewhere.'

He nodded and disappeared. The cupboard doors began to open and close again and she heard the chink of plates, and assumed that he had found the cloth and spread it on the long table.

Stella had never actually made a jelly before. They were a luxury, a treat, and with Christmas so near when she had arrived at Oak Tree Crescent, Celia had been saving such things for the festivities. She had made one for Stella's first weekend and that was all. Still, it looked easy enough. She boiled the kettle on the gas stove, sprinkled the jelly crystals in a bowl and poured the boiling water over them, stirring until they seemed to have disappeared. Then she took the bowl outside to the meat safe that stood by the back door.

William Lacock appeared again.

'I don't think there are enough cups and plates. How many will be here?'

Stella gazed at him. She had only met the family a few times and still hadn't got them properly sorted out in her head. She thought all those who were at Bertram – *Uncle* Bertram, she was supposed to call him – and Aunt Maisie's house yesterday were coming, but what about the other uncle and auntie, Robert (who she thought was William's brother) and Bella, who hadn't been present? And there was another auntie too, Joan, who was William's older sister and lived alone. Was she coming? Stella rather hoped not. She had only once met Aunt Joan, a tall, thin woman very like her brother, with a beaky nose and hooded eyes, and had found her rather forbidding. She had looked at Stella with some disfavour and, not quite out of her hearing, had made remarks in a harsh, grating voice about 'orphanage children' and 'knowing nothing of her background'.

'I don't know,' she said helplessly, and tried to count the numbers in her head. 'There were five of us yesterday, so if everyone else is coming as well today, that would make eight. Have we got enough chairs?'

'If we bring the bedroom chairs down, but there are only six each of plates, cups and saucers in the best tea service. I suppose we'd better use the everyday ones as well. You and I can have those. And what about plates to put the sandwiches and cakes on?'

'And bowls for the jelly,' Stella added, beginning to feel over-whelmed. 'Perhaps there are some in the sideboard.'

She felt uncomfortably as if she were giving him orders, but he nodded and went back. As the sound of cupboard doors and chinking began again, Stella turned her attention to the sandwiches. There were two loaves that would need to be sliced, and this was something else she hadn't much experience of. She had helped both Mrs Mudge and Celia often enough in the kitchen, but neither woman had been keen for her to use sharp knives.

Still, it had to be done, and she got out the saw-edged bread knife and started work, holding the loaf against her chest as she had seen Mrs Mudge do. Somehow, it wasn't quite as easy as it looked and the slices came out thick and uneven instead of thin and smooth as Mrs Mudge's and Celia's did. Sometimes the edges were hard to cut and looked almost chewed as she tore them away. And then the knife slipped and she cried out as it ripped a jagged cut in her finger. Blood spurted out, soaking into her jumper and dripping on to the loaf itself, and tears came to Stella's eyes and rolled down her cheeks.

'What's the matter?' William emerged again from the dining room and stared at her in dismay. 'Oh my goodness! Whatever's happened?'

'I've cut my finger. And I've spoiled the bread.' It all seemed suddenly too much for her, and as she stared at the welling blood she felt sick and shaky, and the kitchen walls seemed first to close in on her and then drift away.

William caught her as she swayed and half carried her into the living room, where he sat her on a chair and told her to put her head between her knees. 'Stay there while I fetch a bandage,' he ordered, going back to the kitchen. He returned a moment later with a cup of water and the tin box that contained bandages and sticking plasters. 'Now, sip this and let me have a look.'

Stella did as she was told and began to feel a little better. She averted her eyes from the blood and tried not to flinch as he examined her finger. 'I was trying to cut the bread ...'

'I know. It's all right. I'll have to wash it and then I'll put a bandage on. Look, hold this hanky against the cut.' He folded his own handkerchief into a pad and pressed it firmly against the cut finger. Stella squeaked a little. 'It'll stop it bleeding so much. I'll fetch some water from the kettle.'

William Lacock might not be much good at such household tasks as laying a table, but he had done a first-aid course as part of his Home Guard training and dealt swiftly and efficiently with Stella's injury. Before long, she had one finger bound with white bandage – 'as thick as a pre-war sausage' her foster father said with a smile – and was ready to start work again. He refused, however, to allow her to slice any more bread.

'You'll never be able to hold the loaf properly with that finger, and you might cut it right off next time. I'll do it.' But he had now retreated into inefficiency again, and his slices were as thick and uneven as Stella's.

Together they stumbled through preparations that Celia could have completed in half the time. Every now and then one of them would slip upstairs to see if she wanted anything – a cup of tea, an aspirin, extra pillows – but she shook her head and said she just wanted to sleep. By noon, they had managed to create a pile of sandwiches any ploughman would have been pleased to find in his dinner box, and Stella had found the tin of cakes she and Celia had made on Christmas Eve and arranged them on the cake stand they had run to earth in the cupboard by the fireplace. They'd also found several large plates there, together with a rabbit-shaped mould that Stella decided to use for the blancmange.

'I ought to make that soon, or it won't set. I'll just put the potatoes in the oven and do it while they're baking.' She went out to the meat safe where the milk was stored with other foods that needed to be kept cool. 'It looks as if the jelly's setting,' she reported as she came back inside. She surveyed the scene in the kitchen, with plates of food set at random amidst the debris of preparation. 'We'd better get tidied up before they all arrive.'

Tidying and washing up took about half an hour, and Stella thought the potatoes should be done by now. 'I don't know how long they usually take, do you? I can't remember how long Mrs Mudge used to put them in for. It was mostly baking I helped her with.' She opened the oven door and put her hand cautiously inside. 'They're still very hard.'

'They'd better have a bit longer then.' William glanced at the kitchen clock. 'Weren't you going to make the blancmange?'

Stella's hand flew to her mouth. 'I forgot all about it! We started tidying up instead. Oh dear, and now I'm going to have to use the saucepan and a bowl and *they'll* need washing, and we haven't even had dinner yet. And Mum hasn't had anything but water all morning.' Her voice trembled. 'What's the matter with her? Why does she feel so ill?'

'I don't know,' he said. 'It's probably just flu. I expect she'll be better in a day or two.' But he sounded worried and Stella gazed at him anxiously. 'If she isn't better by morning, I'll call the doctor on my way to the bank.'

'But will you still go – if she's ill?' Stella couldn't believe she was talking to him like this, as if she were as adult as he. She half expected him to tell her off for being cheeky, but he just sighed and said, 'I have to go to work, Stella. I can't take time off without permission from the bank manager. But I'll ask if I can come home early.' He hesitated. 'Will you be able to manage? I could ask one of the neighbours to look in. Or maybe Joan – Auntie Joan – would come.'

Stella quailed at the thought of being left here with his sister, with her beaky nose and disapproving stare. 'I'll look after Mum,' she said, pouring milk into the saucepan and saving a little to mix the blancmange powder to a pink paste in the bowl. 'You don't need to worry. I can manage.'

The blancmange poured into the rabbit mould at last, she looked into the oven again. The potatoes were now slightly soft round the edges and she wrapped her hand in a tea towel and lifted them out. William had put cold meat on two plates with some of Celia's pickles and chutneys, and Stella gave them a potato each. They sat down at the table.

'Boxing Day dinner!' he said with an attempt at cheerfulness. 'I always think it's even nicer than Christmas Day.' He started to cut his potato and it bounced away from his knife and rolled off the plate and on to the floor. 'Oh dear. I don't think they're quite done yet . . .'

By mid-afternoon, Celia said she felt a little better and would come downstairs. William helped her into her favourite winter frock and she sat in the armchair by the fire he had lit in the front room to wait for their visitors. She still looked very wan, and Maisie, who was first through the door, exclaimed in dismay and hurried over to her.

'Why ever didn't you let us know you were poorly? I would have come round and helped. Or everyone could have come to us again.' She sat down beside her sister-in-law and looked anxiously into her face. 'You do look pale. It wasn't anything you ate yesterday, surely? I don't think anyone else has been upset.'

Celia shook her head. 'No, it's nothing like that. I just felt very shaky and I've got a dreadful backache. William gave me aspirin but it hasn't helped much. He and Stella have been so good. They've got all the food ready and laid the table, and Stella even cooked dinner.'

Stella and William glanced at each other. They hadn't told Celia about the undercooked potatoes, nor their meal of cold meat and pickles with the last few crusts of bread left from the jaggedly cut loaves. She had of course noticed Stella's bandaged finger, but they had made light of it and she hadn't seemed to have the energy to pursue it.

'You must go to the doctor tomorrow,' Maisie declared. 'I don't like the look of you at all. What do you think, Bertie?'

Bertram was saved from replying by the arrival of the other three guests, Robert, Bella and Joan, who had walked round together. They too exclaimed at the sight of Celia, looking so wan in her chair, and Joan followed William out to the kitchen, where he and Stella were making tea for everyone.

'I hope Celia hasn't been wearing herself out looking after the child,' she said sharply, as if Stella were not there. 'I told her when she first said you were thinking of it, you're not used to children and you'll find it too much for you. But of course she wouldn't take any notice of me, and now look what's happened.'

'It's nothing to do with Stella,' William said. 'She's a good girl, no trouble at all and always willing to help. Celia will be better soon. She's had a backache for quite a long time now, on and off, and this is just a worse turn than usual.'

Joan sniffed. 'And it's not hard to see why. All the extra cooking, washing and cleaning, not to mention the war work she does—'

'That's mostly knitting. Do you take saccharin in your tea, Joan?'

'Two, as well you know. Don't try to change the subject, William. Celia's been doing too much for too long. She's not strong. She needs looking after.'

'I can help look after her, Auntie Joan,' Stella said bravely, picking up the teapot to take into the front room. 'I've helped Daddy do the tea for this afternoon, and I'll look after Mum during the school holidays while he's at work.'

Joan turned and looked down at her with as much surprise as if the teapot had spoken. 'Haven't you been taught never to interrupt adults when they're talking, Stella? And what are you doing with Celia's best teapot? You're bound to drop it.'

Stella's hand shook and she put the pot down hastily. She felt as if she had been struck. She looked at William, who said, 'Take the tray into the other room, my dear. I'll bring the pot. Joan, perhaps you'd like to bring the plate of biscuits. I'm sure everyone is ready for some refreshment.'

The rest of the afternoon passed in family conversation, most of it above Stella's head, so she sat on a small stool beside Celia, reading one of the books she had been given. After a while, it was time for tea and she jumped up and helped William set the plates of sandwiches and cake out on the dining table. The family crowded in and sat round, rather squashed together, and Joan stared at the plates.

'Who on earth made those sandwiches? They look as if they've come from a labourers' café. The bread must be an inch thick.'

'Stella and I did them together. We're not very good at slicing bread.'

'I can see that.' She sniffed. 'And what's in this bowl? Jelly? Why haven't you turned it out on to a dish?'

'I thought I ought to do that at the table,' Stella said. 'I've brought the big meat platter and—'

'The *meat* platter? Why in heaven's name—'

'Joan,' Robert said, raising his voice, 'why don't you stop criticising? The child has done her best and to my mind she's made a very good job of it. Those sandwiches are much more to my taste than the prissy little things you usually provide, which wouldn't fill a gnat's stomach.'

Joan drew in an indignant breath, but before she could say any more Celia, who was sitting in her usual chair and looking as if she'd rather be back in bed, said, 'Bob's right. Stella has worked hard all morning and William and I are very pleased with her. I'd thank you to remember that she's our daughter now, or will be in a few weeks when the adoption papers come through, and must be treated as such.' She rested her head on her hand, suddenly exhausted, and Joan flushed a dull red and pressed her lips together but said no more.

Stella put a large tablespoon into the jelly bowl.

'Has it set?' William asked anxiously, and she shook her head.

'I don't think it all has. The top's still soft. The bottom seems all right, though.'

'Turn it out anyway,' Bertram said encouragingly. 'I'm sure it will taste just as good. And is that blancmange in our old rabbit mould? I haven't had a rabbit blancmange for years.'

Joan sniffed. 'If that's meant to be a rabbit, then the jelly ought to be green, to look like grass. That jelly's red.'

'I don't think it matters,' Robert said at once. 'I don't suppose Celia had a green jelly anyway. There *is* a war on, Joan, in case you hadn't noticed.'

'That's right,' Bertram agreed. 'We're lucky to have jelly at all. Go on, Stella.'

Stella turned the bowl upside down over the platter. Red liquid filled it to the edges and some of it dripped on to Celia's best table-cloth. Stella stared at it in dismay.

'It hasn't set at all.'

'Some of it has, at the bottom.' Bertram scooped some of the liquid jelly into his own bowl quickly. 'It'll taste just as good. Give me your bowl, Joan, and I'll serve you some.'

'No thank you. I prefer proper jelly, not a drink.'

'Have some of this, then.' He took the bowl from Stella and scraped out some of the thick jelly that had set like leather at the bottom. 'And make sure you eat it. Now, what about that rabbit?'

The rabbit was slightly more successful. The blancmange hadn't thickened quite enough, but it had managed to keep its shape, more or less, although its ears hadn't formed properly and one got left in the mould and had to be carefully eased out and smoothed on to the head. Joan looked at it with no more favour than she had the jelly.

'What are all those speckles? They look like dust – I hope you washed the mould before you used it, Stella. It's probably been at the back of the cupboard for years.'

Stella gave her a guilty look and she raised her eyes to the ceiling. 'I don't think I'll bother, thank you very much.' She laid down her spoon. 'William, I'm afraid I have to say that I can't imagine why you and this child, who's barely known anything but poor homes and an orphanage and clearly has no idea how to behave, took it upon yourselves to prepare a Boxing Day tea for eight people. You should have asked one of us to help you. I'm sure Maisie or Bella would have been only too pleased.'

The two women opened their mouths to say that of course they would, but William spoke instead, with a severity Stella had seldom heard from him. 'I think the child has done very well, Joan, and what her life has been before she came here is none of your business. As a matter of fact—'

'I *do* know how to behave!' Stella burst out, unable to bear any more. 'I *do*! I lived in a vicarage before my daddy died and I had to go the children's home, and before that I had a proper mummy and daddy and a sister *and* a baby brother, and we lived in a nice house before we were bombed. And we always had jelly for tea on Sundays, and a blancmange rabbit, and Christmas cake and *everything*. And now it's all gone because of the war and they're all dead except Muriel and I don't even know where she is, and nobody cares. Nobody at all!' Tears poured down her cheeks and she stared round the table at the shocked faces, and then turned to Celia, who was white-faced and in tears herself. 'I'm sorry, Mum. I wanted it all to be so nice for you and now everything's gone wrong.'

'Oh, my poor little dear.' Celia put her arms round her and drew her close. 'It hasn't all gone wrong, and none of it is your fault anyway. I'd had those jelly crystals for a long time, they probably just didn't work any more, and the blancmange looks lovely. And so do the sandwiches – they're just the sort men like and anyone who doesn't like them doesn't have to have one. You've been a real little help and a dear, good daughter, and I won't let anyone say another word against you. Isn't that right, William?'

'It is,' he said from the other end of the table. 'Stella has spent all morning working when most children would be enjoying their new presents, and as Celia said earlier, she'll be our legal daughter in a few weeks' time and we consider her as such now. She's one of the family. And now I think we should all get on with our tea. Does anyone want a second cup?'

Chapter Twenty-Four

Celia did not get better. The pain in her back got worse, and one day when she tried to get out of bed, her legs gave way beneath her and she was sick. The doctor, who had already been twice and found nothing wrong, told William that she must go to hospital and be properly investigated.

To Stella's dismay, Joan, being the only unmarried sister, came to stay to look after her brother and his foster daughter. Her regime was strict and even William was cowed by it, although he was able to escape every day to the bank and in the evenings either to the hospital or his Home Guard duties. It fell to Stella to endure the full brunt of her disapproval.

'I always said it would be too much for Celia, taking on a strange child. She should have accepted years ago that if God means you to have children he will give them to you naturally.' She flushed a little, as though the natural way of having children was not much better, and certainly not to be spoken of. 'Now look what's happened.' She stared accusingly at Stella.

'I didn't mean to make her ill,' Stella said in a small voice, horribly afraid that Joan might be right. 'I've helped as much as I could.'

Joan's look said that she doubted if this could be true. 'Well, you'll certainly have to help now. I have business to go to, as you know.' She worked in an office somewhere in town. 'I can't spend my time running around after you.'

She gave Stella a list of jobs. All the washing-up after every meal, much of the vegetable preparation, dusting the furniture and ornaments and brushing the carpet every morning before school, a lengthy task involving saving used tea leaves from the pot and scattering them over the carpet before sweeping them into Celia's dustpan. Since she was home before either William or his sister, Stella was also expected to lay the table for tea and have the kettle on when they came home.

She did all these tasks willingly, telling herself that she was doing them for Celia and William rather than Joan. But they left little time for herself, and she missed the hour she had always been given after she finished her homework to read her book before bed. Now she was told to make her cup of cocoa and go to bed almost as soon as her homework was done, and there was no question of reading. The light had to be put out ten minutes after she had gone upstairs. There was a war on, Joan reminded her tartly, and electricity could not be wasted on one child reading trashy Enid Blyton stories.

Stella missed the evenings she had come to enjoy, with Celia knitting by the fire and William helping with her arithmetic homework. Joan, who believed that education was important for girls who might, as she did herself, have to earn their own living, helped her once or twice, but she was impatient and scornful when Stella did not understand the problems she had been set, and called her wilfully stupid. After that, Stella struggled alone.

She worried too about Celia. She was usually in bed by the time William came home from the hospital, and although she strained her ears she could hear no more than a mumble of conversation between brother and sister. One evening she heard Joan give a cry of horror at something William said, and she got out of bed and crept on to the landing. The living room door was slightly open and she could just hear what they were saying.

'A *growth*?' Joan exclaimed. 'Oh, *William* ... And in her back? I didn't even know you could get growths there.'

'You can get them anywhere,' he said, his voice tired and despondent. 'I saw the doctor himself this evening and he explained it to me. It's cancer—'

'Don't say that word!'

'It's what it is, Joan. It's cancer and he thinks it's spread further than her back. It might even have started somewhere else and only now got as far as there. There are other lumps, too ... One in her ... her bust.' Stella could hear the embarrassment in his voice. 'And under her arms. He says it's as bad as it could possibly be.'

'But can't they do anything? Operate? Take them away?'

'Nothing. There's nothing they can do. It's gone too far, and there's no treatment.' He sounded as if he was about to cry, and Stella heard his armchair creak as if he had just dropped into it. 'He says it's just a matter of time. Weeks – maybe no more than days.'

'Days,' Joan repeated, and for once her severity seemed stripped away and she sounded as shaken as her brother. 'Oh, William. Poor, poor Celia. I must go to see her. I'll ask for time off tomorrow afternoon. They let visitors in during the afternoons, don't they?'

'Yes, from three until four. And Stella should go as well.'

'Stella? Why Stella?'

'Because Celia wants to see her, of course. And I'm sure she'll want to see Celia. Of course she must go.'

'Oh, I don't think so, William.' The coldness was back in Joan's voice. 'That's quite unsuitable. Stella's just a child, and apart from that, she's no relation.'

'No relation? We are about to adopt her!'

'Well, that will have to go by the board now,' Joan said. 'You can't possibly consider adoption if poor Celia ... I'm sure you can see for yourself that anything of that nature will be impossible.' There was a short pause, and then she said in a brisk voice, 'I'm sorry, William. It's been a shock to both of us. We need a hot drink. I'll go and make some cocoa.'

The door began to open and Stella scurried back to her bedroom and crept into bed. She lay shaking in the darkness, trying to make sense of all she had heard.

Celia had a growth. Lots of growths. Stella had heard of these before, usually when people talked to each other in muted voices and mouthed the word 'cancer' as if it must not be spoken aloud. That was what Celia had, and she was going to die from it.

Celia was going to die ... The horror of it had come into the room with Stella and it seemed to fill the air, dark and grey like a winter fog, vibrating with the grating tones of Joan's voice. Celia was going to die, and Stella would not be adopted after all. She was going to lose her second mother and the father she was slowly growing to love, and the home that had become, almost without her realising it, her sanctuary.

What was going to happen to her now?

Celia died just before Easter. For the last few weeks, William seemed to spend all the time he could at the hospital and Stella scarcely saw him. She was not allowed to see Celia at all. Children were not allowed to visit unless in very special circumstances, and even though Celia's illness was as desperate as you could get, Stella wasn't her daughter and it was considered unnecessary for her to go. William tried to explain this to her, but she could see that he didn't really understand it himself.

'I've told them what a help you've been to me,' he said despondently. 'And she wants to see you too. She's asked the doctor and all the nurses but they say no. I'm sorry, my dear.'

Joan, of course, took the hospital's part.

'Quite unsuitable,' she said in her harsh voice. 'Hospitals aren't pleasant places to visit at the best of times, and with all those people so ill ... They don't want a child like Stella staring at them.'

'I wouldn't stare—' Stella began, but Joan's look froze the words on her lips. 'I miss her so much,' she said instead, miserably. 'I just want to see her again.'

William took her hand. 'I'm afraid you'd hardly know her now, my dear. She's changed a lot; she's very thin and pale, and she sleeps most of the time. She probably wouldn't even know you were there.'

'I could sit until she wakes up. I'd sit very still.'

'That's enough!' Joan said sharply. 'You've been told quite clearly that it's against hospital rules, and that's all there is to it. If you really want to be helpful, you'd do better to stop pestering your ... my brother' – she could never bring herself to refer to William as Stella's father – 'and make yourself useful by putting the kettle on. I'm sure we could both do with a cup of tea.'

Stella obeyed, putting the brown teapot ready by the stove and getting out cups and saucers. Tears trickled down her cheeks as she thought of Celia, who had made her so welcome here, putting books and toys in her bedroom, making clothes for her, teaching her to play the piano. Nobody played the piano now. William never touched it – he barely had time, even if he'd wanted to – and on the one occasion when Stella had lifted the lid and begun her practice, as she was sure Celia would want her to do, Joan had slammed it down again, narrowly missing her fingers.

'Most disrespectful! And who gave you permission to play it anyway, with nobody here to see that you don't do any damage? Don't let me see you touch it again.'

School was her haven now. The boys left her alone and she had made a few friends amongst the girls. She enjoyed the work and never forgot that Miss Marsh had said she might be able to be a teacher herself if she set her mind to it. With William at the hospital every evening, she struggled alone with her homework and slowly found that even the dreaded problems began to make sense. When school broke up for the Easter holidays, her report read so well that even Joan couldn't find fault with it, and just sniffed and looked down her nose without comment, which was as near to praise as she could bring herself to come.

'You've done very well, my dear,' William said, and gave her a shilling. 'I know your mother will be pleased when I tell her.'

But whether she would have been or not, Stella never knew, for when he came home that evening, his face was grey and his eyes rimmed with red. Celia had died that afternoon.

'I could have been with her,' he said over and over again. 'If they'd only sent word to the bank, I could have left and gone straight there. I *should* have been with her.' He sank into his armchair and stared hopelessly at his sister and Stella. 'She's gone. Celia's gone. What am I going to do now?'

For the next few days, the house was almost silent. William moved about like a ghost, his eyes no more than dark hollows in the pallor of his face. He scarcely spoke and spent long hours either up in his bedroom or out in the garden, gazing at the vegetable patch Celia had tended as if he was wondering what to do with it. Joan did the housework and cooking with grim efficiency, and Stella tried either to help or keep out of the way, whichever was likely to get her into less trouble. She spent a lot of her time going to the shops, especially as they would all be closed on Good Friday and Easter Day and Monday. Thankfully, nobody molested her now, and when neighbours saw her they crossed the road or hurried by with downcast eyes so that they wouldn't have to speak to her. She wondered sometimes if she had somehow become invisible.

'They don't know what to say,' William said, during one of their rare conversations. Joan had suggested they both go for a walk ('get out from under my feet' was what she meant) and they decided to go to the local park. It was one of the places Celia had enjoyed, but going there turned out to be not such a good idea, since it reminded them both of what they had lost. They sat on a bench, wrapped in misery, and Stella told him how nobody seemed to want to speak to her now.

'I think they think it's my fault. It's not, is it?'

He shook his head. 'No. They're just embarrassed. They feel awkward so they'd rather not say anything.'

'It makes me feel as if they're blaming me,' Stella said in a small voice. 'She was all right until I came.'

He turned to her in distress. 'No! You mustn't think that. Of course it wasn't your fault. She had backaches for a long time, even before you came. We didn't think they were anything important – everyone gets aches and pains at some time. But ...' He stared at the ground for a while. 'I don't suppose it would have done much good if we'd gone to the doctor sooner,' he said at last, so quietly that Stella could only just hear him. 'They can't really cure what she had, and we'd have had months of worry.'

He was given three days' leave from the bank to arrange the funeral and sort out Celia's possessions. The funeral could not be held until after Easter, and Stella was not allowed to attend. She stayed at home by herself until the family came back for a glass of sherry and a piece of cake made by Joan, who had refused Stella's help, and then they all departed and left the three of them alone.

'Well ...' William said, and left his sentence unfinished. He looked round the room as if undecided what to do next, then glanced at his sister. 'I suppose you'll be wanting to go back home yourself now.'

Joan met his eye. She inclined her head towards Stella and said pointedly, 'That's something we need to discuss, William. I thought we could have a talk this evening – once Stella's gone to bed.'

'Yes, of course, if you want to.' He sounded a little bewildered, as if he couldn't think of anything that they would need to talk about, but Joan had a steely look in her eye and he gave in. He seemed to give in most of the time these days, Stella thought. She also thought she knew what Joan wanted to discuss, and after she had gone to bed and her light was out, she crept back on to the landing to listen.

This time, the living room door was closed and she couldn't hear much of what was said. But Joan's sharp voice carried more than William's deeper tones, and she heard enough to send her miserably back to bed, where she lay very still and let the tears flow silently on to the pillow.

'... stay here with you,' she had heard. '... see it as my duty ... can't manage for yourself ... need to be looked after ... only sensible solution ...' And then her own name. '... *Stella* ... the only sensible thing to do ...'

There was room for her back in the children's home, William said. He looked as if he would rather be saying anything else as they sat in the living room, the two of them under Joan's cold eye, but he stumbled on. 'The matron – Miss Marsh – says you'll be very welcome to go back. She understands perfectly how difficult – how impossible – it is for you to stay here with me now that your ... my wife has passed away.' He paused for a moment as if hearing the words he had just uttered. 'Your Auntie Joan is coming to live with me, but because she has business to go to each day, she won't have the time that your ... my wife did. And she feels – we both feel – that you'll be happier and better off in surroundings that are familiar to you.'

Stella stared at him. He could not meet her eye for a moment, but when he looked at her, she saw his distress. She wondered how she could ever have found him detached and even a little unwelcoming. He's just shy, she thought with a sudden flash of understanding. He hadn't known what to say. And now he was upset and he still didn't know what to say.

His sister did, however. In a flat, uncompromising tone, she said, 'You'll thank us in the end. It's just a good thing that the adoption had not yet been finalised. My brother would have been legally responsible for you then, and it wouldn't have done at all.' She froze him as he began to speak. 'No, William, it *wouldn't*. I told you the other day, I can't possibly take on a child, and you certainly couldn't have managed without me.'

'We could,' Stella said. 'We could manage – couldn't we, Daddy?'

Joan sighed impatiently. 'Really, child, you must stop calling him that now. He is not your father and never will be. As for managing – well, if that shambles you called a Boxing Day tea is anything to go by, I'd be surprised if you didn't set fire to the house in the first week, left to your own devices. No, this is the best way. You'll be properly looked after in the children's home, and since you already know the staff and children there, it won't be at all difficult to settle in. Indeed, Miss Marsh seemed quite pleased at the idea. I got the impression you were rather a favourite of hers,' she ended on a disapproving note.

Stella was silent. She knew that it was impossible to argue with grown-ups once they had made up their minds, and with Joan it was impossible to argue at all. She looked again at William, who was staring miserably at the floor, and wondered if he really wanted his sister to live with him. They had seen little enough of her when Celia was alive, and the few times they had invited her to Sunday tea or gone to visit her had always seemed more of a duty than a pleasure. But she was realistic enough to know that Joan was quite right – William could not manage on his own, and with the best will in the world, Stella wasn't sure that she could cope with all that needed to be done. There was the washing and ironing, for a start – he needed a clean white shirt every day, with separate collars that must be starched, and then there were his vests and underpants ... It made her blush just to think of washing such intimate garments.

The more she thought about it, the more she knew that they really couldn't manage alone. And she didn't want to live with Joan any more than he seemed to. All the same ...

'I thought I was going to have a proper home,' she said in a wobbly voice, after Joan had returned to the rooms she rented in a house in town to start packing her things. 'A home with my own room and a mother and father to look after me. Why did it have to happen? Why did she have to die?'

'I don't know,' he said sadly. 'I really don't know. We all have to die sometime, I know, and so many people are being killed in this terrible war, but for my dear Celia to be taken from us so suddenly, and so young – it seems very cruel.'

Stella laid her hand on his knee. 'Will I still be able to come and see you? Can I come to tea sometimes? Or won't Auntie Joan want me?' As she spoke, she realised that the term 'Auntie Joan' would be forbidden her, and even that brought sadness. For a short while, she had had a family, with aunts and uncles who played Chase the Ace at Christmas, and laughed, and were jolly, and even Joan had been part of that family. Now they were all being taken away and she might not even be able to say goodbye.

'I hope so,' William answered. 'But you'll have to ask Miss Marsh that. The children's home will be like a parent to you now.'

'Couldn't you *ask* if you could keep me?' she asked in sudden desperation. 'They might let you, if you said you really wanted me for your girl.'

He said, 'I'm sorry, my dear. Joan's right. We just couldn't manage, and it wouldn't do. You'll be better off in the home, but I'll never forget you. And there's something you must never forget either.' He paused, then went on in a tight, difficult voice, 'You made my wife very happy while you were here. Very happy indeed.'

He looked into her eyes and she knew the truth, and felt that she must have known it all along. It was Celia who had really wanted her. Celia who had longed for a child, a daughter; who had finally brought him to agree that they would adopt one for their own. William had accepted Stella, had been kind to her, had even grown fond of her, but he would never have loved her as Celia had, and he would not be as hurt by losing her. He could let her go because he had never truly seen her as his.

'Yes,' she said in a small voice. 'Yes, I know.' And she knew that there would not be any invitations to tea, nor any family parties at Christmas. William would send her a birthday card and perhaps a present – a book or a postal order – and he might come sometimes to take her for a walk or out to tea at one of the cafés in town. But the visits would dwindle, and even the cards and presents would come to an end, and she would, if not completely forgotten, be remembered only occasionally as 'that child from the children's home that Celia wanted to adopt'.

She went upstairs to the bedroom she had thought would always be hers, and began to separate the books she had been given from the ones Celia had put in the room to welcome her when she had first arrived.

*

'It's a pleasure to have you back with us,' Miss Marsh said. 'The other children are pleased, and so are the staff. I'm very sorry about what happened to your foster mother, Stella, and it's a great pity that you couldn't stay with Mr Lacock and his sister, but you are very welcome here and we're all very happy to see you.'

'I don't want to be adopted again,' Stella said. 'I don't want anyone else taken away from me. I'd rather stay here.'

Dorothy Marsh looked at her with compassion. All the children here had lost so much, and although Stella's losses had been cruel, they were no more than those many of the others had suffered. But they had no option but to go on with their own lives, and it was her job to help them to do that.

'You mustn't make up your mind about that straight away. Things can often turn out much better than we expect. But while you are here, I want you to be happy. And if you do stay – do you remember what I said to you once about being a teacher?'

Stella nodded. 'I've worked hard at school. I want to try to pass the grammar school exam. I'll need to go there, won't I?'

'Yes, you will. And if you really think that's what you want to do, when the time comes to leave the grammar school, and leave here too – well, it may be possible for you to stay on and help with the younger children. You can train as a teacher in that way.' She hesitated. It was probably too soon to talk to the child in this way, but eleven was not too young to have an ambition and work towards it, and she believed that Stella was the kind of child who was happier with a purpose in her life.

Stella looked at her. In Dorothy Marsh, she knew she had found a mentor, someone who would care about her and help her through all the difficulties that lay ahead. She knew that although she might never be part of an ordinary family again, she could find a different kind of family here, with Miss Marsh and the other teachers, with the children who had been her friends before she left and would be her friends again.

'I'd like that,' she said. 'I'll work hard and help all I can, and one day I'll be a proper teacher.' She paused, then said, 'And then I can look for my sister, Muriel. One day, I'm going to find her.'

Part Five

Part Five

Chapter Twenty-Five

Burracombe, September 1943

MADDY

The children's home arrived at Burracombe at the beginning of September. It had taken some time to move all the furniture, most of it to rooms that would be locked up while the home was in occupation, and store the pictures and ornaments, and most of the organisation had fallen to Isobel and Dottie, with help from some of the estate workers. But finally the rooms were empty and swept clean, ready for the few basic pieces the home would be bringing – long tables and benches for eating and school work, old armchairs and sofas for the drawing room and dining room, which would serve as common rooms, and small lockers and narrow iron beds with horsehair mattresses, which would be distributed amongst the bedrooms. The attics would be turned into dormitories for the boys.

The house looked bare and stark as the two women surveyed it. 'I hope they look after it,' Dottie remarked. 'You must feel a bit worried, Mrs Napier. And sad to be leaving, too.'

Isobel sighed. 'Both those things, of course, Dottie, but we all have to make sacrifices, and we mustn't forget that these children have lost their families, one way or another. It's not all due to the war, of course – some of them were in the home even before that started – but it's the war that has forced their move. And they've come to a lovely place. Perhaps Burracombe will give them something special, that they'll remember all their lives.'

'Poor little dears,' Dottie agreed. 'I know that some of the folk who had evacuees that went back home still hear from them from time to time, and of course we've still got quite a few about the village. Trouble is, they never seem to mix all that well with our kiddies. They're town children and come from different sorts of homes, and they sticks together, which is natural, and I'm sorry to say it, but ours aren't always as welcoming as they might be. Why, I caught young Roy Pettifer and his pal Vic Nethercott tormenting a little evacuee girl only the other day – chasing her and pulling the ribbons off her pigtails, they were. I gave them a proper telling-off.'

Isobel frowned. 'Perhaps we should have a word with their mothers.'

'Oh, I don't think so. They're not bad boys, not really. They wouldn't have hurt her, but she was upset. It's just the way tackers are. More like tribes of savages, if you ask me, got to defend their own territory. But they got to learn, we're all on the same side against Hitler and it behoves us to look after each other. Now, Mrs Napier, you'd better let me know how often you want me to come and help you at the cottage. I've agreed to help out in the kitchens here, but you come first, so 'tis up to you to say.'

'Two or three times a week should be enough, thank you, Dottie. It's not exactly large. Oh, and you'll be pleased to know that Miss Forsyth is coming to stay for a while once I'm settled. She's not been at all well since she went away again at the end of July, and her doctor says she needs to rest.'

'Picked up something in one of those foreign parts she's been to,' Dottie said. 'She wrote and told me about it. Pulled her right down, it has. I'll be glad to see her here. We'll have to build her up again – I'll make some scones and bring some of my own jam and clotted cream as soon as she arrives.'

Isobel smiled. 'Your cream and scones would build anyone up, Dottie. Well, she's coming as soon as she's fit to travel – the children should be here by then, so she can help us make them feel welcome. They'll be so excited to see the famous Fenella Forsyth – they'll think Burracombe is the best place on earth.'

'And so it is,' Dottie declared. 'And so it is.'

*

'And this is where you and Eileen will sleep,' Nurse Powell said. 'I know you like to be together. Angela, Janice and Shirley are in here too. Come in, everyone.' She stood back from the door so that the girls could see their new quarters.

'It's a proper bedroom,' Eileen said in awe. 'Not a dormitory at all.'

'That's because it's a big house,' Janice said. 'It's a mansion, isn't it, nurse?'

'I suppose it is.' Megan Powell was almost as overwhelmed as the children. She had already been shown her own room, which she shared with two other staff members, and could not quite believe that she had come to such a beautiful and peaceful spot from her father's tiny terraced cottage in the dark, gritty valleys of South Wales.

The room – which, had the children known it, was Hilary Napier's bedroom – was large enough for the five narrow beds to be squeezed in close together; not in a row, but with three along one wall and two on the other, with their lockers beside them and one wardrobe and a chest of drawers to be shared between them all. The big window overlooked what had been a broad lawn but was now a large vegetable patch, fringed with a belt of woodland, and beyond that the open moors. None of the five girls – apart from Maddy, who had lived in the New Forest – had ever seen such a vast open space, and Nurse Powell, who had grown up with the sight of the hills of Carmarthenshire and the Brecon Beacons rising beyond the slag heaps that surrounded her village, came to stand behind them and follow their gaze.

'That's Dartmoor. It's beautiful, isn't it? So wild and natural.'

'Are there wild animals there?' Angela asked doubtfully. 'Wolves and bears and things?'

'Don't be daft,' Eileen retorted. 'There's no wolves or bears in England now. Are there, nurse?'

'No, there are sheep and deer and ponies. They won't hurt you.'

'Wild ponies? Can we ride them?' Janice pressed her nose against the glass. 'Can we catch them and keep them for ourselves?'

'I don't think you're allowed to do that,' Megan said, smiling. 'But if we go for walks on the moors, I'm sure we'll see them.'

'We had ponies in the woods near Bridge End,' Maddy said.

'But they weren't tame – they wouldn't let us catch them.' She and Keith and Sammy had tried once, and the ponies had gone crashing through the trees to get away from them. One had looked quite fierce and the children had felt rather scared and decided not to do that again.

'I don't think I want to go on the moors,' Shirley said. 'We might get lost.'

'We won't let that happen,' Nurse Powell said. 'Now, you get yourselves unpacked and wash your faces. You know where the bathroom is, and the dining room, so as soon as you're ready, come downstairs and we can all have tea.'

Left alone, the five girls scrambled to choose their beds. Maddy and Eileen picked the two close together and the other three dipped for theirs. 'Dip, dip, dip, my little ship, floats on the water, like a cup and saucer ...' In a few minutes they had unpacked their belongings and put them away in the plain wooden drawers and wardrobe. That done, they gathered round the windows and gazed out again.

'You can see the village,' Eileen said, craning her neck. 'And the church. I suppose we'll have to go there for services. I wonder where the school is.'

'Won't we have our own lessons? Miss Matthews has come too and she's a teacher.'

'Yes, but we had to go to the ordinary school as well before, so I expect we will here. Anyway,' Eileen added impatiently, 'who cares about silly old school? I want to go exploring. There's woods and all sorts, and I bet we can get up on those moors from here.'

'And make friends with the ponies,' Maddy added eagerly. 'I bet we can catch them easy as anything.' She conveniently forgot her experience with the New Forest ponies. 'You just have to give them sugar. Ponies always like sugar.'

The others stared at her. 'Sugar? But we hardly ever get any. We have to use saccharin in our tea and cocoa. How are we going to get enough to give the ponies?'

'We'll give them saccharin, then,' she said. 'We can save that. I don't like it much anyway. I used to sell the vicar my sugar and I never took saccharin then. I quite like tea without it.'

'You sold your sugar to the *vicar*?'

'Yes. When I lived at the vicarage,' she explained. 'He gave us a

158

farthing for every teaspoon. Or maybe it was a ha'penny. Anyway, if we can't get sugar we'll give the ponies saccharin and they'll let us ride them.'

'We don't know how to ride.'

'*I* do,' Maddy declared. 'There was a donkey at the vicarage and we used to ride him. He didn't mind a bit.' In fact, the ancient donkey, who was living out his days in the orchard, hadn't moved much, even with two or three children scrambling on his back, but he had brayed his annoyance so loudly that half the village had heard him and come to see what was the matter, and Mr Beckett had been quite cross and forbidden Maddy and the two Budd boys to torment the poor creature again. But again, Maddy didn't think it necessary to tell the other girls this.

A bell sounded below them and they scurried down the stairs, joining the other children, who were equally impressed by their accommodation and also full of plans for exploring the neighbour-hood. After tea, however, they were all taken to the common room – once Isobel Napier's gracious drawing room – and told to sit down while Matron gave them a talk.

'Just because we are now in the country doesn't mean you can all run wild,' she told them severely. 'There are still rules to be obeyed.' A boy sitting near Maddy muttered under his breath that there would be, wouldn't there, and she giggled and found Matron's stern eye on her. 'For a start, this lovely house is someone's home and they've had to move out so that we can live here. That means we must take great care not to damage it in any way. There is to be no writing on the walls, no kicking the doors or skirting boards, no spilling ink on the floorboards. When the war is over we want to be able to give it back in as good condition as we found it, just as we would like our own homes to be returned to us if we'd had to give them up.'

She paused and the children gazed back at her. Many of them had no idea what she was talking about. For some, the children's home was the only home they had ever known, and the idea of tak-ing care of the walls that surrounded them, the floors they walked on or the doors they banged was something that had never occurred to them. They knew, of course, that they would get into trouble for writing on walls or kicking holes in door panels, but that was simply because it was all too easy to get into trouble, whatever you did. You had to wash the walls clean or help mend the door, but you never had to think that this was someone else's home and one day they would come back to live there.

For those like Maddy who had once had homes and families, the concept was easier to grasp. They had all done their share of scribbling on walls or peeling off wallpaper, and it had always meant trouble, but they'd also seen their fathers or other relatives putting right their misdemeanours, and understood a little more about the value of ownership. Still, Maddy thought, there wasn't really any need for Matron to go on about it as if it were something new. If you did these things, you'd get into trouble, no matter where you were. For herself, she was more interested in what lay outside the house, and especially in the ponies.

Matron's voice cut into her thoughts. 'Maddy! Are you listening? You look as if you're in a world of your own.'

Maddy jerked back to attention. 'Yes, Matron. You're saying we mustn't write on the walls.'

Matron sighed. 'I've said a good deal more than that. Pay attention, please. I'm telling you about the gardens.' She let her gaze travel round the room, making sure she had every child's eye. 'You are allowed into the grounds to play, but only in certain parts. You are not allowed into the vegetable garden or the walled garden, where fruit is grown, unless you are invited by one of the gardeners or when we go out there ourselves to help, which we will do every day. When that happens, you will have either a nurse or a gardener with you to show you what to do, and you must do exactly as you are told. As you know, there's a war on and food is extremely important. The more we can grow for ourselves, the better, and you'll be helping in that important work. But there are some parts where Mrs Napier, whose house this is, has kindly said you may go. You may play in the woods, or in the paddock – someone will show you where that is – as long as there are no horses there.'

'Horses?' Maddy exclaimed. 'Do you mean the wild horses?'

'No, these are horses that belong to Mrs Napier. They live in the stables, and that's another place where you may not go unless the stable boy or groom invite you. You are not, in any circumstances, to approach the horses themselves. Do you understand?'

The children nodded glumly. It seemed as if this place had even more rules than the home they had come from. After a minute or two one of the boys asked, 'Are we allowed on the moors, miss?'

'We shall go on the moors for picnics once a week,' Matron announced, and there was a ripple of excitement. 'Later on, when we can be sure you won't get lost, some of the older children may be allowed to go by themselves.'

'And see the ponies?' Maddy cried, unable to contain herself any longer. 'Will we be able to see the wild ponies?'

'If they are there, I'm sure we'll see them, but you must remember that these are wild animals. You must not chase them, and that goes for the sheep too. Now, I expect you all want to know about school ...'

The children groaned. School was the least of their interests, but they listened dutifully as it was explained that they would go to the village school with other evacuees in the afternoons, and in the mornings they would do lessons here in the house with Miss Matthews and Mr Ballard, who had both come with them. After tea, group by group, they would either help in the gardens or have free time.

'And then we'll be able to go and find the ponies,' Maddy said excitedly as they were released at last to go outside for some fresh air. 'I'm going to have a white one with brown patches. They're called skewbalds.'

'Go on, it's you that's screwy if you think you're going to get a pony,' one of the boys jeered. 'They're wild, didn't you hear Matron say so? They'll kick you if you go near them.'

'They won't. They'll come to me, because I'll have things they like.' Another idea had come to her while Matron was talking. There were bound to be carrots growing in that big vegetable garden, and ponies loved carrots even more than sugar. Certainly more than saccharin, which she wasn't as sure about as she'd tried to appear. All she need do was put one or two in her pocket when she was helping in the garden, and a skewbald pony was practically hers.

She followed the others outside. There was an instant rush to the woods beyond the broad expanse of vegetables growing where once the lawn had been, and she ran with the rest because climbing trees came only second to her desire to own a pony.

I like Burracombe, she thought, scrambling into the branches of an old oak and looking out towards the village. It's a nice place. I'd like to live here for ever.

Dottie Friend had been at the Barton all morning, making sandwiches and rock buns for the children's tea. She left the food ready for the staff to serve, and set off for her cottage just as the children were sent out into the garden.

The poor little dears, she thought, pausing to watch them. Why, it's just like seeing Ted Tozer's cows let out into the meadows after they've been in the barns all winter. They hardly know where to put theirselves. I don't suppose they've ever had such a lovely garden to play in before.

Not that they were all city children, she remembered, not like the London evacuees who had come to Burracombe when the war first started. After all, the home itself had been in Dorset, which was as much country as Devon. But still, they probably hadn't lived in a house like the Barton. The home they came from would have been more like a school.

She walked on down the drive. One of the little girls was scrambling up into the branches of a big cedar tree, shouting something about ponies to two or three of the boys. They ignored her and ran off, and the girl stopped climbing and looked after them.

'You be careful up there,' Dottie called. 'It's a long way down, and you don't want to get stuck and miss your tea.'

The girl turned her head and regarded her. Their eyes met and Dottie felt an odd little quiver somewhere inside. Why, you poor little thing, she thought. Look at you, so brave and laughing, and inside you're crying your heart out for what you've lost. And how I know that from just one look I couldn't say for the world, but know it I do. And you know it too.

She wanted nothing more than to reach out and gather the child against her.

Maddy spoke, her voice rather small.

'I don't think I can get down. I didn't know I'd gone so high. Please – can you help me?'

'Why, of course I can.' Dottie put down the shopping basket she carried everywhere and stepped nearer to the tree. 'You just come

162

down backwards, very carefully, and I'll guide your feet to the best places. There – that's right. Just a bit further over that way, there's a good little girl. Now this way – yes, it's quite firm, you can put all your weight on that foot. Now this one ... and again ...' Within a few minutes, she could catch Maddy by the waist and lift her to the ground. 'Why, my pretty, you'm as light as a feather! There you are, safe and sound.'

She stepped back and they looked at each other again. Maddy brushed back her fair hair, leaving a smear of green on her forehead. Her eyes were grave for a moment, and then she broke into a smile that made Dottie catch her breath, and her laughter bubbled up once more.

'Thank you!' she exclaimed. 'You saved my life! I could have been there all night and nobody would ever have known.'

'Well, I don't see that there's much to laugh at about that,' Dottie answered, chuckling herself, 'and I dare say someone would have found you before bedtime, but you certainly might have missed those nice rock buns I've been making for your tea. Anyway, now we've met, we'd better introduce ourselves. I'm Miss Friend, and you'll see me about the place, helping with the cooking and so on.'

'Miss Friend?' Maddy said. 'That's a nice name. My name's Maddy.' She smiled again and held out her hand. 'Shall we *both* be friends?'

'We will,' Dottie said. She took the small, rather dirty hand in hers and smiled into the blue eyes that she knew held pain as well as laughter. 'We'll both be friends ...'

'The kiddies have arrived,' Dottie told Jacob Prout when she met him near the village green. 'They came on the train yesterday, so we'll be seeing them around the village soon.'

'Hope they knows how to behave, then,' Jacob grunted, pushing back his cap. 'Some of they tackers from the city got no idea how to go on out in the country.'

'I'm not sure all these are city children,' Dottie said doubtfully. 'Anyway, I can't stand here chattering, I've got shopping to do. I want to get to the bakery before George sells out of crusty loaves.'

'Talking of George Sweet,' Jacob said as she made to pass on, 'have you noticed Ivy's hair lately?'

Dottie stopped. 'Ivy's hair? No – should I have? What's the matter with it?'

'Gone a funny sort of red colour,' Jacob said. 'Aggie Madge says she must be using henna, whatever that might be when it's at home. You have a look, see what you think.'

'You mean she's dyeing it? Why would she want to do that?'

'Search me.' He moved a little nearer, glancing both ways as if to make sure he couldn't be overheard. 'Unless it's something to do with that pub she works in, over to Horrabridge.'

Dottie stared at him. 'Why ever should it? The landlord wouldn't ask her to do that. He won't care what colour her hair is, as long as she does her work right.'

'I don't suppose Lennie cares,' Jacob said. 'But his customers might.'

Dottie shook her head. 'I don't know what you be getting at, Jacob, and I don't think I want to know. Ivy Sweet might not be my favourite person, nor yours, but what she does with her hair is her own business and nothing to do with anyone else.' She glanced up at his cap, now pulled firmly over his head again. 'I don't think you'd be too pleased if folk started gossiping about *your* hair, now would you!'

Jacob reddened and turned away. 'Nothing to gossip about,' he said tartly. 'And I wasn't gossiping, neither, just passing a remark, that's all. There's not many women her age would start dyeing their hair red for no reason, specially in a place like Burracombe. Downright common, if you ask me.'

Dottie gave him a look that said she wasn't asking him, and walked on. But she couldn't help wondering, as she approached the baker's shop, just why Ivy had started to dye her hair. Jacob was right: it wasn't something many women around forty years old would do. In towns, perhaps, but not out here. And it wasn't as if Ivy was much of an oil painting anyway, with her pinched mouth and face that could turn milk sour. Maybe Jacob was right and Lennie, who ran the pub she worked in, had asked her to smarten herself up a bit now that they had all these foreign airmen coming in from Harrowbeer aerodrome.

As she went into the shop, Ivy came out from the back to serve her. She usually worked there in the mornings, so that George could have a sleep after his night's baking, dealing with the customers who came in for fresh bread and morning goods – rolls and occasionally things like doughnuts, if George had had time to make any, that would be starting to go stale by dinner time.

She mumbled a hello. 'What can I do for you?'

'A cottage loaf, please, Ivy, and does George need any of my scones today? I've just got time to make a few before I go back to the Barton to help with the kiddies' dinners.' Her eyes strayed to Ivy's hair. It certainly looked very red, but not a natural red, more a kind of coppery shade with a bit of purple mixed in.

'I don't know what you're looking at,' Ivy said sharply, taking a cottage loaf from the rack behind her. 'Didn't nobody tell you it's rude to stare?'

'I'm sorry, Ivy, but I couldn't help noticing your hair. I mean, it's a bit different from your usual colour.'

'And what's wrong with that? Plenty of people dye their hair.'

Not Burracombe people, and not people your age, Dottie thought, but to say so would have really set Ivy going.

'I'm not saying there's anything wrong with it. Just that it's ...' she searched for a word that wouldn't offend, 'unusual.'

Ivy considered this and seemed to decide not to take offence. 'Well, I like to be a bit out of the ordinary,' she said at last. 'And Lennie thinks it's good for trade.'

'Yes, he must be busy these day, with all the foreign airmen coming in.' Dottie put the loaf into her basket. 'Easy to get on with, people say they are.'

Ivy's chin went up. 'And just what do you mean by that?'

'Why, nothing,' Dottie said, startled, although you never know what might touch Ivy on the raw. Then she remembered that Ivy had been a bit prickly when she had mentioned the foreign airmen before. 'Only what I've heard a few folk say. I dare say Lennie's glad of the extra custom.'

'He seems pleased enough,' Ivy said grudgingly. 'But that's nothing to do with my hair, which I see you still can't keep your eyes off.'

Dottie looked at her carefully. There was an edge to Ivy's voice that she hadn't noticed before, and she looked pale and tired. I don't think she's all that well, Dottie thought. Maybe it's too much for her, working in the pub several evenings a week and then here in the bakery.

'Are you all right, Ivy?' she enquired. 'You do look a bit washed out. I'm sorry if I've said anything to upset you.'

'Nothing you could say would upset me,' Ivy said untruthfully. 'I don't give tuppence for what people think. And I'm perfectly all right, thank you, so no need to lose sleep over either my health or my hair. And now I see I've got other customers coming in, so if you'd like to pay for the loaf ... And George left word that he'd like three dozen scones if you got time to make them, so perhaps it would be a good idea to go home and make a start, since you're so busy up at the Barton these days.'

Dottie drew in a breath, but handed over the money and left without another word, passing Aggie Madge and Mabel Purdy in the doorway. Both, she noticed as she walked away, had their eyes riveted by Ivy's hair.

At the Barton, she found herself working with the cook-housekeeper who had come with the rest of the children's home staff. Mrs Hatch was a tall, angular woman who was always brisk and busy, and had very quickly made it clear that she was in charge.

'I know you've worked for the family here, Miss Friend, and know your way about the kitchen, and I'm glad to have your help a few days a week, but you'll find that cooking for thirty children and staff is a very different matter from providing for smart dinner parties. As long as you understand that, I'm sure we'll get along very well together.'

'Yes, I'm sure we will.' Dottie wasn't quite so certain, but had made up her mind to co-operate. It was part of the war effort that everyone was required to make, after all. And if Mrs Napier could give up her home and move into an estate cottage, all without complaint, then Dottie was determined that she too could play her part.

'You just tell me what to do and I'll get on with it,' she said. 'I can turn my hand to pretty well anything. Is there anyone else to help you?'

'The older girls are expected to give a hand. They'll all need housework and cooking skills when they leave here, and it's no more than they'd do in an ordinary family home. It would be useful if you don't mind showing them what to do when they need it. Matron doesn't like too many cut fingers.'

'I'll be glad to help the little dears,' Dottie said warmly. 'Poor souls, losing their families as they have. I suppose a lot of it is to do with the war.'

'Some of them, yes. Little Maddy, for one. We don't know all their stories, of course – it's thought best that the kiddies are helped to forget – but she told me herself once how her mother and baby brother were killed in an air raid and then her father was lost at sea. And not only that ...' The housekeeper paused. 'Why, what is it, Miss Friend? You look quite upset.'

'Maddy?' Dottie repeated. 'The little girl with fair hair and big blue eyes? Or is there another Maddy?'

'Oh no. They don't allow more than one child with the same name, to save confusion. Why, have you seen her?'

'Yes,' Dottie said, tears coming to her eyes as she thought of the child she had rescued from the cedar tree. 'Yes, I believe I have ...' She turned away for a moment, but the other woman had noticed nothing and continued to talk.

'They're not all war orphans, mind. There are two or three whose mothers died when they were born, and a few foundlings. Babies whose mothers were young girls who got into trouble and left them on the doorstep, you know. It's not at all uncommon. There's one here now, in the nursery, just a few months old.' She shook her head. 'You can't help wondering how anyone could do it, abandoning her child to strangers, but there, I suppose the sort of girls who get into that situation don't think about the consequences.'

'They must wonder about it all their lives,' Dottie said thoughtfully. 'Imagine never knowing where your child was, whether it was happy and well treated. You might pass it in the street one day and never know it was yours ... Did you ever have children, Mrs Hatch?'

'One. He's in the army, somewhere in India. I don't know what we're doing out there, when we're supposed to be fighting Germany, but then this war has spread all over the world and I don't think anybody really knows why. And it's gone too far to be stopped now.' She shook her head at the hopelessness of it all. 'But nobody asks our opinion, Miss Friend, so all we can do is get on with the task the good Lord has set us, and just now that's to make cottage pie for thirty in these big enamel trays. Two of the girls will be coming in soon to help do the potatoes, so perhaps you'd be good enough to put out some bowls for the peeling.'

Dottie did as she was asked. She looked forward to helping teach the girls housework skills. It was something she had always longed for, a daughter to pass on her home-making abilities to. A three-year-old standing on a chair, stirring cake mixture and licking out the bowl; a five-year-old learning to crochet; an older girl making bread and cutting out material for her own frocks ... But Dottie had never married, though she'd had her chance – and thrown it away, she thought with a sigh – and so there had never been a daughter.

Now, she thought as two twelve-year-olds came into the kitchen and gave her an appraising stare, she might have that chance. It was a shame they wouldn't be able to do anything fancy, like ice cakes or make trifles, but she could help Mrs Hatch teach them the basics, and when they left here they'd be ready to go into service with someone like Mrs Napier and work their way up to cook or housekeeper. They'd be able to look after their own families and give them good, honest meals like cottage pie and toad in the hole that everyone liked, and they'd be able to knit and sew. All the things women ought to be able to do.

She thought of the little girl she had rescued from the cedar tree. There had been something about that child – Maddy – that had caught at Dottie's heart. She could not forget the look in those blue eyes, the hint of pain and sorrow hidden beneath the mischief. That's the sort of little girl I'd like to have had, she thought. It was a pity she wasn't old enough to come and help in the kitchens yet, but maybe Dottie could help in some other way – teach sewing, perhaps. The child wasn't too young to learn to sew clothes for her dolly.

She would ask Matron, she decided. Helping these little lost souls was to be her own special war work, and helping little Maddy the most special of all.

Chapter Twenty-Six

Maddy and Eileen soon made themselves at home at the Barton, exploring all the rooms that they were allowed in and then ranging further afield outside. Apart from the woods, there was the paddock, where the children were allowed to play, and a bigger field where the horses grazed. They were not allowed in there, but the two girls climbed up to sit on the gate, gazing at them wistfully

'I bet they're ever so tame,' Maddy said, the first time they did this. 'People ride them, so they must be. I bet if we bring apples or carrots out, they'd come over and we could get on their backs. We could ride round and round the field like bareback riders in a circus.'

'Or a Wild West film,' Eileen agreed. 'I used to go to see them with my brother.'

Eileen's brother had been lost at sea in the second year of the war, soon after being called up. Her mother had been a widow and died shortly afterwards, leaving Eileen with nobody to look after her. Many of the children at the home had similar stories to tell, but they seldom talked about them. They were kept busy all day, doing lessons either at the Barton or at the village school, helping in the house and garden – apart from the babies, all had duties of some kind – and making the most of their limited playtime. They barely had time to dwell on their own sorrows, and buried them deep in their hearts.

Anyway, there was far too much to interest them at Burracombe Barton. As well as the paddock, where the boys spent hours kicking an old football from end to end, scoring goals between the piles of coats or jumpers that served as goalposts, there were great areas of shrubbery where sprawling rhododendrons formed caves and tunnels that could be used as secret passages, dens and hideaways. The boys crawled along them holding bent sticks like pistols or larger ones like machine guns and rifles, imagining themselves as commandos or Secret Service agents, while the girls held dolls' tea parties in hidden clearings. They disappeared into the network of natural pathways every evening after tea, when they were allowed to run loose for an hour before bedtime, and came in looking like Red Indians, with faces and hands covered in red Devon soil, their knees roughened and grazed and their clothes torn.

'You'll all be banned from the grounds if you don't take more care,' Matron told them sternly. 'Clothes don't grow on trees. And who is going to mend them all?'

'Us, probably,' Eileen said gloomily when they had been sent to wash. 'The girls get all the boring jobs. The boys will be able to go out into the sheds with Mr Crocker and learn woodwork, and we'll have to stay indoors and mend their things. It's not fair.'

Dottie, who had seen them troop indoors, dirty but beaming, offered to come two evenings a week to sit with the girls and take mending sessions. Nurse Powell and the other staff, who already had quite enough to do, welcomed this offer and the girls were delighted. They had all taken to Dottie and were happy to sit sewing even the boys' short flannel trousers and blue shirts, while she entertained them with stories of Burracombe and the London theatre where she had worked for a while as a dresser to the famous Fenella Forsyth.

'Fancy you knowing someone famous,' Maddy marvelled as Dottie, her mouth full of pins, showed her how to turn a shirt collar. 'Does she ever come to see you in Burracombe?'

'Of course she doesn't, silly,' Eileen said. 'She's overseas, entertaining the troops, and anyway she wouldn't want to come to a little place like this.'

'As a matter of fact, she does,' Dottie said. 'She's very friendly with Mrs Napier, whose house this is, and comes down quite often – that's how I came to meet her myself. She's coming again quite soon, I believe.'

The girls stared at her. 'Fenella Forsyth? Coming here?' ...

'When?' ... 'Will we be able to meet her?' ... 'Can we get her auto-graph?' ... 'Will there be a concert?' ... 'Will she sing one of her songs?'

The hubbub rose until Dottie raised her hands for silence. 'Quiet, or we'll have Matron coming in to see what's going on, and I won't be allowed to come and help you any more. I don't know exactly when she's coming, but I know she means to, and that's all I can say. As for singing and autographs, well, you'll have to wait and see.'

'My daddy liked Fenella Forsyth,' Maddy said as they went back to their sewing, brimming with excitement. 'He had some of her records, to play on the gramophone. I know all the songs by heart.' She began to sing and the others joined in.

Dottie sat in her chair, listening and watching them, and she felt her heart grow warm. All these children, robbed of everything a child needed most – a home and family of their own – comforted, just as the men so far away were comforted, by the songs of a woman who had only her voice, her beauty and her own generous spirit to give, but gave them all freely. And they're worth giving, Dottie thought. She cheers people up, makes them stronger, whoever they are. Wherever Fenella went, she made people feel better.

And look at these little ones now – they didn't even have to see her to feel it. They just had to sing her songs, to remember who she was and what she did. And every time they sang them, they grew a little bit stronger.

'I'll ask her to come and see you,' she said. 'She's a very nice lady and I'm sure she'll make time for you.'

'These new kiddies up at the Barton,' Alice Tozer said. 'I reckon us ought to lay on some sort of party for them. Welcome them to the village, like.'

The members of the Women's Institute turned in their seats to stare at her. So far, the discussion had been mostly about such regu-lar events as the harvest supper, the monthly soup lunches held in the chapel, and the village whist drives. None of these were strictly WI business, but they had all been busy making jam and preserv-ing fruit, which hardly needed discussing at all, and the knitting and sewing circles had already laid out this month's production of gloves, scarves, balaclavas and socks (mostly navy blue or khaki) on a side table to be viewed before being sent off. So, as they were all concerned with one or other of the other village events, they felt justified in discussing them.

It wasn't as if there were all that many events, these days. Before the war, the village would have been planning for the Deanery bell-ringing festival, Bonfire Night, at least two entertainment evenings when anyone who could sing or tell a story would get up on the stage they made out of pallets, and a pantomime in the new year. But bonfires and bell ringing, apart from some Sunday services if ringers were available, had been forbidden since the war began, and there were not enough young people left to run a pantomime.

'A party?' Aggie Madge said doubtfully. 'Won't that put our own youngsters' noses out of joint? It don't seem to take much to set them all against each other.'

'Well, we'd ask them along too. It would help them get to know each other better. We'm all on the same side, when all's said and done.'

'I don't know as it's a good idea,' Ivy Sweet said, but as she always automatically opposed anything Alice Tozer suggested, nobody felt inclined to take much notice. 'I've heard they're a lot of ragamuffins up there, and doing heaven knows what damage to the place. Poor Mrs Napier must be at her wits' end with it all.'

'Well, you've heard wrong, then,' Dottie said indignantly. 'I'm up there every day, pretty well, and I can tell you they're just the same as any other kiddies, some good and some bad, but on the whole they're no worse than any of ours. Some of them are little dears. And you got to remember they've all lost their mothers and fathers, and it's only right us should try to make up for it a bit. Alice is right – us ought to give them a party.'

'But where's the food going to come from? You know how things are, Dottie. We're all putting by a bit for Christmas now, and my George can't make enough cakes and such for forty or fifty children.'

'We can all put in a bit,' Alice said. 'We can make some sandwiches and cakes each with what we've got, and there's still some fruit about – apples and plums and blackberries and such. We could make a few pies between us. Anyway, 'tisn't the food that matters so much; 'tis the company and letting them see we're pleased to have them here.'

She saw from their faces that not everyone was pleased to have the children there. They had suffered from the evacuees who had arrived after the Blitz had hit Plymouth, although in Alice's opinion that was as much the village children's fault as the evacuees'. Resentful at having to share so much with the townies, they had made little effort to befriend them, and the evacuees, many bombed out of their homes and left with no possessions of their own, had been sullen and bitter. There had been many a battle between them in the fields and woods or up on the moor, and even some real damage before the head teachers of each faction had taken a hand and settled things down. That was why she felt it important to get them off on the right foot now.

'It's not the same as last time,' Dottie said, understanding their reaction. 'Those children were just spread around the houses willy-nilly and nobody had any choice. And even though a lot went back after a while, the ones who are still here have settled in all right. But these new kiddies are all in one place, like a school, and they have to obey the rules. Matron's very strict and so is the boys' housemaster, as they call him. They don't stand any nonsense, I can tell you.'

'I think we should do it,' Constance Bellamy declared. She was a tiny woman of around seventy, who lived in a large house at the other end of the village from the Barton and moved in the same circles as the Napiers. She commanded a good deal of respect in Burracombe and had the last word in much of what was decided. 'We haven't suffered too badly from the war here and it behoves us to do the best we can for these unfortunate little ones. I was thinking of having them to tea myself, three or four at a time, but a party all together is a much better idea.'

Miss Kemp, the head teacher at the village school, nodded. 'I know them, of course, because they come to the school, and I agree with Miss Friend that although they have their difficulties, they're no worse than any of our own children, and they need to be shown that they're welcome.'

'Just think if it was our own little ones, left homeless and with no family,' Nancy Pengelly said. 'I couldn't bear to think of my Bob and Terry sent away to live with strangers and having folk turn their backs on them. Why, 'tis cruel.'

'I don't think any of us have turned our backs on them,' Aggie

Madge said at once. 'That's not Burracombe's way. Dottie and Alice are right – we got to make an effort. I reckon it ought to be done as soon as possible.'

'What about Saturday week?' someone suggested. 'It's the last week of September and there'll still be a few blackberries – us won't be able to pick them after that anyway, the Devil will have spat on them – and plenty of apples. We can give them blackberry and apple pie with a bit of custard, and maybe pasties to start with.'

'That's two lots of pastry,' Dottie pointed out. 'The home don't like giving them too much pastry, say it's not healthy.'

'Stewed fruit, then. It'll be easier anyway. And a few rock cakes to fill them up. I don't mind making a dozen or two.'

Now that the decision was made, the meeting became more enthusiastic and other suggestions began to be offered. Miss Kemp volunteered to make a list. 'I'll help with the organising if you like,' she said diffidently. 'It might be easiest for me, since I know all the children.' Someone gave her an old envelope and she began to write on the back of it, and soon had quite a lot of names.

'That ought to be enough,' Aggie Madge said, peering over her shoulder. 'There'll be plenty more to do besides stew blackberries and apples and make pasties. They'll want squash to drink, and there'll be tables and chairs to set out, and someone ought to be in charge of the games. That had better be one of the men. And maybe us could put up some decorations – string a few flags and a bit of bunting around the walls. It always looks nice to come into the hall and see some bunting, makes it look special.'

The party looked like becoming a celebration as much as a welcome. Alice and Dottie talked about it as they walked back through the village together afterwards.

'It was a good thought of yours, Alice. They're nice little tackers on the whole, and been given a rough time, and it will be good for them to think they'm welcome here. Kiddies in children's homes always feel a bit different, I reckon, and the other children feel it too and don't always know how to be kind to them.'

'Children never do take to others who live different lives to them,' Alice observed. 'Look at what happens when the gipsies come with Goose Fair. Our kiddies always like going to Tavi for the fair all right, but they don't like the gipsy children coming out here, and the gipsies don't like them much either.'

'Well, gipsies have never been popular, have they? Folk always think the worst of them – though if you ask me, kiddies are kiddies whoever they are.' Dottie paused. 'Talking of foreigners, have you noticed anything about Ivy Sweet just lately?'

'Ivy Sweet? Can't say I have, but as you know, we've never had much to say to each other, not from right back when I first came to the village.'

Dottie laughed. 'That's right! She was after your Ted then and proper got her nose put out of joint when he fancied you instead. But I was thinking the other day when I was in the shop that she looks a bit peaky lately.'

'It's that awful colour she's dyed her hair. It would make anyone look peaky.'

'You're right, but I don't think it's just that. I don't think she's all that well, Alice. I can't pretend I've ever liked her much, and I've known her since we were toddlers, but I wouldn't wish her any harm. I think maybe us should go a bit careful with her, just in case.'

'In case of what?' Alice gave her a sideways glance. 'Maybe you don't know the signs like I do, Dottie, but whatever's making Ivy look peaky, I don't reckon it's any illness. I know it'd be a surprise at her age, and seeing how long she and George have been married, but I wouldn't be surprised if Ivy Sweet don't make an announcement before many more weeks have gone by.'

'An announcement?' Dottie paused with her hand on her garden gate and stared at her friend. 'What do you mean?' She saw Alice's raised eyebrows and her puzzled expression cleared, to be replaced by astonishment. 'You mean she might be *expecting*? Ivy Sweet? Never!'

'No reason why not,' Alice retorted. 'I dare say she and George thought it would never happen, but like they say, life's full of surprises, and this could be one of them. Anyway, us'll soon find out, even if Ivy don't deign to tell us officially. But why she should suddenly start to dye her hair is anyone's guess.'

Yes, it is, Dottie thought as she said goodnight and went into her cottage. And there would be plenty of people guessing, too.

*

Isobel Napier, who had missed the WI meeting, heard about the party from Dottie, who was making steak and kidney pudding, and had her own suggestions to make.

'It's a lovely idea. Alice Tozer's a very kind woman to think of it. I'm sure it will make a lot of difference to the children.'

'Our own kiddies will be asked too,' Dottie said, cutting the meat into cubes. She put them into a saucepan where a chopped onion had been gently frying for several minutes, and turned them over with a wooden spoon to brown them. 'It's to help them get to know each other. They all seem to keep themselves to themselves now, you see, village children and home children separate, and it don't help that they don't all go to school at the same time. We want them to be friends.'

'Yes, of course.' Isobel thought for a minute. 'Dottie, why don't we have the party at the Barton? We could have it in the paddock – it's still warm enough and there's that big marquee in the barn that we used to use before the war, so it won't matter if it rains. It would be lovely to get that out again. We could have games out there too – races and so on. And the children could help prepare it all, couldn't they? What do you think?'

Dottie gazed at her. 'You wouldn't mind? I mean, a lot of young tackers running wild all over your garden ...'

'Well, they're doing that already! And it's only in the paddock. They can't do much harm there. We could keep the horses in the stables that day, so they could use the field as well. It would be so much nicer than the village hall. Why don't we ask the other WI ladies?'

Dottie made up her mind. 'They'll say yes, for certain. I'll pop round to Alice Tozer on my way home and see what she thinks, but I reckon everyone would be pleased. We'll need to get the trestle tables and chairs up from the hall.' She started to mix the flour and suet together.

'No, we've got our own somewhere. One of the old estate workers will know. Anyway, now that's settled, let me tell you my other news.' Isobel's eyes were bright with excitement. 'I heard from Fenella this morning. She's coming to stay at the end of next week! Her doctor says she needs a few weeks in the country to recuperate before she goes abroad again.'

'Oh, that *is* good news.' Dottie's round face flushed with pleasure. 'Why, that means she'll be here for the party! Do you think she'll come along, Mrs Napier? Some of the girls were asking about her the other day. There's one little dear knows all her songs and started to sing them, in such a sweet voice, and before I knew it they were all singing.'

'We'll have to see how she is. She's been quite poorly, you know, and I don't want her overtaxing herself.'

'No, us got to look after her,' Dottie agreed. 'I dare say she's as thin as a stick too and will want fattening up.'

Isobel looked amused. 'Well, we're not planning to sell her in the market, Dottie. You make her sound like a spring lamb!'

'And so she is, a dear lamb,' Dottie declared, mixing water into the flour and suet. 'There, that'll be a good dinner for you and ... who did you say was coming?'

'The vicar and his wife, and Miss Bellamy. She probably doesn't feed herself properly, just grubs up a few vegetables from her garden and stews them with an Oxo cube. I like to make sure she has a meat meal now and then.'

'She buys as much meat as her ration gives her, and liver too, when Bert Foster's got it,' Dottie said, rolling out the suet pastry and spreading the meat on top. She formed it into a ball and wrapped it in a square of white cotton, torn from an old sheet. 'But I reckon she gives most of it to those dogs of hers. Fat as butter, they are. There, I'll just pop this into some boiling water and you can leave it until you're ready. Just keep the water on the simmer, and make sure it don't boil dry.' She washed the flour from her hands and dried them on the roller towel hanging on the back of the kitchen door. 'You'll be all right doing the vegetables, will you? Only I promised to go up to the Barton this evening to help with the little ones' baths.'

'I'll be quite all right,' Isobel said with a laugh. 'I did learn to cook at finishing school, you know. Look at all that jam I made last week!'

'It's a wonder to behold.' Dottie smiled. 'Young Stephen will be asking to take some back to school.'

'He did take a couple of pots when term started, but that was plum and he's not so keen on that. He likes the blackberry and apple best. And strawberry, of course, but I can never get that to set properly.'

'It needs more pectin,' Dottie said. 'You make it by stewing apples and straining out the juice. Trouble is, strawberries and apples don't come at the same time.' She took her jacket off the hook and thrust her arms into the sleeves. 'Well, if that's all you need me to do, I'll be on my way. I'll go and talk to Alice about the party. I'm sure she'll be pleased, and we might slip round to Miss Bellamy and see what she thinks, too. Then we can just let the members know, and start planning.' She paused. 'And I know we're not allowed to ice cakes these days, but it would really be the icing on *our* cake if Miss Fenella would come along and give the children a song. I'll write and ask her myself, this very afternoon.'

News of the party spread quickly through the village, and the newcomers issued invitations as grandly as if they had lived at the Barton all their lives. Not all the village children were impressed.

'That's *our* place,' Roy Pettifer said jealously as the two factions encountered each other on the village green. ''Tisn't yours, to go asking people to parties.'

'Well, we're living there,' one of the boys retorted. 'So it's ours now. But you don't have to come to the party if you don't want to.'

'It's not your party anyway,' Jackie Tozer pointed out. 'My mum says the WI thought of it and it's Burracombe people are doing all the work.'

'It's *for* us, though,' Eileen argued. 'To welcome us to the village and show we can all be friends. That's what Matron said.'

'It still don't mean you can say who can come and who can't.'

'We can *all* come,' Maddy declared. 'That's what Miss Friend said. It's going to be a big party for everyone in the village and there's going to be a great big tent we can all sleep in, and—'

'*Sleep* in?' Vic Nethercott echoed. He was Roy's best friend and the two were seldom seen apart. 'I never heard nothing about sleeping there.'

'Well, it must be true, or why would we be having a tent?' Maddy had heard nothing about sleeping either, but wasn't going to back down easily.

'That's in case it rains, stupid!' The boys began to jeer at her and she ran at them, waving her fists. Vic laughed and grabbed her wrists, holding her away from him so that she couldn't even kick his shins, and Roy began to tickle her under her outstretched arms.

Maddy squealed and tried to wriggle away. 'Don't do that! Stop it!' She was half laughing, half crying, and stamping her feet with temper. '*Stop it!*'

Jackie grabbed Roy's arm and tried to drag him away. 'Leave her alone. You can see she doesn't like it.'

'She's laughing, isn't she?'

'Everyone laughs when they're being tickled. It doesn't mean they like it. Let go of her, Roy.' She pulled his arm and gave him a kick.

'Ow!' Roy let go and Maddy skipped out of his reach. He bent to rub his leg. 'You shouldn't kick, Jackie Tozer.'

'You shouldn't bully little girls,' she retorted. She went over to Maddy, who was standing with Eileen, sniffing and rubbing her face. 'Don't take any notice. They're the stupid ones. Not worth bothering with. Especially that Roy Pettifer.' She scowled at him and he stuck out his tongue.

'We're coming to the party anyway. You can't stop us.'

Jackie turned her back. She took hold of Maddy's arm. 'You come with me. I'll show you our chickens.'

Maddy and Eileen followed her along the village street to the drive leading to the Tozers' farm. Maddy, who had been on farms when she lived at Bridge End, looked about her with interest, but Eileen, who had rarely been outside Southampton, hung back, casting nervous glances at the cows that were being led through the yard.

'What are they doing?'

'They've just been milked,' Jackie explained. 'They're going back to their field. They won't hurt you.'

Eileen still hesitated. 'How do you know that? They've got horns, and that one's looking at me as if he doesn't like me.'

'Don't be daft. They're as gentle as lambs. And they're shes, not hes.'

'All of them?'

'Of course. You can't get milk from bulls.' Jackie rolled her eyes and Maddy giggled.

'It's all right,' she said to Eileen. 'I used to go to the farm when I was evacuated before. I saw them being milked and one day the farmer let me try myself. I couldn't get much out, though.'

'I often help,' Jackie said offhandedly. 'It's easy when you know how.' The cows had all left the yard now and the girls went through the gate.

'It's a bit mucky,' Eileen said, looking down. 'We'll get into trouble if we get our shoes dirty.'

'They're only our playing shoes.' Maddy was following Jackie eagerly. She was pleased to have been singled out and hoped they would be invited into the farmhouse as well. More than most of the children, Maddy missed being in a real home, with a family, and craved the feeling of sitting in a warm kitchen with a motherly woman to look after her. She thought of Mrs Mudge at the vicarage, and sighed wistfully.

Jackie took them across the yard to where a flutter of hens was pecking busily at the ground. She went into a small barn and came out with three buckets of chicken feed.

'Here, you can help me feed them. Just throw it on the ground.' She gave the two girls a bucket each and they began to scatter the feed. The hens rushed at them, squawking and squabbling for the food, and Eileen laughed.

'I like them! Do they lay eggs?'

'Well, we wouldn't keep them if they didn't.' Jackie was throwing in a businesslike, experienced sort of way. 'We'll go and look for some in a minute. They're supposed to lay in their boxes, but they go all over the place. My mum once found twenty in a pile between two bales of hay in the barn. Every one the hen laid slipped down the crack and she didn't even know they were there. They were too old to be any good, though.'

'Do you keep them all for yourselves?' The children at the Barton rarely saw a fresh egg and seldom got a boiled one to themselves. Most of their eggs were dried, which were only good for making cakes or scrambling.

Jackie shook her head. 'We're not allowed to. We have to sell most of them.' She didn't say that they probably kept a few more than was really permitted, just as most people did who had chickens. Even the authorities couldn't tell precisely how many eggs a hen would lay.

Alice Tozer came out of the house and looked across the yard. 'Who's that you've got with you, Jackie?'

'It's Maddy and Eileen,' Jackie called. 'From the Barton.'

'The Barton? Well, ask them in. Your granny's just made some biscuits.'

The girls crowded into the big farmhouse kitchen and Maddy closed her eyes in bliss. The warmth coming from the range, the smell of biscuits fresh from the oven, the gentle hiss of the big kettle and the sight of a ginger cat curled up on an older woman's lap in a large wooden armchair gave her an instant feeling of being at home. I wish I could live somewhere like this, she thought. A proper home, instead of a children's home.

'Are you all right, my dear?' Alice Tozer asked, a little anxiously, and Maddy opened her eyes. 'Not feeling faint, are you?'

'No, I'm all right. I was just ...' She didn't know how to explain what she was feeling; instead she smiled at Alice, and the farmer's wife drew her close to the range and held both hands out to the fire to warm them before rubbing Maddy's own hands. 'You'm cold, that's what it is,' she declared. 'This September weather can be proper treacherous. Here, come and sit by Jackie's granny and I'll make you a cup of cocoa.' She moved the kettle across to a hotter part of the range to bring it to the boil.

Maddy sat down obediently on a stool beside the big armchair. Minnie Tozer smiled down at her and stretched out a foot to move her footstool for Eileen to use. The two girls sat close, suddenly shy.

'You both like cocoa, don't you?' Alice asked, and they nodded. 'And the biscuits are nearly ready. They need to cool down before they go crisp.' She stirred cocoa to a paste in three cups, with a teaspoon of sugar and some milk. The kettle was boiling now and she poured hot water on the mixture. 'I'll put in a drop more milk. You two look as if you could do with it. Are they looking after you over at the Barton? Feeding you proper and all that?'

'Yes, thank you,' Eileen said. 'We have milk every morning. And porridge.'

'That's good. Porridge is good for you. And once you've been out here in the fresh country air for a few weeks, you'll start to get those roses in your cheeks and look just like Burracombe children do. Now, here's your cocoa, my dears. Jackie, fetch some plates out for the biscuits, there's a good girl.'

'They're ginger,' Minnie Tozer said, her wrinkled hands stroking the cat on her lap. 'Same as Ginger here. Like cats, do you?'

The two girls nodded. Maddy had never had a cat of her own, but there had been one at the vicarage, living mostly in the kitchen as this one probably did. 'My friend Sammy had a parrot,' she said.

'A parrot?' Minnie echoed. 'Well, that's a funny pet! And who was Sammy?'

'Sammy Hodges. He was evacuated, like me, and he was my best friend. It wasn't really *his* parrot,' she added, anxious to tell the truth. 'It belonged to Mrs Purslow that he lived with, but it was just like his. We took it out on a picnic in the forest one day.'

'On a picnic? Weren't you afraid it would fly away?'

'It was tied to its stand,' Maddy explained. 'But then some big birds came and frightened it, and it fell off. Mrs Purslow was really cross, and Sammy's dad came that night and nearly took him home again.'

The two women gazed at her, evidently suspecting that there was more to this story than Maddy was telling them. Jackie produced the plates and Alice put some biscuits on them and passed them over.

'Well, I hope it all ended happily and Sammy took better care of the parrot after that. He probably shouldn't have taken it outside.'

'No, he shouldn't,' Maddy agreed, not mentioning that she had more or less bullied him into doing so, just as she had cajoled him into many of the other scrapes they had got into. She sighed heavily, remembering those days that seemed so endlessly happy now, and wondered if she would ever see Sammy again.

'Ginger used to get into a lot of trouble when he was a kitten,' Jackie observed, settling herself on another stool and munching a biscuit. 'He got right up on the kitchen roof one day and wouldn't come down. Dad had to get a ladder and put it up, and he just went higher. He was up there ages.'

'How did you get him down in the end?' Maddy enquired.

'Dad put a plate of food on the lower part of the roof, and Ginger jumped down and upset it, and it went all over Dad's head. It was really funny.'

'Your father didn't think so,' Alice said, picking up some knitting. 'Now, what time do you two girls think you should go back to the Barton? I wouldn't like them to be worrying about you.'

'I don't expect they'll do that.' Maddy licked her finger and dabbed at some crumbs on her lap, then put them in her mouth. 'They might be cross, though. We were only supposed to be out for half an hour.'

'Half an hour? And what time was that?'

'I don't know. About half past three?' She glanced interrogatively at Eileen, who nodded.

'We were supposed to be back for tea, and tea's at four o'clock.'

'But it's gone half past four!' Alice exclaimed. 'Of course they'll be worried! You must go at once. You'd better tell them you came here with Jackie and forgot the time.'

Maddy stood up. 'Come on, Eileen, or we'll miss tea.' She turned her smile on the two women. 'Thank you for having us, and thank you for the biscuits. They were lovely.' She glanced casually at the plate. 'It won't matter so much if we miss tea, since we've had those, but we might still be a bit hungry ...'

Alice laughed. 'Take another two each to eat on the way back, and tell your teacher – Matron, is it? – that we're sorry we kept you here but we didn't realise ... And come again, won't you? We'll always be pleased to see you at Tozers' Farm.'

The girls ran out, and Alice turned to Minnie with a smile. 'That one's a real little monkey; you can see it in her eyes. And she knows how to turn the charm on, too! A proper little heartbreaker she's going to be.'

Minnie nodded. 'I wonder what sort of home she came from, and what happened to her family. That's the sad thing about these little ones, Alice – they've all lost the people most dear to them, and they probably don't even understand why.' She shook her head. 'It's a cruel thing, war, and it's the little ones who suffer the most, and I don't reckon the men who start wars even give that a thought.'

Chapter Twenty-Seven

To everyone's relief, the day of the party was fine and almost the entire village made its way to the Barton to prepare for it. Since Alice had made her first suggestion, the idea had taken on gigantic proportions and there was much to be done and a lot of help needed to do it.

The marquee, which in the days before the war had usually been erected on the wide, sweeping lawns in front of the house, was put up – not without a struggle – by those of the estate workers who had not been called up for military service and who were mostly of an age when hauling vast lengths of heavy canvas about was a task they thought they had left behind them. They were helped by the local Land Girls, who had never put up anything larger than a bell tent at Girl Guide camp, and most of them not even that.

'These long poles slot together for the roof,' Jacob Prout declared, taking charge. 'We got to lay them out first. And those over there, they make the doorway. Who's got the guy ropes?'

'Who hasn't?' Ted Tozer's cousin Norman demanded crossly, trying to disentangle a mass of rope that had probably been put away neatly coiled but had, in the way of all ropes, cables and wires when left to themselves, mysteriously tied itself into knots. Several such masses had been unearthed from the barn where the marquee was kept, and as they had now had several years in which to carry out their evil task, they were not only tangled but stiff with damp and, in some cases, turning green.

'I don't reckon half of this belongs to the marquee at all,' Norman said. 'Us'll never get all they sorted out.'

'Yes, we will,' Joanna, the Tozers' Land Girl, said cheerfully.

'It's no worse than a skein of knitting. Come on, girls, we'll do this while the men spread out the canvas. Our fingers are more nimble than theirs.'

Nimble or not, their fingers were sore by the time they had finished, although they had to admit there did seem to be more rope than was needed. They laid it out in new coils along the side of the paddock while some of the Burracombe boys, delighted to have the chance to nose about in the Barton outbuildings, discovered several boxes of tent pegs for the guys to be fastened into the ground.

The marquee was finally erected, as perfect as you could expect in wartime, Jacob declared – although why it should be any less perfect in wartime than when peace prevailed he didn't explain – with just one bulge along one side and a corresponding ruckle in the other where popular opinion had it the guys were wrongly placed. Two or three of the Land Girls, overseen by Jacob, tried altering the positions to correct this, only to find that the bulge and ruckle had also apparently changed places, and Jacob thought it had looked better in the first place so wanted it changed back; at which point Norman and Ted Tozer, who were rather tired of Jacob's officiousness, advised him that if he wanted anything else changed about he was welcome to do it himself, but they were ready for their tea and in any case had cows to milk. They didn't exactly throw their tools at his feet, since the only tool they had between them was a clump hammer for knocking the pegs into the ground and Ted wanted to take it back to the farm to make sure it didn't get lost, but the look on their faces convinced Jacob that everyone had done enough and it was time to call a halt.

''Tis only for a kiddies' party, anyway,' he muttered, loudly enough to be heard. 'Not as if it was for summat smart and got to be done proper.'

'And "thank you everybody" would have been nice, too,' Ted grumbled to his cousin as they made their way back to the farm. But they knew Jacob and his moods, and it had been a hot and difficult afternoon, so they didn't hold it against him. You couldn't hold too much against Jacob, anyway – he was too useful around the village.

Nobody noticed either the bulge or the ruckle as they crowded into the marquee. The women had come early, bringing tablecloths and old sheets to drape on the long tables that had been used so many times for harvest suppers, returning home once the cloths were spread for plates of sandwiches, buns and jam tarts ('I always think a plate of jam tarts cheers a table up,' Dottie remarked) and jugs of orange and lemon squash. The long benches that had always been kept with the tables having apparently vanished, Miss Kemp had got some of the bigger boys to carry the forms used at the school dinner tables through the village, stopping several times along the way to rest. Just before they arrived, old Mr Crocker remembered that the benches had been moved to a different barn, and they were brought out and set up, so the boys had to turn round and carry theirs back.

George Sweet had made a huge cake, big enough for a royal wedding, which stood in the middle of the top table with a paper flag on top saying 'Welcome to Burracombe'. Ivy had stuck it in on a meat skewer and stood back to admire the effect.

'Nobody can say we haven't tried our best,' she said to Aggie Madge and Dottie, who had come to stand beside her. 'I just hope they're grateful.'

'I'm sure they will be,' Dottie said, trying not to steal covert glances at Ivy's shape. No announcement had been made yet, but she was pretty sure Ivy's waist looked thicker, and her hair was definitely redder, although what that might have to do with her being in the family way she had no idea. 'It's a lovely cake, Ivy. George has done a good job.'

'Well, he's the only one got a big enough tin and oven. And you needn't keep gawking at me like that, Dottie. I know what you're thinking.'

Dottie felt her cheeks redden and quickly averted her gaze. 'I'm not thinking anything!'

'Oh yes you are, and so is every other busybody in the village.' Ivy stared at her defiantly. 'Well, since you're so interested, you might as well know, and you can spread it about too, since everyone will be able to see for themselves soon. I'm expecting, and there's nothing to be ashamed of in that. My George is as pleased as Punch.'

'My goodness,' Dottie said faintly, almost lost for words, and then, rallying, 'Congratulations, Ivy. What a surprise. I mean – you must be really happy about it, after all these years.'

'And what does that mean?'

'Why, nothing. Only that – well, you've been married quite a while, and we all sort of thought ...' Dottie floundered to a stop, quelled by Ivy's glowering look. 'We thought perhaps you didn't want children. Not everybody does.'

'So the whole village has been talking about us behind our backs,' Ivy said bitterly. 'It's no more than I'd have expected, mind. Well, now you've all got something else to chew the fat over, and you can do it to your hearts' content. Why me and George haven't started a family before now is our business and nobody else's, and why we're doing it now is ours too, just the same. And you can tell that to anyone else who asks, Dottie Friend.'

'I'm sorry, Ivy,' Dottie said. 'I didn't mean to offend. I'm really pleased for you, and so will everyone else be. And it's a lovely cake. It really is. You've done Burracombe proud.'

Ivy gave her a suspicious look, then sniffed and said, 'I'd better get back. There'll be customers in, party or no party, and my George needs his rest after being up baking all night.' She turned and marched away, her back stiff.

'My stars,' Aggie Madge said. 'So Ivy's expecting, is she? I don't know how it struck you, Dottie, but it didn't seem to me she was as happy about it as she'd like to pretend. There was a funny look in her eyes – almost like she was hiding something. I wonder if George is as pleased as she says, too.' She chuckled. 'I wouldn't have minded being a fly on the wall in the bakery when Ivy gave him the good news, would you?'

'I don't know, Aggie,' Dottie replied slowly. 'And I don't think us ought to talk like that. I hardly like to say it, but Ivy's right – there *is* too much gossip in Burracombe, and sometimes it can be downright harmful. If Ivy says she and George are pleased, I think us ought to believe her. Give her the benefit of whatever doubt we might think there is.' She sighed. 'The trouble with Ivy is that it's all too easy to put her back up, and she's no better at accepting an apology than she is at giving one.'

By three o'clock that afternoon, the party was in full swing. Isobel Napier had made a speech welcoming the children to Burracombe and hoping their time here would be happy, and thanking the villagers for making this party possible. Basil Harvey, the vicar, who hadn't intended to say anything but felt he ought to respond, made a rather hesitant little speech, saying that he was still quite new to the village, but he felt sure that everyone was more than grateful to Mrs Napier – and Colonel Napier too, of course, who was away helping to win this dreadful war – for allowing them to use her lovely grounds for the party and providing the marquee and doing so much for the village in general and the children in particular, and ... At which point, sensing that he was about to flounder, his wife, Grace, tugged at the hem of his jacket and whispered that he'd said enough now, so he sat down thankfully and everyone applauded, more because they hoped the speeches were over than because it had been a good one.

Not that the speeches *were* over, because Matron felt there should be a response from the children's home, for whom, after all, the party was being held, so she got up and gave the gathering a potted history of the home, which in most cases went in at one ear and out of the other, and after that the boys' housemaster, not to be outdone, rose to his feet as well, but by this time the audience had decided enough was truly enough and begun to talk amongst themselves, and he was wise enough to utter no more than a few words of thanks before capturing the final moment of glory by announcing that the afternoon's games would now begin, which got the biggest cheer of all.

Miss Kemp and Jacob Prout then came forward to organise the races, starting with running from one end of the roped-off track (the extra ropes had come in handy for this) to the other. Running races were always good as time fillers, because they needed no equipment and you could divide the children up into a number of groups according to age, as well as separating the boys and girls, so a good half-hour could pass just on these. There was a lot of rivalry between the village children and the visitors, as the newcomers were termed, and loud cheers for the winners. Maddy won the race in her age group, with Jackie Tozer a close second, and they sat down together and shared Maddy's prize – a small Crunchie bar, which had cost Miss Kemp fourpence and one point of her sweet ration.

After the running races came sack races, with sacks provided by Ted Tozer and smelling strongly of chicken feed, and three-legged races in which the legs for each couple had to belong to one village child and one Barton child. This caused some reluctance amongst the participants, but eventually they were all paired off, and apart from Vic Nethercott, who was partnered by a large boy with black hair and thick eyebrows and a glowering look about him, they accepted their fate with fairly good grace and by the time they reached the finishing line were laughing and punching each other good-humouredly. In the case of Vic and Bertie Blake, however, the punches were not good-humoured and the two had to be separated and sent to different parts of the paddock.

The last race was the egg and spoon, in which Maddy, who had a steady hand and understood that this was the one race in which the slowest had the best chance of winning, was confident of success and, possibly, another Crunchie bar. The eggs were the china ones Alice Tozer used to encourage her hens to lay, and they were balanced on dessert spoons. Miss Kemp blew her whistle and the racers set off, most far too quickly and dropping their eggs almost as soon as they started.

Picking the egg up was as much an art as the actual race, since you were not allowed to touch it, only to scoop it up with the spoon, which on the trampled and uneven grass was a tricky proposition. Maddy, moving at little more than walking pace (which was also forbidden), passed the others smugly, holding her spoon out at arm's length and keeping her eyes firmly fixed on it – so firmly fixed that she tripped on a tuft of grass, staggered, and dropped the egg within inches of the finishing line. As, half weeping with frustration, she tried in vain to scoop it back into its spoon, the rest of the racers passed her, and by the time she had finally captured her egg, she was so far behind the others that the rest of them had wandered off and only Miss Kemp waited sympathetically for her to straighten up and take the final step or two over the line.

'Never mind,' said Jackie, who had actually won. 'You can share my prize this time. It's a Kit Kat.' She flourished a bar wrapped in dark blue paper. 'It's plain chocolate, though. It says on the wrapper that they'll start doing their usual chocolate when milk is available again. We could have let them have some of our milk, if they'd said.' She unwrapped the bar and broke off a finger to hand to Maddy. 'Anyway, that's the races finished. I wonder what's next.'

The rest of the afternoon passed in ball games – football for the boys and rounders for the girls. Maddy and Jackie sat together on the long bench, where Eileen joined them, and the three ate sandwiches and buns and swapped stories about their homes.

'I wish I could stay in Burracombe for ever,' Maddy said. 'I like villages better than towns. Towns get bombed too much.'

'Not in peacetime,' Jackie argued. 'It's only in wars that you get bombing.'

'Yes, but some people say this war's never going to end. It's just going to go on and on, until everyone's dead.'

'Don't be daft,' said Roy Pettifer, who was sitting opposite. 'We're going to win. Mr Churchill says so.'

'Mr Churchill doesn't know everything,' Eileen said, and there was a shocked silence. 'Well, he *doesn't*. Nobody does.'

'Mr Churchill's helping us win this war,' Roy said dangerously, 'and then there'll be no more fighting. And anyone who says he's not is going to have to fight *me*.'

'That's right,' chimed in Vic, who was sitting beside him. 'That's the trouble with you evacuees, you only see the bad side of everything. And what I always say is—' But they never heard what Vic always said, because at that moment Mrs Napier, who was sitting at the top table with some of the other grown-ups, stood up, rapped on a plate with her spoon and called for silence.

'I hope you've all had a lovely afternoon here,' she said, smiling round at them, 'and enjoyed the races and games and now this lovely tea. I hope you've made some new friends and will go on playing together. We all want the children now living in the Barton to be happy after their sad experiences, and this is Burracombe's chance to show what a friendly and welcoming village this is. And now I have a very special surprise for you.'

She stepped away from the table and made her way towards the entrance to the marquee. Dottie, who knew what the surprise was, looked at her friends, smiling with suppressed excitement.

'What is it?' Aggie Madge hissed. 'What's going to happen?'

Dottie twinkled at her. 'Wait and see. She'll be here directly.'

'Who will?' Aggie stared at her. 'You don't mean ... Oh, you do! You *do*, don't you? It's—'

'Ssh. Here she comes now.' Dottie looked towards the doorway, where Isobel Napier was returning, leading a vision of such glamour that everyone gasped. And then a huge cheer went up.

Fenella Forsyth, looking as if she were about to step on to the London stage, seemed to float as if her high-heeled shoes were tapping on clouds. She wore a filmy dress of speedwell-blue chiffon and silk with a jacket and scarf of the same material, so that you couldn't see where one ended and the others began. The blue matched her eyes and turned her blonde hair almost silver in the September sunlight, and her face wore the radiant smile that won the hearts of everyone who saw her and had made her famous throughout the theatres of London – and now, the theatre of war, as she went abroad to entertain troops enduring the most basic and primitive of conditions, conditions that Fenella, for her all finery and glamour, was happy to share with them.

The children of the Barton, who had heard so much about the famous singer and actress but had never seen her, except in photographs and on film, were spellbound, and even the residents of Burracombe, who had often seen her about the village, were awed, for she had never appeared like this during her visits to Isobel Napier. The Fenella they knew, while glamorous enough by Burracombe standards with her well-cut London clothes – even those she herself considered countrified and simple – had never come amongst them in this almost magical, fairy-tale guise.

'Isn't she lovely?' Dottie breathed, feeling quite proprietorial. 'And she's just as nice as anyone else, you know, even though she looks as fine as a queen. No side to her, never puts on airs, talks to everyone just the same. She's a lovely lady.'

'Is she going to sing for us, do you reckon?' Aggie whispered, and it seemed that she was. The tumult of cheering and excitement was beginning to die down now as Isobel raised her hand, and when all was quiet at last she said: 'I can see that I don't have to introduce my very good friend Fenella Forsyth – you all know her, either from the films she's been in, or from the songs she sings on the radio and the records she's made. And those of you who live in Burracombe will have seen her when she's come to visit us. Indeed, one person in this village knows her almost as well – probably better, in some ways! – as I do myself, and that person is Dottie Friend.'

Everyone turned to look at Dottie as if they'd never seen her before, although most of them knew perfectly well that she had worked for the famous actress.

'And you all know,' Isobel continued, 'that Miss Forsyth is now doing some wonderful war work, going abroad – often to dangerous places – to entertain our troops. But today, to make this day extra special for all of us, she has come to Burracombe to entertain *us*.' Another huge cheer went up. 'And this is for *all* of us – Burracombe people and our visitors.' She stepped back slightly and said, in the manner of a radio presenter introducing an act, 'Miss Fenella ... *Forsyth*!'

The cheer this time would have lifted the roof off the marquee, if Jacob and his cohorts had not fastened it on so firmly. Everyone was on their feet, clapping wildly and shouting at the tops of their voices, and Fenella Forsyth stood, smiling and waiting, until eventually, when it seemed that the noise would never cease, she raised both hands and they gradually fell silent.

'Thank you all so much.' Her voice was as melodious as if she were already singing. 'I want to say how happy I am to be here this afternoon, helping you make friends, and I hope that after today that's just what you will be – all friends together. Because that's what this war is about, you know – people who didn't want to be friends beginning to quarrel and fight and letting it go too far until now it seems almost impossible to stop.' Roy and Vic, as well as some of the other boys, glanced sideways at each other, looking rather shamefaced. 'But it *will* stop,' she went on, 'and it's people like us – all of you, and me – making up our minds that friendship is better than fighting that will help stop it, and stop other wars happening in the future. Will you promise me you'll try to do that?' She waited as a huge 'Yes!' sounded around her and then, smiling, said, 'And that's why my first song for you in Burracombe today is going to be a new one that nobody has ever heard before. It's your very own song, and it's called "Friends Along the Way" ...'

After singing for nearly half an hour, Fenella said, 'Now it's your turn. I'm sure some of you know lots of other songs, as well as the ones I sing, and there's nothing like a good sing-song with everyone joining in, so let's have a few of our favourites. We'll start with "Run Rabbit Run".'

Nobody needed telling twice, and they all bellowed out the words. 'He'll get by without his rabbit pie, so run rabbit – run rabbit – Run! Run! Run!' After that, it was natural to go on to 'Roll Out the Barrel', 'Yes! We Have No Bananas', 'Lili Marlene' and all the other songs that had become popular during the war. It began to look as if the sing-song would go on late into the evening, and Matron started to glance at her watch.

Maddy, who had left her seat and crept forward to the front row during the singing, sang more loudly and enthusiastically than any of them, and when Fenella stopped and asked, 'Is there anyone who would like to come up and sing with me?' she leapt up and waved both hands in the air, crying out, 'Me! Me! *Me!*'

'*Maddy* ...' Matron began in a reproving voice, but Fenella smiled down at the eager little girl and held out her hands.

'Come along, then. You can be first. Stand on this chair so that everyone can see you. In fact, why not stand on the table? Take your shoes off so that you don't make the tablecloth dirty.' Disregarding Matron's disapproval, she helped Maddy off with her shoes and lifted her on to the table. 'What a little featherweight you are! Now, what would you like to sing?'

Maddy gazed at her dumbly. She seemed to have lost all power of speech, and Matron tutted and murmured something about making a show of the child, but Dottie, who was sitting at the next table, leaned over and said, 'Why not sing the one you sang when we were sewing? "The Old Oak Tree", wasn't it? This little girl's daddy had all your records, before the war,' she explained to Fenella. 'She knows them all.'

'Oh yes, let's sing that,' Fenella agreed, and took Maddy's hand. 'It's one of my favourites. We'll sing it together. I'll start, and you join in when you're ready.' She began to sing softly, and after a few seconds Maddy began to sing as well, very quietly at first and then with more confidence. The two voices rose together in harmony and the audience listened, with more than one eye shedding a tear or two before it was over. At the end of the song, there was a moment's silence before they all applauded.

'That was lovely,' Fenella told her. 'And now let's have one of the boys join us. Who sings in the church choir?' Two or three boys put up their hands. 'Come along then. Yes, all of you. And when we've sung, everyone can join in again, because that's the best singing of all – when everyone sings together, no matter whether they've got a good voice or not. In fact,' she said, looking more serious, 'I want you all to remember that *everyone* has a voice, and everyone has a right to use their voice. So don't let anybody, *ever*, stop you singing. It's the best way in the world to keep us all happy.'

The party was over at last and Matron was finally permitted to declare that it was well past her charges' bedtime and they must all go back to the house at once. The village children were also chivvied home by parents who were all too aware of the clearing-up that still needed to be done, and Isobel took Fenella's arm and told her she was looking tired and must come home to the cottage.

'You've done far too much – you must have a good rest tomorrow. I shan't let you do a thing.'

'You're looking tired too, Mrs Napier,' Dottie declared. 'It's been a long day for us all. But what a lovely party it's been. It wouldn't have been half as good in the village hall, and that's a fact. The children ought to be proper grateful to you.'

'We should be grateful to them,' Isobel said quietly. 'They may be far too young to have fought, but so many of them are casualties of the war just the same. They each have a sad story to tell.'

'That little girl who sang,' Fenella said. 'What did you say her name was? Madge? Maggie?'

'Maddy,' Dottie replied. 'Yes, she's just the sort of kiddie Mrs Napier means. Lost all her family in the Blitz except for her big sister, and then they were separated and sent to different children's homes, if you can believe it. At least that's what she says. She might have got it wrong, of course. I think some of them hardly know what's really happened and what they've dreamed or been told by other kiddies.' She lowered her voice. 'And I heard Matron telling Mrs Hatch a little while ago that she'd heard the sister had died too. It was all very vague, but it seems she was at another home – near Southampton, I think it was – and Matron knows the matron there and asked after the girl and was told she'd gone. So if that's true, little Maddy really is all on her own in the world.'

Fenella stared at her. 'But that's terrible. And have they told Maddy herself?'

'They've hinted at it,' Dottie answered. 'Not told her straight out, but I think she understood what Matron meant all right. Went very quiet for a few days, and slipped away on her own quite a bit. She came down to the cottage but I couldn't get much out of her. To tell you the truth, I don't think she could quite bring herself to believe it, and maybe it's better that way. Knowing for certain would be just too much for the little scrap to bear.'

'Poor little soul,' Fenella said. 'She seemed very sweet, and has such a nice little voice.'

Dottie laughed. 'Oh, Maddy's sweet all right! But don't let those big blue eyes fool you, Miss Fenella. Artful as a barrowload of monkeys that one is, always in and out of trouble of one sort or another. Not that there's a speck of malice in her,' she added quickly. 'It's just that she's full of life, despite what's happened to her.' She chuckled and shook her head, then said more thoughtfully, 'I tell you what, though. If there's one child in the entire home who ought to be with a family, it's little Maddy. She looks so lost sometimes it could break your heart. And she always seems to need someone to cling to, someone to be specially fond of, if you know what I mean. It used to be Nurse Powell, but since I've been going to the Barton to teach a bit of cooking and sewing, I reckon she's started to get fond of me.'

'Is that a good thing?' Isobel asked as they made their way along the track. 'Should children in the situation that these are in be allowed to attach themselves to one person? It seems to me that it must lead to more disappointment in the future.'

'I worry about that too,' Dottie admitted. 'But what can you do when a kiddie who's lost everything looks to you for a bit of comfort and love? I reckon I've got enough to give them all, and I can't hold it back when I know how much they need it. I just hope it's helping to make them stronger, not weaker.'

'And I'm sure it does,' Fenella said as they paused to say goodbye before going their separate ways. 'Now, I will see you again soon, won't I, Dottie? You won't be spending all your time at the Barton?'

'Goodness me, no! I work at the Bell Inn too, a few hours now and then to help out behind the bar, and then there's the baking I do for George Sweet. But I'll always find time for you, Miss Fenella. Anyway, tomorrow's my day for helping at the cottage, so I'll be there first thing in the morning and see to breakfast for you both. Neither of you is to do a thing, mind. Don't even get out of bed if you don't want to!'

They laughed and parted, Dottie hurrying along the twilit village street to her own cottage, and the two others towards the estate cottage where Isobel lived now, with Stephen when he was at home from school. Both were, as Dottie had said, tired and looking forward to a cup of cocoa and bed. They walked in companionable silence, mulling over the events of the day, and as Isobel opened the cottage door they stood for a moment breathing in the evening air.

'This is such a lovely time of year,' Fenella said softly. 'The leaves beginning to turn, the autumn flowers like Michaelmas daisies taking their own place as all the summer ones begin to settle down for the winter. It's sad to see the swallows leave, but we know they'll come again next spring, just as the snowdrops will appear in February and then the primroses and daffodils in March and April. And so it goes on. The world keeps on turning, Isobel, whatever we humans do to spoil it. We can't ever destroy it completely. I hope we never will.'

'I hope so too,' Isobel said soberly. 'We've done almost the worst we could ever do, with this awful war.' She looked up as a dark shape fluttered above their heads. 'The bats are out already. Baden used to love watching for them, you know. When he was a little boy, he thought they were night birds, flying round to look after the house.' Her voice quivered. 'I miss him so much, Fenella. My boy – my firstborn. No other child is quite like that, you know – the first one you carry, the one who first looks you in the eye. I don't think I shall ever get over losing him at Dunkirk.'

Fenella took her friend in her arms. 'I don't see how you can, darling. All you can do is learn to live as he would have wanted you to. And I think you're doing that already. He would be very proud of what you've done today.'

For a while, both were silent. Isobel wept without sound, and Fenella held her close and did not speak. But as she stood there, feeling her friend's grief, her thoughts turned to the children she had never had, perhaps never would have. At least I am spared this, she thought; spared this terrible anguish – one of the worst of all griefs – of losing a child.

And yet in her heart, she knew that she would rather suffer such pain, however harsh, than never know a child's love at all.

Chapter Twenty-Eight

L ate summer passed into autumn, and then winter. The
American air force, based mostly in East Anglia, was making daily bombing raids over Germany, but so many planes
were lost that towards the middle of the month the raids stopped
until fighter planes could be brought in to use as escorts. At about
the same time, Italy, which had been on Germany's side, did an
about-turn and declared war on their former ally, creating some
confusion amongst the Italian prisoners of war and their captors.
The fighter planes arrived and took to the air and the raids began
again, causing huge losses and even firestorms. Dottie and some
of the other village women saw the newspaper headlines in Edie
Pettifer's shop and shook their heads.

'I know they did the same to us in the Blitz,' Dottie said, 'but
it don't seem right somehow. I mean, we know what it's like. We
saw Plymouth in flames and we know what people suffered then. It
must be the same over there. And all of us, Germans and British
alike, saying we'm Christians. I don't understand it at all.'

'Yes, but like you say, they did it to us,' Jacob Prout pointed out,
passing them in the doorway with his daily packet of Woodbines.
'Anyway, us've talked like this before and it always boils down to
the same thing – all's fair in love and war.'

'I'm not sure I agree with that. Two wrongs don't make a right,
and killing little children is *never* fair.' She folded her lips together.
'I'm not sure I even want this newspaper now, Edie. 'Tis nothing
but bad news.'

'You shouldn't have started to read it, then,' Edie told her. 'I
reckon you owe me a penny for the front page anyway, so you

may as well take the lot. And there's a nice knitting pattern in the middle, worth anyone's money, that is.'

Dottie smiled apologetically and handed over her money. But as she went out, her smile faded. I'm sick and tired of this old war, she thought, picking her way back along the muddy lane to her cottage. Sick and tired. And it wasn't as if they were getting the worst of it in Burracombe. Plenty of folk would say they were getting the best. But when you thought about it – half the world bombed to smithereens, young people's lives wasted fighting for something they never wanted to start, babies being killed in their cots and little children like those at the Barton robbed of their mothers and fathers ... where was the sense in it? Where was the sense in *any* of it?

She looked up at the sky. It seemed full of dark clouds and ominous threats. There'll be snow, at the very least, she thought, and then we'll have all that malarkey to contend with, even though I suppose it will please the youngsters, but I'm just about fed up with it *all* ...

However, to the disappointment of the children, there was little snow, and with no Bonfire Night or fireworks to brighten the sky, November seemed a cold and dreary month. The party had brought the village children and the evacuees together, but it was an uneasy alliance, and although they played well enough on the whole, scraps and fights were liable to break out at any time, as much from boredom as from real hostility. Some friendships were forged, however, most notably between Maddy, Eileen and Jackie Tozer. They could not become truly inseparable, since the Barton children were only allowed in the village at certain times of day, but at every opportunity Maddy and Eileen would turn up at the farmhouse door, certain of a welcome, and with Jackie would set off into the fields and woods, and sometimes up the little path that led past the charcoal burners' cottage to the standing stones that overlooked the village from their grassy plateau up on the moor itself.

'This is the best place in the whole world,' Maddy declared, throwing pebbles at the tallest of the stones. 'I'm going to stay here for ever and ever.'

'You can't,' said Eileen, who, sometimes feeling a little excluded on these outings, was inclined to be grumpy. 'When the war's over, we'll go back to Southampton and you'll never come here again.'

'I will. When I'm grown up, I'll be able to do whatever I like. I'll come back here to live. I could live at the farm with you,' she said to Jackie. 'You've got lots of bedrooms.'

'Yes, but when the war's over, my sister Val and my brothers Brian and Tom will come back, so we'll need them. And don't throw things at the stones. If they get angry, they'll come down to the village and throw themselves at the houses and knock them down.'

The two girls stared at her and backed away slightly.

'Is that true?' Eileen asked dubiously. 'Has it ever happened?'

'I don't know, but it could, easy. My dad told me, anyway, so it must be true. They've been there thousands of years and they look after Burracombe. There's stones like this all over Dartmoor and nobody knows why, but some people say they're witches that have been turned into stone. Or people that witches have turned into stone,' she added doubtfully. 'I can't remember which, but it's best not to make them cross, whichever they are.'

Maddy shivered. 'I don't want to stay up here anyway. It's too cold. Let's go back to the farm and do a jigsaw or something.'

They scurried down the hill, past the charcoal burners, who were hard at work with the huge mound of turf that held their fire, and along the lane to the farm track. Jacob Prout, busy clearing ditches, gave them a wave, and they waved back and ran past him and through the yard, heedless now of the cows that had so alarmed Eileen on her first visit. At last, breathless and with glowing cheeks, they burst into the big kitchen, to find Dottie Friend enjoying an afternoon cup of tea with Alice and Minnie.

'Well, you three look very bright and rosy, I must say,' Dottie exclaimed. 'And what have you been getting up to?'

'Just walking,' Jackie replied airily. 'We went up to the standing stones, but it looks as if it might snow so we came home.'

'Don't think there's any snow on the way,' Alice said, mixing cocoa in three cups. 'Rain, more like, bitter cold though it be. And how's little Maddy, and Eileen? Us don't seem to have seen you for a few days.'

'We've been busy making Christmas decorations for the house,' Maddy said, sitting down on a footstool beside Dottie and leaning against her legs. 'When are you coming to help us make our puddings?'

'Ah, that be all arranged. I'm coming on Sunday, and do you know why?' The girls shook their heads. 'Because it's Stir-Up Sunday, that's why! We put all the flour and dried fruit and milk and such, and whatever eggs we might be lucky enough to get' – she winked at Alice – 'into the biggest bowl we can find, and we stir it round and round with a wooden spoon. And everyone who wants to help can have a stir as well, and as they stir they make a wish. Only you mustn't tell anyone what your wish is,' she added sternly, 'because if you do, it won't come true.'

'That will take all afternoon,' Maddy said. 'And I don't think there's a big enough bowl at the Barton for all of us.'

'There isn't. We're going to use one of they old tin tubs that the Napier children used to have their baths in by the fire when they were little tackers, before the squire put in proper bathrooms with geysers for hot water. And that's why everyone has to have a turn at stirring – it'd be too hard for one body to do all that work.'

'Will there be silver threepenny bits?' Jackie enquired. 'We always have two in ours. I got one last year and Joanna got the other.'

'As to that, I couldn't say. It would need a lot of threepenny bits for everyone to get one, and it wouldn't be fair not to have enough. No, I know *everyone* doesn't have to get one,' she added as Jackie opened her mouth, 'but we'd need more than two, anyway. There might be a few, perhaps.' She made up her mind to save any silver threepenny bits that came her way, to slip into the mixture. She could ask her cousin Jessie at the post office and Edie in the shop to keep some back from their change, too. These little ones needed all the brightness that could be given to their lives.

'I hear some of the children might be going to Australia,' she remarked conversationally. 'That'll be a good chance for them to start a new life. Get a bit of sunshine too – I hear it's a lot warmer there.'

The three girls stared at her. Eileen found her voice first.

'*Australia?* But ... why?'

'Well, like I said, to give them a new chance,' Dottie said. 'Mostly boys, I think. They'll go and work on farms and such. I heard it on the wireless this morning.'

'But what about their mothers and fathers?' Jackie asked. 'Will they go too?'

Dottie shook her head. 'These are the children from places like the Barton, who haven't got mothers and fathers any more.' She glanced at Maddy and Eileen, not wanting to distress them by referring to their own state. 'I think they'll be adopted out there, so they'll have new families and new lives. I think it sounds lovely for them.'

Maddy looked around at the others, then turned back and put her hand on Dottie's knee. 'I won't have to go, will I?' Her voice was frightened and trembling. 'I don't *want* to go to Australia. I want to stay here. They won't *make* us go, will they?'

'I'm sure they won't.' Dottie wasn't really at all sure. In her experience, children got very little say in what was to happen to them, especially those in children's homes. 'I think it's mostly the older boys, the ones who can work a bit. But they might not be going from our home here anyway. It was just something I heard on the wireless. It might not even happen at all.' She was wishing she had never mentioned it. You ought to know better, Dottie Friend, she scolded herself. It was bound to upset these poor little girls. They'd had too much change in their lives already, and not much of it good.

'Well, I won't go,' Maddy stated. 'If they try and make me, I'll run away.' She looked at Dottie again. 'I'll come and live with you. You'd have me, wouldn't you?'

Dottie stared down into the huge blue eyes and felt her heart melt. You poor little dear, she thought, I'd have you in a minute. And for a moment or two, she wondered if it might be possible. Could she offer to take this little girl, so loving and needing love so much? Could she even, perhaps, adopt her for her own?

No. It would never be permitted. Herself, an ordinary little countrywoman with no schooling to speak of, with no man beside her, adopting a child? Dottie had very little knowledge of adoption laws, but she felt sure it wouldn't be allowed.

'I'd like nothing better,' she said at last, folding Maddy's hand in hers, 'but I don't think they'd let me. You'll have to stay in the home till you're old enough to leave. But you can come and see me any time you like, just as you can come to the farm, and Eileen as well. You'm always welcome, in either place, isn't that right, Alice?'

'Of course it is. You come along here, or down to Dottie's, whenever you've a mind. And I don't think they'll send you to Australia. Like Dottie said, it's mostly the boys, and there might not be any going from here anyway. You're safe in Burracombe.'

'I want to stay here always,' Maddy said, holding Dottie's hand tightly. 'I want Burracombe to be where I *live*.'

'I don't!' Jackie said, surprising them all. 'I want to go to lots of other places – places abroad. France, and America, places like that. *I'd* go to Australia if I got the chance, see if I wouldn't!'

Alice turned on her. 'And that's just silly talk. As if you'll ever be able to do those things. You know nobody's allowed to go abroad now unless—'

'Our Val's gone abroad,' Jackie interrupted. 'She's in Egypt. *I'd* like to go to Egypt, and I'd—'

'*Unless* they've been sent there because of the war,' Alice went on, raising her voice to override her daughter's. 'And even when the war's over you won't be allowed abroad, not for a long time. Anyway, it's too expensive. People like us don't go abroad for our holidays.'

'I didn't mean for a holiday,' Jackie retorted. 'I meant to *live*.'

'And *that*,' her mother said repressively, 'is even sillier. Your father will never let you.'

'He can't stop me, after I'm twenty-one. I can do what I like then.'

'You'll be married by then.' Alice was beginning to get angry, and Jackie's face was turning red, her eyes bright with defiance.

'I won't! I'm never going to get married, not if it means I can't do what I like. I'll—'

'Oh for goodness sake, Jackie!' Alice's patience snapped. 'Leave it alone, you silly girl. A lot's going to happen before you turn twenty-one, and you'll forget all this nonsense. It's this war,' she added, turning to the other women. 'It's giving girls ideas, and no wonder. Look at our Val, out in Egypt with nobody to supervise her. And engaged to be married she might be, but she never sees her Eddie now, and that's a bad situation. It's never good for engaged couples to be apart, even when the girl's at home where she should be, getting her trousseau together.'

'And there's Hilary Napier,' Minnie chimed in. 'She's out there too, driving army officers about like they're too grand to drive their own cars. Nothing but a chauffeur! It don't seem right, somehow.'

'I don't see why,' Jackie argued. 'Not if girls can do the jobs just as well as men. I'm going to join up when I'm old enough, and I'll—'

'*Jackie!*' Alice exploded. 'Will you stop all this *I'll do this* and *I'll do that*! We've all heard quite enough for one afternoon. Now, Maddy and Eileen, do you want another biscuit? And I think you should be going back to the Barton soon; it's starting to get dark.'

'Yes, we'd better,' Eileen said, accepting another home-made ginger biscuit. 'Matron gets very cross if we're late and she'll say we can't come out again. Come on, Maddy.'

The two girls stood up and put on their coats, scarves and gloves. Maddy turned back to Alice.

'Thank you for the cocoa and biscuits,' she said politely. She looked at Dottie and said, 'I know what my wish is going to be when I stir the pudding, but I'm not going to tell you. I want to make sure it comes true.'

They ran out into the yard and the two women looked at each other.

'Poor little mite,' Alice said sadly. 'All any of them want is a mother's love. And 'tis easy to see what her wish is going to be, Dottie.'

'I know.' Dottie sighed. 'If only I could make it come true.' She smiled a little, but her eyes were damp. 'Maybe I ought to make that *my* wish, when I'm stirring the pudding myself ...'

Maddy took Dottie at her word and came to visit her in the cottage whenever she could. It wasn't quite as often as she'd have liked, since there always seemed to be something else to do – playing hopscotch on the terrace in front of the Barton, exploring the woods with Eileen and the other children, helping Jackie to feed the hens that were her own special responsibility, even occasionally sitting on a three-legged milking stool with her face pressed against a cow's warm flank, trying to squeeze milk from a full udder. But her fingers were too small to be of much use with that, and after a while Norman Tozer said he would 'just finish old Daisy off' for her, and she would watch as he drew off a whole bucketful to add to the inch or so she had managed.

She liked being in the milking parlour. It was warm in there, sheltered from the raw December cold, and the cows seemed to enjoy it too, their heads nuzzling in the long trough that she had helped to fill with feed before they came in. They shifted gently from hoof to hoof as Norman and Ted sat close to them on their stools, and uttered soft, murmuring moos that sounded as if they were talking to each other.

They all had names – Bluebell, Daisy, Rosie, Bess – and Maddy soon knew them as well as the Tozers did. She loved to sit on the gate to their field, watching them and learning their ways.

On cold, wet days when they weren't allowed outside to play, the Barton children made more Christmas decorations. Isobel had brought them a box full of coloured paper strips to make paper chains with, enough to festoon the whole of the hallway and the big sitting room with festive colour. Because, like the marquee ropes, they would tangle together almost by themselves if put back in the box, they were hung up straight away, and the Barton seemed ready for Christmas before the village had even thought about it.

People were, of course, thinking about it, though, and Miss Kemp and her new young assistant, Miss Gray, were planning a Christmas party at the school for all the children at once – both village pupils and those from the Barton.

'It will be our thank you for the lovely party they gave us in September,' Miss Kemp told the Burracombe children. 'And I want you all to try to think of some way of making it extra special. Remember, when we're all enjoying Christmas dinner at home with our families, these children have no homes to go to, no mothers or fathers. So we have to be particularly kind to them.'

Some of those who had made friends amongst the orphanage children nodded earnestly, but others looked more doubtful. Roy and Vic, who had a running feud with Bertie Blake who had been Vic's reluctant partner in the three-legged race, scowled at the thought of being extra kind to him – or, indeed, being kind to him at all.

'My mum heard that some of them are going to be sent to Australia to live with kangaroos,' Vic said as they walked home. 'Hope Snaky Blake goes. The further away the better.'

'Maybe a kangaroo will jump on his head,' Roy suggested, and they laughed and pushed each other as they ran.

Nothing had been said about the Barton children being sent to Australia. It seemed that quite a lot had gone from other parts of the country, though, and the general opinion was that it was a good chance for them, better than some of them probably deserved. Just because they'd lost their families didn't mean they were all good, and some of the villagers still regarded them with suspicion.

'They're nothing but little tackers,' Dottie told Alf Coker, the blacksmith, when he complained that a couple of the boys had been hanging around his forge. 'They're just interested, that's all. What harm have they done?'

'It's not what they've done, it's what they might do that bothers me,' he answered. 'I've seen the way they look at my tools. I take care to lock 'em up at night now, I can tell you.'

Dottie was disturbed to hear this. Nobody in Burracombe had ever locked their doors, and she still didn't. It would be a shame if people got so distrustful that they turned their keys on each other, when Burracombe had been such an open, friendly place.

Perhaps Alf would be a bit more understanding when he had children of his own. His wife Peggy was expecting now, and Dottie knew he was hoping for a boy, to take on his business. Perhaps he'd realise then that there was a difference between badness and ordinary boyish mischief. But then Alf had been a boy himself once, and ought to know. A proper little scallywag he'd been too, now she thought about it. In fact, that was probably why he was so suspicious of other small boys.

She went home and found Maddy sitting on the back doorstep, playing with Alfred, Dottie's cat. He was still young enough to enjoy darting after the fluffy pompom hung on a few inches of wool that Maddy was dangling over his head, and Dottie stopped to watch them for a few moments before Maddy looked up and saw her.

'That's a lovely toy,' Dottie said, admiring the pompom. 'Did you make it yourself?'

'Yes, I made it for Alfred. It's supposed to be his Christmas present, but I won't see him on Christmas Day so I brought it now.' She stood up and followed Dottie into the cottage.

Christmas Day, Dottie thought, putting on the kettle. Wouldn't it be lovely to have this little dear here that day, sitting at the table all rosy and smiling, waiting for her Christmas dinner? Seeing her opening her presents – Dottie had already knitted her a Fair Isle cardigan and bought a new Rupert book, and she knew that Alice was making some mittens and a woolly hat – and enjoying the pudding they had stirred together. She thought of the wish she knew Maddy had intended to make, and the one she hadn't dared make herself, and a great sadness washed over her as she reminded herself that none of this could ever come about. Maddy belonged to the children's home, and although some of them did get adopted, and it might well happen to Maddy herself – a stab of jealousy pierced her as she thought of someone else taking the child away to be their little girl, when Dottie so passionately wanted her for her own – it would be a family with money who took her, not an ordinary woman living in a simple country cottage with an earth privy at the bottom of the garden and a tin bath, dragged into the kitchen on a Saturday night to be filled with hot water from a series of kettles and pans.

I ought to hope that someone nice, with enough money to give her a good home, will come along and take her, she thought, making tea. But I don't. I *can't*. This dear little soul has stolen my heart, and I couldn't bear to let her go ...

The school Christmas party was held as usual on the last day of term. That gave the two teachers and Mrs Purdy, the school cleaner, time to clear up afterwards and remove all the decorations strung about the room. This year, with double the number of children attending, there was bound to be more to do than usual.

'I wouldn't mind,' Mabel Purdy said, leaning on her broom next morning to survey the devastation, 'but that's good food trodden into the floor, that is, and that's waste. Whatever happened, Miss Kemp? It looks like there was a riot.'

'I don't quite know,' the headmistress said ruefully. 'It all went very well to begin with. Our children were here first, ready to welcome the evacuees, all those who have been with us ever since the Plymouth Blitz as well as the Barton children, and everyone seemed happy enough then. We played several games – Miss Gray was a great asset,' she added, smiling at the assistant teacher. 'She knew some different ones as well as the usual ones we always play.

But of course it was very crowded and some of the children got their toes trodden on, and there was a bit of pushing and shoving, so we thought we'd better have tea to calm them down.'

'Only it didn't,' Sheila Gray added. 'There wasn't enough room at the tables unless all the children squashed together, and someone spilt someone else's orange squash—'

'It was Bertie Blake. I'm afraid he is rather a troublemaker.'

'Yes, and it went all over Jackie Tozer's frock, and Jackie is never one to let a boy get the better of her, so she punched Bertie, and then Bertie's friend Gerald Mitchell pushed her off her chair, and then Bob Pengelly punched *him*. Gerald called Bob an ugly mug and said he looked like a chimpanzee—'

'Well, 'tis true he'm not the best-looking tacker in the village,' Mrs Purdy interjected. 'Takes after his father, he do. They say whoever made those old gargoyles on the church tower used a Pengelly as a model, hundreds of years ago. But nicer folk you'd never wish to meet, all the same for that.'

'Yes, but calling him a chimpanzee was going too far,' Miss Kemp said. 'Anyway, it started a fight between the lot of them, and before either of us knew what was happening, they were all at it – hitting, punching, throwing food at each other, the girls as much as the boys, and it was complete bedlam. It took us ten minutes or more to put a stop to it. And that was only because I rang the bell and threatened to call the village policeman.'

'Well, he wouldn't have been much help,' Mrs Purdy said caustically. 'Old Simeon's never had to stop more than a dog fight in the whole of his days. Those Southampton boys would have made mincemeat of him.'

'It wasn't just them,' Sheila Gray said fairly. 'Our children were just as much at fault. I'm afraid they all went home with their tails between their legs, after a good telling-off. Such a shame, just before Christmas.'

'Be that as it may,' Miss Kemp said grimly, 'they can't be allowed to behave like that. It was like watching wild animals. And there'll be another telling-off awaiting them when they return to school after the holidays. I am simply not going to tolerate it. I seriously considered making them come back to help clear up, but I'm not sure we would have achieved much.'

'I'm glad you didn't,' Mrs Purdy declared. 'I'm better doing it on me own. I know how everything should be and where things go. Don't you worry, Miss Kemp. It'll be like a new pin when they come back, and I'll be waiting for them too, that first morning, and ready to give them my own opinion of their carrying-on. If you don't have no objection, that is,' she added belatedly.

'You'll be very welcome to give them your opinion,' Miss Kemp said, knowing that the cleaner would do so anyway. 'I dare say their parents will do just the same. And the matron at the Barton. I don't think any of the children will be in any doubt about it. Not to mention the fact that they ruined their own party.' She sighed. 'I can't help feeling sad about that. They're nice children, on the whole, and I don't like to think of their Christmas being spoilt.'

'Why don't we try again in the new year?' Sheila suggested. 'Have another party, just to make things better? They won't expect quite as much as they do at Christmas, so they won't be overexcited as they were at this one, and it will probably be a much happier occasion. Maybe we could make it a spring picnic – we often get quite nice days in February, and we could look for snowdrops and pussy willow or something. And there won't be all the clearing up to do afterwards,' she added with a glance at Mabel Purdy's face.

Miss Kemp looked at her. 'Well, I was going to say that you were a glutton for punishment, but that might actually be a good idea. Yes, why not? But we'll think about it later – just for now, we need to clear up after *this* party. And we'll help you with that, Mrs Purdy,' she added. 'It's the least we can do, to take out all the rubbish, and that includes these paper chains the children took so long to make and which are now lying all over the room. *They* certainly can't be saved for next Christmas.'

Chapter Twenty-Nine

Even in wartime, Burracombe could still celebrate Christmas in style. There were no bells rung at midnight on Christmas Eve now, nor for the service next morning, but Minnie Tozer and her son Ted were not going to allow the villagers to forget their sound. Two nights before Christmas, they got together the handbell ringers (mostly Tozers), who accompanied the carol singers round the village, sounding their music over the cold, clear air. It was almost, Constance Bellamy said, coming to the door and carefully closing it so that no light should escape and lure German bombers to Burracombe, as if the stars themselves were singing. She'd half a mind to join them, she declared, and went back for her winter coat and scarf, wrapping them around her as she stumped along with the rest of the crowd. In fact, so many of the villagers joined the throng that there was hardly anybody left in the village to sing to, and by nine o'clock they were all crowding into the warmth of the Bell Inn for the sausage rolls and mulled cider that Bernie and his wife Rose provided by tradition.

The village hall was in use every evening that week for various Christmas parties – the fur and feather whist drive, the WI supper, the Mothers' Union tea, the country dance club's treat night – and the fact that it was mostly the same people at each event didn't matter at all. They were meeting to do different things, so each evening had its own flavour and character, and different people took charge. Nobody wanted to be left out. It was Christmas, after all.

Even Ivy Sweet went along to the WI supper and the fur and feather. She was a sharp whist player and usually went home bearing a rabbit or pheasant, but on this occasion her mind didn't seem to be on her cards and she won no more than half a dozen eggs, smuggled in by Alice Tozer. As they walked home together, George said, 'You feeling all right, Ive? You don't seem yourself just lately.'

'I'm quite all right, thanks,' she said rather sharply. 'Why shouldn't I be?'

'I don't know, do I, or I wouldn't have asked. Only some of the others been asking me about you, seem to think you look a bit peaky.'

'Well, you can tell them from me to mind their own business! And while you're at it, tell them to find someone else to gossip about. I suppose they're casting aspersions about my hair again.'

'I don't think it's so much your hair, Ive. It's more that – well, they know you're expecting, and after all the time we've been married they're a bit surprised, that's all.'

'And what's *that* supposed to mean?' She stopped dead and turned on him. There was a moon that night and it shone on their faces. 'I hope you told them there was nothing to be surprised about!'

'Of course I did.' But he didn't sound entirely convinced, and she felt a beat of panic in her chest. 'Look, Ive, that's more of an aspersion on me than you, when you come to think about it. Hinting that I can't ... well, do my duty by you any more. I don't suppose they even meant it that way, though. It's just the way folk talk.'

'More's the pity. If you ask me, they talk too much.' She walked on quickly and George kept silent pace beside her. After a few minutes, she stopped again and turned to him. 'George ... *you* don't think there's anything in what they're hinting, do you?'

There was a moment of silence. George looked down gravely into her face and then took her arm.

'Ive, to me 'tis nothing but cause for celebration,' he said quietly. 'You know how much I've always wanted a family. It's been a long time coming, but now I reckon us've been blessed, and I'm not going to look for fault where I don't believe there's any to find. By next Christmas us'll have a little one to rejoice in, and for me that's the best Christmas present you could ever give.'

Christmas at the Tozers' farm was, as in so many homes during those years of war, tinged with sadness.

'It never seems right without the boys and Val here,' Alice said, looking at the empty chairs where Val, Brian and Tom would normally have sat. 'I do miss them something awful, Ted.'

She and Ted had come down early on Christmas morning, he to start the milking and she to put the goose into the oven. Alice kept half a dozen geese, fattening one each year for their own dinner, one for the Napiers and one for Dr Latimer. She was making stuffing now while a couple of rashers sizzled in the frying pan for the sandwich Ted would take with him to the milking parlour.

'They'll be back, large as life and twice as ugly,' he said, not wanting her to be sad on Christmas morning. 'The war's taken a turn now. What with the Americans carrying out all these raids over Germany, and Italy turning round and coming in with the Allies, we'm set fair on the road to victory. It might take a year or two, but—'

'And what could happen in that time?' she broke in. 'You know as well as I do, Ted, there's thousands being killed every day. Our boys aren't immune. It could be them any time. They might even be lying dead somewhere this very minute.' She grabbed a tea towel and held it over her face.

Ted moved closer and put his arm around her shoulders. 'Here, come on, my bird. This is no way to carry on of a Christmas morning. You know none of our young ones would want us to be miserable. Val's safe enough where she is, by all accounts, and wherever the boys are, I reckon they'm doing their best to celebrate and have a good time – you know the armed services always look after their men and give 'em summat special at Christmas. And they'd want us to do the same. Us can't do any more for them than us have done already, sending out they parcels you and Mother put together, so what us got to do now is make it a good Christmas for the family around us here. Our Jackie – her's only a kiddie still, and deserves a Christmas she can look back on as a good family time. And there's Joanna, too – her's like another daughter to us. Us don't want her to feel in the way.'

'I'd never let her feel that.' Alice wiped her face and nodded. 'You'm right, Ted, I know. I won't let it spoil Christmas. It was just ... for a minute, thinking about it all – well, it just came over me what us've been missing all this time.'

'And if the good Lord wills it, us'll have it again,' he said quietly. 'There's plenty of folk won't, though, and some of 'em not a million miles from here.'

Alice nodded. 'The little ones up at the Barton. Some of they have lost everything and everybody, and they'll never get it back. We'm the lucky ones, Ted, and what us should do is share our luck. I know us can't have any of them over here today, because they've got their own Christmas, but afterwards Jackie can invite a few of them round. That little Maddy that pops in to see us, and her friend Eileen, and a few more as well. They can share our fireside for a few hours and have a bit of a sing-song round Mother's harmonium, and remember what 'tis like to be part of a family.'

'That's a good idea, maid,' Ted approved. 'And now we got that sorted out, maybe you can finish making my bacon sandwich, before it goes up in flames. I got the milking to do, remember, and if our Norman's out there already and got half the cows done before I even show me face, he'll never let me hear the end of it. And don't forget him and his lot will be back here for their Christmas dinner too, so there'll be plenty of us to help celebrate.'

'Oh my dear days, the bacon!' Alice rescued it from the pan and slapped it on to the bread she had put ready. 'Well, 'tis proper crispy, I'll say that for it. There you are, Ted, and wish Norman a happy Christmas from me, and when you come back in, we'll hold Christmas proper.' She handed him the sandwich and gave him a kiss. 'Happy Christmas, Ted, my dear. I won't forget what you said. Us'll make this a Christmas we can be pleased to look back on, and I hope our boys and Val will be doing the same.'

Ted went out into the darkness of early morning and Alice continued with her work. It wasn't long before Minnie and Joanna appeared in the kitchen, and then they all laughed to hear excited squeals coming from Jackie's room.

'Bring her down here, so us all can see her open her presents,' Minnie suggested as Alice opened the door to the stairs. ''Tis nice and warm here as well.'

Jackie came down towing the stocking she still begged for, and the pillowcase that was filled with bigger presents. It wasn't easy finding presents these days – no toys were being made, and Jackie was too old now for the assortment of knitted animals that had been made for her over the years – but Alice and Ted had been into Tavistock and bought her some books. There was the Rupert annual she insisted she was not too old for, a story by Enid Blyton and a 'Book of Wonders' containing stories and articles that Alice had thought Jackie would enjoy. 'See, there's a bit from *A Christmas Carol* and one of the *Just So Stories*, and a lovely piece about the Northern Lights and a bit about Canada, and some poetry and – look at this, Ted, a bit about farming! I reckon this'll keep her interested for hours.'

Jackie unwrapped the book now and started to look through it immediately, but her grandmother said, 'You'll have plenty of time to read that later, maid. Open your other presents now, so us can all see.'

The other presents comprised a cardigan that Minnie herself had knitted from one of her own old ones, the wool unpicked and washed so that it didn't knit up crinkly; two pinafores Alice had made, which were glanced at briefly and then put aside, Jackie not considering these worthy to be called Christmas presents; and a game of Lexicon from Joanna, which the family agreed they would play together later. Tom, Brian and Val had all sent postal orders, and she took these back to her bedroom to be put away until they could be cashed at the post office.

The rest of the day went as Christmas always did at the farm. Apart from essential jobs like milking and feeding, no work was done, and with morning service at the church at eleven and dinner on the table by one, the family had plenty of time for a leisurely meal. They started with oxtail soup, made by Minnie the day before Christmas Eve, strained and left to cool in the pantry so that the fat could be taken from the top; followed by the goose – which everyone declared to be the biggest and finest yet – accompanied by potatoes roasted in the goose's own fat, a bowl of carrots as orange as a sunset, another of dark green cabbage and some mashed swede and turnips. Alice had also put an onion each to roast around the bird, and made rich gravy in the pan while the bird was resting, while Minnie had fetched a jar of her own redcurrant jelly from the cupboard.

After this, they all needed a rest of their own before Alice produced a pudding that looked as good as any pre-war one – and so it should, she said, for she'd used half the entire family's dried fruit ration in it, the other half having gone into the cake – and a bowl of crusty yellow clotted cream to go with it. There was one silver threepenny bit, which Jackie found in her helping, and after the pudding there was a mince pie each, which they all denied they had room for but managed just the same, and then, as Alice lit the lamps against the darkness beginning to creep across the sky, Ted poured a last helping of cider into each glass. 'I know wartime Christmases don't match up to the ones we used to have,' he said, holding his tankard up to catch the light, 'but to my mind, that was as good a dinner as any us could ever have had in peacetime. So I want to propose a toast to my dear wife Alice and my dear mother, for working so hard to cook it for us.' He smiled at them both. 'I don't reckon anyone in the land has had a better meal than we have here, not even the King and Queen in Buckingham Palace, so here's to Alice and Mother.'

The others raised their glasses, using their own names for the two women so that it sounded a bit muddled, and everyone laughed. But Ted hadn't finished.

'And there's others us must remember specially at this moment. We all know who they are. Our boys, Tom and Brian, away fighting us hardly knows where; our girl Val, out in Egypt nursing wounded soldiers; and my brother Joe, and his family that us've never even met, in America. A toast to them and everyone else who's far from their homes on this Christmas Day.' He paused, and said quietly, in a voice that was suddenly a little creaky, 'To absent friends.'

'To absent friends,' they all echoed soberly, and there was a moment or two of silence.

Alice cleared her throat. 'That was very nice and suitable, Ted, and thank you for your kind words. And now I think you and Norman ought to go into the sitting room and see that the fire Joanna lit is still burning well, and have half an hour in an armchair before you has to go out and do the afternoon milking. Us women will see to the clearing up, and when you come in again there'll be some tea on the table before us has a few games and a bit of a sing-song round the harmonium. Carols and some of the old songs – that's what I like at Christmas.'

It was what they all liked, and the rest of the day passed in its comfortable, traditional form until at last, tired out but reluctant, Jackie went to bed and the others sat round the embers of the great fire that had been burning in the inglenook fireplace since mid-afternoon, enjoying Ted's mulled cider and talking peacefully of Christmases gone by and, mostly with optimism, of those yet to come.

'It can't be much longer before it's all over, surely,' Alice said wistfully. 'Ted reckons the war's turned a corner, and I hope he's right.'

'Of course I am,' Ted declared. 'Look at it this way. Us've had four Christmases with Hitler hammering on our door, and he's not got in yet, and now that we've got the Americans over here ...'

'And you know what they say about that!' Norman said with a grin, but Ted frowned at him, and although Norman winked at Joanna, he said no more.

'... and the Italians on our side – yes, Norman, I know what they say about the Italians as well, thank you very much – well, I reckon there's light at the end of the tunnel and it might not be quite such a long tunnel as we think.'

'Hang on,' Norman said. 'Where exactly d'you reckon we are – in your farmhouse, with Hitler in the yard banging on the door, or in a train going through Grenofen Tunnel? Only I'm a bit lost.'

'Well, I hope you can find your way home then,' Ted told him sharply, but with a twinkle in his eye. 'Because much more cheek from you, and that's where you'll be heading, before you know where you are.'

'That's where we'll be going anyway,' Norman's wife said, nudging him. 'Look at you, tipsy from all that cider. Let's get our coats on while you can still find your sleeves.'

Norman laughed and stretched out his legs. 'There's still a glass or two in that old jar, my bird, and I reckon Ted was on the point of pouring some of it into my tankard, weren't you, Ted? And I need it, because I want to propose a toast of my own.' He waited while Ted shared around the last of the cider, and then raised his tankard high. 'To all of us Tozers, and especially to Ted, Alice and Auntie Minnie. You've given us a fine Christmas and we'll remember it whatever happens next. It's been a good day. To Tozers – wherever they may be.'

'To Tozers!' they echoed. 'To Tozers all over the world.'

*

A rather more decorous tea party than that at the school was held at the estate cottage where Isobel Napier now lived. As cottages went, it was quite large, and she was able to accommodate Fenella as well as Stephen, home for the holidays. The day before Christmas Eve, she told them that she was thinking of inviting a few of the Barton children to tea on the day after Boxing Day.

Stephen made a face. 'Do we have to? Do I have to be here as well?'

'Of course you do,' his mother said sternly. 'These are children who have no homes of their own, and it's no hardship to us to offer them the hospitality of our own for a few hours.'

'They've already *got* our home,' he pointed out. 'That's why we've got to live in this poky cottage.'

'Goodness me, it's not all that poky,' Fenella said. 'You should try living in a tent with a dozen other men, and the nearest latrine a hundred yards away. I think it will be a very good idea to invite some children to tea, but how are you going to decide which ones to ask? You can't have them all. And how will you entertain them?'

'I thought a few board games, since it's dark so early now and they won't be able to play outside. But I expect they've got most of them – Ludo, Sorry, backgammon and things.'

'Pencil and paper games,' Fenella declared. 'Consequences is always fun. And a sing-song round the piano. The one we had at your big party went very well.'

'I'm not sure it will go so well with only a few of us, but if you're here it's more likely to be a success. As for how we choose – well, we can't really, can we? Not without causing some jealousy. We will have to ask Matron to draw lots.'

'I suppose so, although I was hoping that little girl who came up and sang with me would be one of them. I quite took to her and I know Dottie thinks the world of her. She often pops into the cottage.'

'We'll just have to take the chance, I'm afraid,' Isobel said. 'We can't show any favouritism.'

The children greeted the news that four of them were to be invited to tea with Mrs Napier with less enthusiasm than she might have expected.

'We'll have to wear Sunday suits and have extra baths,' one of the boys said gloomily.

'And sit up straight and have teeny-weeny sandwiches and put them on our plates first before we take a bite,' added another.

'And say "yes please, Mrs Napier", and "no thank you, Mrs Napier", and not speak until we're spoken to.'

'And not drop crumbs.'

'And not ask for sugar in our tea.'

'And take the cake nearest us on the plate, even if we don't like it.'

'I don't want to go,' Gerald Mitchell said finally. 'I'd rather we had another party at the school. I liked that one.'

The other children, remembering the chaos of the school party and the tongue-lashings they had received, first from Miss Kemp and then from Matron, were silent. But none of them was much keener to attend than Gerald – except for Maddy, who had heard from Dottie that Fenella was to be there but was keeping the knowledge to herself. If the others knew, they would change their minds at once, and that would lessen her own chances. Unlike them – and because of her secret knowledge – Maddy was desperate to be invited.

Unfortunately, when the lots were drawn, she was not one of the chosen ones.

'Eileen Baxter, Gerald Mitchell, Susan Jenkins and Stanley Brown,' Matron announced, secretly dismayed to find Gerald's name amongst the chosen. 'You'll all be allowed a bath that morning, whether it's your turn or not, and please report to my office at half past two, neat and clean in your best clothes and with your hair brushed. I shall be inspecting fingernails as well, and anyone who is not up to my standard will be ...'

'Not allowed to go,' Gerald muttered hopefully, deciding immediately to dig his fingers into the blackest mud he could find.

'... sent back to wash all over again,' Matron continued, knowing exactly what he intended. About Stanley Brown, a quiet little boy who hated getting dirty at any time, she had no fears. Nor about the girls, because although Eileen was rather a tomboy and almost as likely as Gerald to come in covered in mud and with grass and twigs in her hair, she could be relied upon to look clean and tidy in her

Sunday frock. Susan Jenkins could equally be trusted to present a creditable appearance, and she had good table manners too. One of the casualties of the war, she had grown up with parents who insisted on correct behaviour at all times and had never yet been seen even to put her elbows on the table.

By and large, Matron thought, they could have done worse, although she still regretted Gerald's good fortune and so, she suspected, did he.

However, despite the initial reluctance, there were a surprising number of disappointed faces after the lots had been drawn, for tea out was a rare treat for most of them and there had been much speculation about the kind of cakes there might be on offer. But no one was more disappointed than Maddy.

'I really wanted to go,' she wept, sitting on her bed with Eileen perched uncomfortably at her side. 'Fenella Forsyth is going to be there, and she *likes* me. Nobody else wanted to go as much as me. Why did it have to be Gerald? *He* doesn't want to go.'

'But it if hadn't been him, it would have been another boy,' Eileen pointed out. She felt guilty at having been chosen and would have offered to swap with her friend if she hadn't wanted quite badly to go herself.

'Well, Susan then. I don't suppose she'd mind not going. Shall I ask her to go to Matron and tell her I can take her place?'

'No, because Matron won't let you. It has to be fairly drawn. And I think Susan does want to go really. She looked ever so pleased when her name was read out.'

Maddy sniffed and looked mutinous. 'She ought to let me go instead of her, after I gave her my liquorice toffees. I had no sweets all week apart from that barley sugar you gave me.'

'You don't like liquorice toffees. You wouldn't have given them to her otherwise.'

'That's not the point. Susan does, and I gave her mine, so she owes me. I'm going to ask her.' Maddy got off the bed and set off towards the door, but Eileen caught her by her skirt.

'No! Don't – it's not fair, and Matron won't let you anyway. Don't be selfish, Maddy. You go to Miss Friend's a lot, *and* the farm, and Susan hardly ever goes anywhere in the village.'

Maddy glared at her. 'I'm not being selfish!'

'You are. You know you are.'

'All right, then, what about you? *You're* being selfish – you've got a place too, and you've never offered it to me. *You* could swap. You say you're my best friend, so why don't you?'

Eileen gazed at her. She had never seen Maddy in this mood before and didn't know how to deal with it. Doubtfully, she wondered if she ought to do as her friend was demanding, but then she shook her head.

'It'd be just the same. Matron wouldn't let us change. She'd say the lot had to be drawn again, and then neither of us could go. Anyway,' she added, 'I *want* to go, and I won it fair and square, so why shouldn't I?'

Maddy stared back. The two girls met each other's eyes, neither willing to back down. Then, with a little cry of fury, Maddy flung herself away and buried her face in her pillow. Alarmed, Eileen put a tentative hand on her shoulder, but it was shrugged impatiently off.

Eileen sat beside her for a minute or two longer, staring at the shaking body. Tears began to brim from her own eyes and slide down her cheeks. She sniffed and rubbed them dry with the back of her hand.

'Maddy?' she said uncertainly. 'Maddy, don't be like that ...' She touched her friend's shoulder again, but Maddy twisted away.

'Go away! I hate you! You're not my best friend any more. I'm never going to speak to you again – *never*!'

Fenella was disappointed with the result of the draw too.

'I know there mustn't be any favouritism,' she said to Dottie, who had come along in the morning to make sandwiches and cakes. 'But that boy Gerald is a really rough sort of child, and I don't even know Stanley and Susan. Eileen's nice enough, but I was hoping one of them might be her friend Maddy. I quite took to that little girl.'

'She is a dear,' Dottie agreed, taking two sponge cakes out of the oven. 'Often pops in to see me on her way back from school. You could always come down to the cottage about that time, if you really want to see her.'

'Oh, it doesn't matter that much,' Fenella said. 'I'm only here for a few days this time anyway, so I probably won't get a chance.'

Dottie turned the cakes carefully out of their tins on to a cooling rack. 'You'm not still thinking about adopting a kiddie, then?'

Fenella sighed. 'I don't know, Dottie. It wouldn't be easy. I can't even offer a settled home at present. And what would be the point of taking a child from a children's home and sending her to a boarding school, where she'd have to start all over again? It would be cruel – and there'd still be the holidays to think of.' She cut a pile of sandwiches into quarters.

'I could always look after her for you,' Dottie offered diffidently. 'I've got the room now, and never had an evacuee. 'Twould be a pleasure to have a kiddie about the place.'

'But you've already got enough to do. You work at the Bell two or three evenings a week, you help Isobel here, you even help cook at the Barton. How could you possibly manage a child as well?'

'I suppose not,' Dottie agreed regretfully. 'Unless I changed my hours at the Bell for dinner times. But no, you're right – it wouldn't really do. It's a shame, though, when you think of all those little ones just needing a proper home and someone to love them.' She slid a tray of flapjacks from the oven and marked them into squares with a sharp knife. 'I hope they all like peanut butter. I always think putting a tablespoon of that into the mixture makes flapjacks easier to cut as well as tasty.'

'They look delicious.'

'The children seem to like them, and the oats are good for them. They do take up quite a lot of sugar and marge, but there's no eggs in them, and the golden syrup isn't rationed, which helps a lot.' She was aware that she was chattering, to hide her disappointment. The idea of a child – a little girl – living with her at the cottage had been much on her mind lately, and Fenella's hints about adopting had seemed a solution for both of them. Now it seemed that Fenella had decided against it. I'll have to write to the billeting people and see if there's any evacuees needing a place, she thought, but she knew it was unlikely now. Most children were already settled, and some had even gone home now that the bombing seemed to have stopped. But with all the raids on Germany now, who knew what it might start again, in retaliation?

Dottie sighed and tested the sponge cakes to see if they had cooled. She spread raspberry jam on one and positioned the other on top. There was no icing sugar, of course, but she had kept back a few precious cherries from her own dried fruit ration, and she cut them into quarters and placed them around the edge. 'There. That looks all right, I reckon.'

'It looks lovely. If there's any left, you must take a slice home with you.'

Dottie laughed. 'Any left! You haven't seen those children eat, Miss Fenella! It's not often they see a tea like this. I guarantee there won't be a crumb left.'

'It's going to be a lovely tea,' Fenella said. 'And mostly due to your efforts. You know, Dottie, if it were possible for me to adopt one of those children, I couldn't do better than to leave her with you. In my opinion, she'd be the luckiest little girl in the world!'

To everyone's surprise – and considerable relief – the tea went without a hitch. Stanley and Susan, overawed by the presence of the famous Fenella Forsyth, sat almost mute for the whole time, steadily munching their way through the sandwiches and cakes and remembering to say 'please' and 'thank you' and take the cake nearest them on the plate. Eileen, still upset by the quarrel with Maddy, spoke only when spoken to at first, but cheered up after a while and sat close to Fenella, answering questions about the home and school and even volunteering a little about her own parents, who had been killed in the Portsmouth Blitz. She had been sent after that to live with an aunt in Southampton, but the aunt had become ill and unable to take care of her.

'So you do still have some relatives?' Fenella asked, and Eileen nodded, her mouth too full of sponge cake to speak for a moment.

'My Auntie Betty and Uncle Brian, and I've got three cousins, too. They said I could go to them for Christmas, but Auntie Betty's in hospital now so I couldn't. I've got a granny too, but she's ever so old, nearly a hundred, I think.'

Fenella doubted this, but knew that to a child of Eileen's age anyone over fifty was in their dotage. She went on talking to Eileen and asked about her friend Maddy.

Eileen's eyes filled with tears. 'Maddy's not talking to me now. She's cross because she couldn't come this afternoon.'

'Oh dear.' Fenella was taken aback. 'But it's not your fault. Didn't Matron draw lots for you to come?'

'Yes, but Maddy knew you'd be here and she wanted me to give her my place. But I wouldn't have been allowed to. They'd have drawn again if I'd said I wanted her to come instead of me.'

'We had to come anyway, even if we didn't want to,' Gerald Mitchell butted in, breaking off from his conversation with Stephen. The two had already become fast friends and were quietly plotting to escape into the woods as soon as tea was over. There would still be half an hour of daylight left, just enough to build a makeshift den and start a game of commandos.

'I hope you all wanted to,' Isobel Napier said, wondering if she really wanted her son to make friends with this brash, loudly spoken boy. 'We want you to enjoy your time at the Barton.'

'I'm going to leave the first minute I can,' Gerald told her. 'I'll join the army and go and fight. That's what I want to do.'

'You're too young,' Eileen argued. 'You can't join up till you're sixteen, Nurse Powell said so.'

'She don't know nothing about it. You can lie about your age, and if you're big enough they'll take you.' He lifted one arm and bent it to show off his biceps. 'I'm going to be a commando.'

Isobel noticed Stephen's admiring glance and said, 'I'm sure you'd be a very good soldier, Gerald, but I'm afraid she's right. They'll check your age and you won't be allowed. Anyway, the war will probably be over by the time you're old enough.'

He lowered his arm and looked sullen. 'It won't. It's going to go on for years and years. And even if it is over, there'll be another one starting up somewhere. There's always a war going on somewhere.'

This was so depressingly true that the conversation was halted. Fenella glanced quickly round at the faces and said, 'If you've all had enough, why don't we play some games and then have a sing-song? Do you all know how to play consequences?'

Gerald, who had been hoping to be allowed out into the garden with Stephen, said, 'I'd rather play football. So would Stanley, wouldn't you, Stan?' Stan, afraid to say no, nodded. 'Can we go outside?'

Isobel caught her son's eye and gave in to the inevitable. After all, the whole point was to let the children enjoy themselves. 'You boys go out, then, and we'll stay in by the fire. There aren't really enough of us for a good game of consequences,' she added apologetically, but Fenella had another idea.

'I'll read you a story. What books have you got? I'm sure there must be some of Hilary's on the shelves.' She got up and went to the bookcase that stood in the corner of the room. 'Look – *The Wind in the Willows*! What could be nicer?'

'I've read that book,' Susan said, speaking up so suddenly that they all looked at her in surprise. 'I liked the bit where Mole went back to his home best. Can we have that?'

'Of course.' Fenella thumbed through the book and came to sit by the fire. They gathered round her as she found the place and began to read the story of Mole and Ratty's long winter walk, and Mole's realisation that they were passing near his very own home, still with the stepladder and whitewash left just as he had abandoned them on the spring day when he had cried, 'Hang spring-cleaning!' and set off on his adventures. Fenella's beautiful tones brought the tale to life as she gave each character their own distinctive voice, and when the mice came to sing carols she paused and said, 'Let's sing with them, shall we? What do you think they would have sung?' and after that the little gathering passed naturally into carol singing of their own, the book was laid aside and they moved over to the piano, where Isobel played for them, and eventually even the boys returned, glowing from their games in the cold air, and joined in.

'It was a lovely party,' Isobel said later as they cleared up after the children had returned to the Barton. 'But it was you who made it so lovely, Fenella. You have a real gift with children. It's such a shame you've never had any of your own.'

'I know,' Fenella said, piling up plates that had once held cakes, sandwiches and flapjacks and now bore nothing but crumbs. 'And now it's almost too late. And yet ...' She stood still for a moment, her thoughts going back to the party. Little Susan, with her big brown eyes and shy good manners. Eileen, bright and sharp as a needle, yet kind-hearted too, worrying about her friend Maddy, who had so badly wanted to be here. And Maddy herself, with her sweet voice and her tragic story of loss. 'Maybe it isn't, after all.'

There must be some way for her to adopt a child. But which should she choose? And how, even with Dottie to help, could she manage?

Chapter Thirty

With none of his own friends living nearby during the school holidays, Stephen Napier spent as much time as he could with Gerald Mitchell. The Barton children were allowed into the grounds to play, as long as they kept away from the vegetable gardens and stayed within earshot of the house so that they could hear the bell summoning them back; and also, provided they asked permission, into the village. Stephen, who knew every inch of the countryside within walking distance, disdained the idea of staying near the house and led Gerald into far-distant shrubberies and woods. There, they built dens and became commandos, seeking out the enemy and making traps out of sticks tied across shallow pits and covered with leaves.

'We need more of us,' he said after a couple of days. 'It's all right being commandos, but if we're going to do proper sabotage and catch prisoners, we need some Germans. It's not much fun if there's nobody looking for us and nobody to kill.'

'It was better in Southampton,' Gerald said. 'We had bomb sites there, and you could go in the ruined houses and look for unexploded bombs. I had a friend who found one and it went off in his hands.'

Stephen stared at him. 'What happened? Was he hurt?'

'Well, he was blown to bits, of course,' Gerald said nonchalantly. 'So I suppose it hurt, only we couldn't ask him, could we? After that, they said we couldn't play there any more.'

'I don't think I want to play on bomb sites,' Stephen said, although he felt a tremor of sick excitement in his stomach. 'It's better in the woods. But we still need enemies. Can't you bring a few from the Barton? What about that other boy who came to tea?'

'Stan? He's nothing but a drip. Still, I suppose he would do for a prisoner. We could tie him up and leave him in one of our dens until his mates came to rescue him.'

'Has he got any mates, if he's a drip?'

'No, not many. So he'd probably be there for ages!' Gerald laughed. 'Why don't we have a battle instead? We used to have some good battles in Southampton. One boy had to be taken to hospital. Trouble is, you need a lot on both sides to have a really good battle, and there are only twelve of us big enough. The rest are just babies, really.'

Stephen, half awed and half daunted by Gerald's tales, was beginning to wonder if this was such a good idea. He said, 'What about the girls? Can any of them fight?'

Gerald snorted derisively. 'Fight? Girls? Don't be a twerp! They're *girls*. There's one or two not bad, mind. That Eileen, that came to tea with you, and her friend Maddy. Maddy's nearly as good as a boy at climbing trees.'

'I've seen her. She looked nice.'

Gerald gave him a look, as if 'nice' wasn't a word he had much use for. 'She's all right, I suppose. She can get round Nurse Powell easy as anything.'

'Miss Friend likes her, anyway,' Stephen went on. 'She said Maddy goes to see her sometimes. Tell you what, we could go down there if we wanted. Miss Friend says I'm always welcome at her cottage.'

'Is that the old girl that comes to the Barton and cooks our dinner sometimes, and helps the girls with their sewing? Can I come too, next time you go?'

'Don't see why not. We could go this afternoon. She'll probably give us a bun or something.'

'She's doing our dinner today. It's my turn to help wash up, so I won't be able to get out till about three o'clock.'

'We could go then. I'll meet you there. You could bring Maddy too, if you like.'

Gerald snorted again, and Stephen realised that he wouldn't want to be seen walking through the village with a girl, even if she was nearly as good as a boy at climbing trees. Still, at least he had got Gerald off the subject of battles and bomb sites. Stephen was all for mock battles, but he had a feeling Gerald wasn't too bothered if people actually got hurt – even killed – and although something in him was drawn to the danger the other boy treated so casually, something else held him back. Perhaps it was the shadow of his own older brother, killed during the retreat to Dunkirk, and the knowledge that his father was also fighting somewhere. And once a week at school morning prayers, the headmaster would read out a list of names of former pupils who had been killed. It made the war very real to him, and he didn't like being reminded of it.

He was home in time for lunch. Fenella had gone into Tavistock to meet a friend, and he did a jigsaw puzzle with his mother until she said it was time for her WI meeting. They left the half-finished puzzle on the card table and she went upstairs for her hat and coat.

'What are you going to do, Stephen?' she asked when she came down. 'You should go outside for an hour or so, since it's turned fine again. Why not go for a walk?'

Stephen did not think it was necessary to tell her of his and Gerald's plans to visit Dottie. He knew she wouldn't object to his going, but he wasn't at all sure that she would approve of his taking Gerald. He had been well aware of her doubts about the other boy during their tea party, and had managed to avoid any mention of their friendship since.

'Yes, all right,' he said, surprising his mother, who knew that Stephen rarely went for a walk just for the sake of it. 'I'll see if I can find you any snowdrops.'

It was too early for snowdrops, but Isobel doubted if her son knew that. Still, it would do him no harm to be outside looking for them, and she gave him a quick kiss before opening the front door.

'Be home by dark, darling. I'll probably bring back some sausage rolls for tea. Miss Friend said she'd take some to the meeting for me.'

She closed the front door and Stephen stood in the small hallway, feeling baffled. He had forgotten – if he had ever known – that Dottie would be attending the WI meeting. In fact he hadn't even known she was a member. Why should he? He had never taken the slightest interest in the WI before, and had no idea what went on there.

All he did know was that on WI afternoons his mother was seldom home before four thirty and that presumably Dottie wouldn't be at her cottage until then either. And he had arranged to meet Gerald Mitchell there at three …

Well, it didn't matter. They could go and do something else instead, and visit Dottie another day. He would probably meet the other boy on the way, so they needn't even go as far as the village.

Stephen fetched his coat, and the gloves and balaclava helmet Dottie had knitted for him, and went out, looking for Gerald. There was no sign of the other boy, but as he was passing the end of the Barton drive, he caught sight of Maddy and Eileen coming towards him.

The two girls had made up their quarrel. Maddy had felt ashamed afterwards, knowing that Eileen had won the lot fairly and that she could not have given up her place at the tea party. She had not been able to go as far as saying so and apologising, but when their sweet ration was handed out next day she had offered Eileen the bag – 'You can have these if you like. I don't really want them' – and Eileen, who knew a peace offering when she saw one, had accepted it and then held out her own. 'Have mine instead.'

Nothing more had been said, and they had shared their sweets as they normally did, and then resumed their friendship as if nothing had happened. Maddy knew that Eileen would tell her about the tea party later, and it wouldn't seem half as important as it had at the time.

Stephen stopped. 'Hello,' he said to Eileen. 'You came to tea with us.' He looked at Maddy. 'You're Maggy.'

'Maddy. Where are you going?'

'Well,' Stephen said a little awkwardly, 'I was going to see Miss Friend at her cottage, but she won't be there because of the WI meeting, so I don't really know.'

'Come with us instead,' Maddy offered. 'We're going to the bridge to see if we can see any fish.'

Stephen hesitated. He still expected to bump into Gerald at any minute and didn't want to be seen with girls. He said, 'I've got to go to the cottage anyway. I'm meeting someone there.'

'How can you, if she's not going to be there?' Eileen asked, and Maddy said, 'I bet it's Gerald Mitchell. He said he was going out to tea in the village this afternoon but he wouldn't tell us where. He was ahead of us, anyway, so he'll be nearly there by now.'

'We'd better go and see,' Eileen said, and they set off, Stephen walking slightly behind the two girls so that if Gerald saw them he could claim not to be with them.

The village street was quiet. Most of the men were at work in the fields and the women either indoors or, if WI members – as most of them were – at the meeting. The three children met nobody until they arrived at Dottie's cottage. There was no sign of Gerald, either along the way or at the door.

'He's gone somewhere else,' Stephen said with some relief. He had found the company of the two girls oddly calming after the somewhat apprehensive excitement of being with Gerald. He decided that he would ask his mother to hold another tea party, and this time to make sure Maddy came too. She was, as Gerald had said, nearly as good as a boy anyway.

Maddy, however, was frowning a little.

'He's been here, look. The gate's not properly shut and Miss Friend always makes sure the catch is fastened in case the dog over the road comes in and chases Alfred.'

'Perhaps he's in the back garden,' Eileen suggested. 'We'd better go and see, in case he's waiting at the door.'

Gerald was not waiting in the garden, but the back door was ajar. The three children looked at each other uncertainly.

'He can't have gone in,' Stephen said doubtfully. 'Not if Miss Friend isn't here.'

Maddy glanced at him as if to say he didn't know Gerald as they knew him, and said, 'We'd better go and see.'

'We can't do that,' Eileen protested. 'Its burglaring.'

'No it isn't. We're not going to steal anything. Anyway, if Gerald's there ...' She left the sentence unfinished, and after a moment or two of hesitation, Stephen stepped forward and pushed the door open.

'Come on. We'd better make sure he's all right.'

Nobody could imagine what harm might come to Gerald in Dottie's cottage, but the two girls followed him into the room. Eileen, who had never been there before, looked round with interest at the small scullery and the living room that served also as kitchen, with a neat little range built into one wall and two wooden armchairs, piled with cushions, standing one on each side.

'That's where Alfred sleeps,' Maddy said, pointing to one of the chairs where a crocheted blanket was covered in cat's hairs. 'I wonder where he—' She was interrupted by a sudden unearthly screech and she stared at the other two, her face suddenly white. 'That's him! That's Alfred – he sounds as if he's hurt!'

With no more hesitation, the three of them crowded through the door and into the little passageway leading to Dottie's tiny parlour. Even Maddy and Stephen had never been in here before, for it was seldom used, but now they pushed the door open without ceremony and rushed in.

Maddy gave a cry of horror.

'*Gerald!* What are you doing to Alfred? You're *torturing* him!'

'I've made up my mind,' Fenella said as they were walking back after the meeting had been concluded. It had been a short meeting today, there not being much business to discuss, and everyone was glad to be going home before dark. 'I'm going to see the matron at the children's home and ask if there's any possibility that I might adopt that sweet little girl.'

'The one who came to tea?' Isobel asked. 'I agree, she seems a very nice little thing, and so well mannered. Never forgot to say "please", and thanked me so nicely for having them.'

'No, not that one,' Fenella said, not sure whether Isobel had meant Eileen or Susan and not bothering to find out. 'The one who sang at the big party – Maddy. You know her, Dottie. She comes to see you at home sometimes.'

'A dear little maid.' Dottie nodded. 'And she seems so lost, somehow. As if she's always looking for someone to love. They separated her from her sister, you know, and I think the sister's died since. They've never told Maddy, straight out, mind, and I don't think even Matron knows for sure. It's like a lot of kiddies in that position – they break off all contact, so she'll probably never really know.' She was silent for a moment, then looked at Fenella. 'But do you reckon they'd let you adopt her?'

'How could you, anyway?' Isobel asked. 'You'll be going abroad again soon, and you could never take her with you. Besides, she needs to be at school. Would you send her to a boarding school?'

'Oh no, I wouldn't do that. The child needs a home life with someone who'd look after her.' Fenella turned to Dottie. 'I'd need your help. I know we talked about it before, and you do have so much to do, but if you could give Maddy a home while I'm away, I'd pay you for her keep and enough extra for you to give up your work at the pub – in the evenings, anyway. Do you think you'd be able to do that? I know you'd love to have a child about the place.'

'It's true, I would,' Dottie said thoughtfully. 'And I'm proper fond of the little scrap. I'd been thinking of letting the billeting people know I had room, if they'd got any evacuees needing somewhere, so I'd have had to give up the evening work anyway ...' She remained silent for a few moments, with her hand on her front gate, while Fenella gazed at her anxiously. But before she could speak, a shriek sounded from inside the cottage and they all jumped and stared at each other.

'Why, what's that dreadful noise?' Isobel gasped. 'Is there someone in there?' She caught her breath as screams and a sudden crash were added to the shrieks. 'Dottie, whatever's happening?'

'That's not a person,' Dottie gasped. 'That's a cat – it's my Alfred! He sounds as if he's in pain. Oh my stars, whatever can be the matter?'

'Let him go!' Maddy stormed, pushing her way in. 'You're hurting him! Let *go*!'

Gerald Mitchell, standing in the middle of the room with Alfred clutched to his chest, turned quickly away from her, but not before they had all seen that the cat was trussed up like a chicken, his paws bound tightly with string and a half-knitted khaki sock pushed down over his head. He was squirming desperately in Gerald's arms, emitting screech after screech, and Gerald was hard put to it to keep hold of him. When Maddy flew at him, her fists flailing and legs kicking, he was forced to let go, and Alfred fell in a heap on to Dottie's grandmother's rug, where he lay lashing out as best he could with his tied legs, his claws scoring deep scratches in whatever they could touch.

'You're a beast! A horrible, cruel *beast*! Poor Alfred! You've nearly killed him. Oh, Alfred, *Alfred*!' She was upon the startled boy, forcing him to the floor, where he almost fell on the shrieking cat and came within reach of the scrabbling claws. He added his own yells to the noise, and Maddy, now pummelling him with her fists, continued to shout, while Stephen and Eileen, trying to pull the two apart at the same time as rescuing the terrified cat, joined their own voices to the clamour.

'Get this flaming bitch off me!' Gerald bellowed. 'She's worse than the bleeding cat! Get her *off*!' He began to fight back, his bigger fists landing squarely in Maddy's face, and she screamed with pain and fury.

Stephen left Eileen to grapple with the frenzied cat while he attacked Gerald. 'Stop that, you bully! You're hitting a girl, and she's a lot smaller than you anyway. Stop it at once!'

'Who's going to make me?' Gerald sneered, turning on him. 'You? You're just a posh sissy! Whose side are you on anyway?' He aimed a punch at Stephen's face, but Stephen ducked smartly and knocked him flying with a blow to his chin.

Gerald fell back against the display cabinet housing Dottie's mother's best tea service, handed down through the family. There was a crash and a sound of smashing china that seemed somehow to continue for far longer than anyone might have expected. Eileen, who had finally managed to quieten Alfred and begun to untie his paws, yelped and dropped him, and Alfred shot past her, with his head still swathed in khaki wool and trailing string from his back paws. Stephen, astonished and dismayed by the success of his punch, stood staring at the destruction, and Maddy, who had stumbled against a small table on which had rested a large china jug – now in smithereens on the floor – climbed unsteadily to her feet and wiped blood from her nose with the back of her hand.

There was a short, appalled silence and then another voice sounded from the doorway.

'What in the name of all that's wonderful has been going on in my parlour? Who said you could come in here and have a free fight? *And what have you been doing to my Alfred?*'

Order of a sort, considering the havoc that had been wreaked, was restored eventually and the four reprobates were made to sit in a row on Dottie's settee, where they made a sorry picture, their faces stained with tears and blood, and bruises already beginning to appear round Maddy's eye and nose, and all over Gerald's sullen face.

Alfred had been caught and gently released from his bondage but had refused to stay indoors, even when offered a saucer of milk. He had escaped into the garden, where he could be seen on the roof of the coal shed, washing himself frantically and then crouching in a furious heap, glowering at the creeping shadows.

The three women surveyed the shamefaced children.

'Well?' Dottie asked eventually, and even Fenella had never heard her use that tight, angry tone of voice before. 'What do you have to say for yourselves? Whose idea was it to walk into my house uninvited, tie up my poor dear little cat and make free of my parlour? You realise that's my granny's best tea service you've smashed, not to mention Aunt Dorothy's bedroom jug that she left to me in her will special? And I don't reckon I'll ever get they bloodstains out of my rug. What did you think you were playing at, the four of you?'

The children glanced at each other. Gerald gazed woodenly back at Dottie while the others stared miserably at the floor. There being no immediate answer, Isobel added her voice. 'Stephen? Have you nothing to say? I'm ashamed of you, thoroughly ashamed. You know perfectly well that you do *not* walk into other people's houses uninvited. And to go into Dottie's *parlour*, of all places ... As for poor Alfred – words fail me. I always thought you were a *kind* boy!'

'I *am*!' Stephen burst out, unable to bear this slur. 'I *am* a kind boy! And I didn't do those things. I never—'

'You were in here,' his mother stated. 'You can't deny that, so don't try.'

'But it wasn't like that!' Even now, Stephen couldn't bring himself to tell tales on someone who had been his friend, although he knew very well that their friendship had ended the moment he had come into the parlour and seen Gerald with Alfred clutched to his chest. He looked desperately at the others, and it was Maddy, who had no loyalty towards Gerald, who came to his rescue.

'It wasn't Stephen!' she said hotly. 'It was that horrible Gerald Mitchell. He's a bully, and a thief as well, probably, and we weren't even *here* when he came in. We were outside. All of us.'

Fenella, who had been wondering ever since she had come in and

233

seen the devastation whether her decision to adopt Maddy was after all a wise one, said in a disappointed tone, 'So why *did* you come in, Maddy? I'm sure you know better than that really. Even if you do often come to see Dottie, you shouldn't come in if she's not here, now should you?'

'No! And I didn't – not at first. None of us did. But we thought Gerald would be here, because Stephen said he was bringing him to see you and we knew he would have got here first, and so we went round the back and the door was open and then we heard ... we heard ...' Her voice broke and she began to sob. The women looked helplessly at her and then at Eileen, who was crying in sympathy, and at last Isobel said grimly, 'I think you'd better tell us the whole thing, Stephen, and never mind any nonsense about telling tales. None of you is leaving here until we know the truth.'

'All right,' he said, not looking at Gerald. 'We heard Alfred crying, that's what it was, and we thought he sounded as if he was hurt or frightened, so we came in. Gerald was in the parlour and he'd got him tied up, and Maddy ... well, Maddy sort of went for him, and made him let Alfred go,' he finished uncertainly, not sure whether this counted as tale telling or not.

'*Maddy* went for him?'

'She's like a bleeding tiger,' Gerald said, speaking for the first time. 'She's mad. Ought to be locked up, she did, in a loony bin.'

'*Maddy* ought to be locked up?' Fenella exclaimed. 'You walk into someone else's house and torture their cat and you say that a little girl with more courage in her little finger than you have in your whole body ought to be locked up? Why, you're a coward as well as a bully, and you deserve all you got!'

It was dark before the children were returned to the Barton, where a grim-faced Matron and anxious Nurse Powell awaited them. Dottie's attempts at an explanation were waved away as Matron and the boys' housemaster ordered baths, attention to the bruises and black eyes that both Maddy and Gerald were displaying, and then early bed after a supper of bread and milk.

'You're lucky to be getting even that,' Matron told them sternly. 'I shall want to see all of you in my office at eight o'clock sharp in the morning, and meanwhile you are to speak to nobody. Nobody at all. Not even each other,' she added to Maddy and Eileen. 'In fact, I've a good mind to separate you for the night.'

'Please, Matron, don't do that,' Maddy begged. 'We promise we won't talk to each other, don't we, Eileen?'

'It really wasn't their fault,' Dottie added. 'And Maddy was a brave little girl and saved Alfred from whatever that dreadful boy was going to do to him.'

Matron, who had no idea who Alfred was and didn't want to know just now, brushed this aside. 'The point is that you say they entered your house without permission, and they've obviously been fighting. I can't tolerate that kind of behaviour and I'll be the judge of who was at fault when I've heard their explanation in the morning. Thank you for bringing them back, Miss Friend – and Mrs Napier.' She favoured Stephen with a look that said quite clearly that she thought it a pity that he too wouldn't be reporting to her office at eight o'clock sharp. 'You can leave them in my care now.'

Dottie, however, was not to be dismissed so easily. Standing with her feet planted firmly on the doormat, she said, 'If you don't mind, Matron, I'd like to have a word with you now, without the children. There's things you ought to know before you talks to them tomorrow.'

'I would, too,' Fenella said, equally firmly. 'I have something important to discuss with you, and I'm afraid it won't wait. I'll be going away again soon and there are things I need to do before I leave.'

Matron looked at them helplessly, then shrugged. 'Very well. Nurse Powell, see to these children, please, and have them ready for me immediately after breakfast in the morning. They are not to speak to anyone else and they can have their breakfast in the kitchen, away from the others. I mean to get to the bottom of this before I decide how to deal with them.' She looked at Isobel. 'Mrs Napier, I know this is your house, but I am in charge here now and it's my duty to see that there is no damage done to your property. What happened in Miss Friend's cottage this afternoon is very disturbing to me, as I'm sure you'll understand, and I will make every effort to ensure that it never happens again.' She glanced at Stephen. 'No doubt you know how to deal with your own son. And now, Miss Friend and Miss Forsyth, if you would like to follow me . . .'

Isobel, feeling almost like a small girl herself to be so summarily dismissed from her own house, put her hand on Stephen's shoulder and turned away. 'Come along, Stephen. Let's go home and get you cleaned up. We'll see you later, Fenella. And thank you, Dottie, for being so understanding.' She turned back and looked after the subdued little group now climbing the stairs after Nurse Powell. 'Goodnight, Maddy and Eileen, and don't worry. It will all be sorted out tomorrow, I promise.'

She and Stephen walked out through their own front door and down the steps. The moon was now rising and gave them light to see their way back to the estate cottage, and as they started along the track, Stephen took his mother's hand.

'It wasn't Maddy's fault,' he said in a small voice. 'Gerald was really going to hurt Alfred. He's a horrible boy and I'm never going to play with him again. I'd rather have Maddy any day. I hope she doesn't get sent away.'

'I think you're right,' his mother said, smiling down at him. 'She's a brave little girl and a good friend. I hope we shall see quite a lot more of her.'

'You want to *adopt* her?' Matron repeated, staring at Fenella.

'Yes, I do,' the actress said firmly. 'I've been thinking about it for a long time, and I made my decision today. I must admit,' she added with a smile, 'I did waver a little when I saw what had happened in the cottage, but once I understood the facts, they simply confirmed my feelings. I felt a bond between us the moment she came up to sing at the party in September, and every time I've seen her since, it's become stronger. And Dottie here knows her well and is willing to take care of her while I'm away.'

'More than willing,' Dottie added eagerly. 'It'll be a pleasure to have her round my feet. She can stay with me as long as Miss Fenella wants her to.'

Matron looked from one to the other. 'I hardly know what to say. I do see, of course, now that you've explained what happened at the cottage, that neither of the girls was at fault. Nor Mrs Napier's son, although if I had known he was spending so much time with Gerald, I would have warned her. He's a bad influence, that boy, and I'm going to have to discuss with his housemaster what is to be done about him. I'm not at all sure we can keep him here after this. But that's for us to decide, and of no particular interest to you,' she went on hastily. 'I have to admit, Miss Forsyth, that this is most unexpected. We do receive offers to adopt from time to time, of course, but this is an unusual one. For a start, you're not offering Maddy a normal family life.'

'No, but—' Fenella began, but Dottie broke in.

'I can give her that, Matron, while Miss Fenella's away entertaining the troops and such. She'll have a good, sensible upbringing in my cottage, with no airs and graces, just a simple country life, and there's plenty of families in Burracombe will welcome her through their doors. Why, she's up at the Tozers' farm with young Jackie every chance she gets as it is. She'll get a lot more normal life than she gets here in the home, if you don't mind me saying so.'

Matron sighed. 'I'm afraid that's true. We do our best, but there's no denying that we are an institution and, until they're grown up, most of these children will never really know what it is to live in a normal house.' She looked at Fenella again. 'Are you quite sure it's Maddy you want? Wouldn't you like to consider any of the other children? Susan Jenkins, for instance, who went to Mrs Napier for the tea party – she's a quiet little girl, and very biddable. I have to tell you, Maddy can be quite a little spitfire, and if there's any mischief going on, she'll be at the heart of it. But in all fairness, she's never malicious and she's a bright, intelligent little thing.'

'And she's the one I want,' Fenella stated. 'As far as I'm concerned, she's the daughter I've always longed for, and I have only two questions to ask. The first is, would she be available for adoption? She doesn't seem to have any family, apart from the sister who was separated from her and who I understand may be dead, so would the authorities agree to let me have her? And the second is, would she *like* me to adopt her? I don't think it would be right to force her.'

'I'm sure she would like it, and I don't think there will be any objection from the authorities,' Matron said. 'They'll be only too pleased for someone to take on the responsibility and expense. There are plenty of other children needing the kind of care we offer here.' She thought for a moment. 'I think the best thing for me to do is make contact with the right person tomorrow and set things in motion. It might not take very long at all. Once we know if it's possible, you can talk to Maddy yourself.' She glanced at the clock. 'Meanwhile, we do have a routine to adhere to, so if you don't mind ...' She rose and held out her hand, and Fenella stood up too and shook it warmly.

'Thank you very much, Matron. It's been a pleasure to meet you and I'm looking forward to hearing from you again. Dottie here will always know how to find me, if you need to contact me while I'm away. Don't say anything to Maddy, though – I'll want to do that myself.'

She and Dottie left the room and walked down the wide hallway to the front door. Neither of them spoke until they were halfway down the drive and out of sight of the big house. Then Fenella stopped and flung her arms around the little countrywoman.

'Oh, Dottie! It's all going to come right, I know it is! We're going to have a little girl! I know she'll be mine officially, and once the war is over she'll be coming to me, but until then she'll live with you – it will be as if we're sharing her. It's going to be so wonderful.'

'It is,' Dottie said, returning her hug. 'The most wonderful thing that's ever happened to me. I'll do my very best for the little dear, Miss Fenella, I promise you that. The very best I could ever do.'

Part Six

Chapter Thirty-One

April 1944

A CHILD IN BURRACOMBE

It was just before Easter when the adoption finally came through. Fenella, back in Burracombe again for a short time, took Maddy to church for the Easter Day service – her first appearance in the village as the actress's adopted daughter. They sat in the Napiers' pew at the front, so that everyone could see them, with Dottie just behind. Maddy, dressed in a new spring coat of pale green tweed that Dottie had made from one of Fenella's own coats, sat between her new mother and Stephen Napier, with Isobel on his other side. Colonel Napier, who was also home on leave, sat beside his wife. It was almost, the villagers murmured to each other, like old times to see the family pew nearly filled, although it broke your heart to think that one member of the family would never sit there again.

It was good to hear the bells ringing, too, as they had done for special occasions ever since Mr Churchill had said they could be rung last Easter. With so many of the younger men away, it had been difficult for Ted Tozer to muster a team, but they had practised and performed well, and to hear the bells pealing out made you feel that things were looking up and the war might yet be over before too long.

'And we'm going to win it,' Bert Foster murmured to Edie Pettifer, as they sat together in the back row – almost, one or two people whispered, as if they were a courting couple at the pictures! ''Tis only a matter of time now, mark my words.'

Dorothy Doidge, playing the organ, launched into the first hymn, and Basil Harvey, who was well settled in as vicar now and loved almost as much as the old vicar – who had died in the vestry at the age of seventy-two after giving the most fiery sermon of his life – led the procession of six choir men and four boys up the aisle to begin the service.

Maddy felt strange and conspicuous in the front pew. The Barton children were in the side aisle, as usual, and she could feel their eyes upon her in her new coat and hat. Since it had become known that she was to be adopted, there had been mixed reactions amongst the other children and she knew there had been some jealousy. Why should she be chosen, above all the rest? Why should a famous actress and singer, who could pick any child in the whole world, want little Maddy Simmons? Why couldn't they have drawn lots, like they had for the tea party – a party Maddy hadn't even attended? 'Not fair,' some of them muttered. 'Just not fair . . .'

But others were pleased for her good fortune, and to Maddy's relief, these included Eileen, who had been her friend from the day of her arrival and had always stood by her in the many scrapes they had got themselves into.

'You're ever so lucky,' Eileen had said without a trace of envy. 'You'll have a lovely time, living with Miss Friend.'

'I'm to call her Auntie Dottie now,' Maddy said. 'I'm going to have my own bedroom, all to myself, and I can have friends to tea whenever I like. You can come first. I'll have Susan too, sometimes. But I shall never, ever have that horrible Gerald Mitchell.'

'He's not staying here anyway,' Eileen told her. 'I heard someone say he's being sent to another home that's just for boys, where it's a lot stricter than here. Good riddance!'

Fenella had, true to her word, made sure that Maddy was happy with the arrangements before going ahead. Dottie had asked them both to tea in her cottage one day, and after eating their fill at a table spread with her best embroidered cloth and laden with plates of sandwiches, scones and a Victoria sponge at least three inches thick, Fenella had turned to Maddy, who was cuddling a purring Alfred.

'Maddy, darling, I've something to ask you. Something very serious, so you need to think carefully before answering.' She paused, while Maddy fixed her with huge, slightly alarmed blue eyes. 'You see, I've been thinking for a long time that I would like to have a little girl of my own. But while I'm travelling so much, it's never seemed possible. However, my dear friend Dottie here has been thinking almost the same—'

'I always wanted an evacuee, you see,' Dottie broke in. 'But it never seemed to happen at the right time.'

'And what we've decided is this.' Fenella paused, surprised to find her heart thumping madly. 'If – and *only* if – you like the idea, Maddy, I would like you to be my little girl. It wouldn't be just for a few months or even a few years – it would be for ever. I would like to adopt you.'

She stopped. Maddy was staring at her, her mouth open. She looked from Fenella to Dottie, whose own eyes were brimming with tears. At last she said, 'You mean you'd be my *mummy*? You want me to be your little girl?'

'Yes!' Fenella exclaimed, her voice high with emotion. 'Yes, that's exactly what I mean. I'd be your mummy!'

Maddy frowned a little, as if trying to assimilate the idea. 'But where would I live? Would I have to go away and ... and entertain the troops, like you do? Would I have to live in a tent?'

'No indeed!' Fenella laughed, a little hysterically. 'You'd never have to do that. You'd stay here in Burracombe. You'd live with Dottie. With Miss Friend, I mean.'

'With Miss Friend? And Alfred?'

'Yes, my little dear, with me and Alfred.' Tears were now on Dottie's cheeks. 'And you wouldn't call me Miss Friend any more, either. I'd be your Auntie Dottie. And you could stay here as long as you like.'

'Until you leave school, anyway,' Fenella amended. 'But by then the war is sure to be over and you can come and live in London with me. So ... what do you think?' There was a hint of anxiety in her voice now. 'You don't have to decide straight away. You can think about it for as long as you like.'

Maddy got up from her chair and put Alfred carefully on the floor. She came over to the two women and put her hands on their knees. When she looked up into their faces, her eyes were large and solemn.

'I want to be your little girl,' she said. 'I want you to be my mummy, and I want Miss Friend to be my auntie.' And with only the smallest pause, she added, 'And I want Alfred to be my cat!'

The formal arrangements had seemed to Maddy to take an endlessly long time, but at last they were over and here she was, in church, making her first appearance as Fenella's adopted daughter. Afterwards, she and Fenella would go to the estate cottage for a small sherry party given by Isobel and Gilbert, who was on a short leave, to welcome her to their circle, and then return to Dottie's cottage for Sunday dinner. This was the right thing to do, Fenella had said firmly when Isobel had protested that she would have liked them to stay with the Napiers for the meal as well. Dottie's cottage was to be Maddy's home for the time being, and Dottie so much wanted to give them this first celebration that Fenella could not have refused.

'Well, Maddy will always be welcome here, you know that,' Isobel said at last. 'Dottie will give her a good home and a sensible upbringing while you're away, but she'll need to be able to mix with the kind of people you and I know as well, as she grows up.'

'I feel quite sure that Maddy will be able to mix,' Fenella replied. 'She has a lovely quality of happy confidence that will endear her to everyone she meets. I feel very blessed to have found such a delightful daughter.'

The hymns and prayers almost over, Basil climbed to the pulpit for his sermon. He looked down kindly at the little girl in the front pew and then began.

'The subject for my sermon this Easter Day is taken from St Paul's Epistles to the Hebrews, chapter thirteen, verse two: "Be not forgetful to entertain strangers; for thereby some have entertained angels unawares" ...'

''Tis a happy day for us all,' Alice Tozer said as the congregation made their way out of the church. 'And it were a lovely way for the vicar to remind us that it behoves us all to be kind to these little souls who have fetched up amongst us. They've all got a sad story

244

to tell, and who knows what they've got lying ahead of them? 'Tis up to us to make their time in Burracombe a time they'll look back on with a smile.'

'I dare say you'll be seeing quite a bit of young Maddy yourself,' Aggie Madge commented. 'She's pretty thick with your Jackie, I've noticed.'

'Yes, she is, and always welcome at the farm. Such a sunny little face she has, 'tis always a pleasure to see her come through the door.'

George and Ivy Sweet were walking just behind. Ivy's pregnancy was well advanced now, and although there was still a hint of anxiety in her eyes, and her hair was still red, she carried herself well and George looked proud of her. He took her arm in his and said in a low voice, 'If things had been different, Ive, I'd begun to think about adopting a kiddie myself. One of they young tackers, to learn the bakery business and take over from me one day. But as things are now, us don't need to do that. It won't be long now before us is a proper family.'

Ivy turned to him. 'Would you have wanted to do that, George? Take on someone else's child?'

George's eyes were steady as they met hers. If he saw the shadows in them, he gave no hint, but replied, 'I don't reckon it would have made all that much difference, Ive. I'd have taken it for my own and welcomed it as such. Just as I will this little one you'm carrying now, only this one will be *our* baby, and will call us mother and father.' He kept his eyes on hers and added firmly, 'And that's all that matters.'

It was evening at last. Fenella had decided to stay at Dottie's cottage with Maddy for the rest of the holiday, before she returned to London and set off again on her travels. She would be away for several weeks, and Maddy would be well settled by the time she came home.

'Time for bed now, darling,' she said, giving Maddy a kiss. 'You go up and get into your nightie, and I'll come and tuck you in. And when you wake up tomorrow, I'll be there in the other bed and we'll go for a picnic up on the moor, just like all the other families in Burracombe.'

Maddy kissed her and then Dottie. She bent to stroke Alfred, whom she had already planned to smuggle upstairs into her bed once Fenella had departed, and climbed the steep, narrow cottage stairs to her room.

No lights shone from the windows of the other cottages. When the war was over, the lamps would be lit and the curtains not yet drawn, and a warm glow would shine across the village street, but as yet it was still dark. But Maddy stood gazing down, and slowly a procession of memories formed in her mind, memories of other bedrooms and other streets.

Her first home, in Portchester Avenue in Portsmouth, which had been completely destroyed by one of the earliest bombing raids of the war. She could still just remember her mother's shock at seeing it, and the misery of the first few days living in a corner of the church hall, with two camp beds the only space they had to call their own, surrounded by other homeless families. Her sister Stella had done her best to look after her, but nothing could console Maddy for the loss of her doll, Princess Marcia.

From there, they had gone to the neglected squalor of the little house in October Street, where Jess Budd had helped them to scrub and clean until it was fit for them to live in. They'd been happy enough there, surrounded by the good neighbours of October Street and April Grove, until they were bombed out yet again, and this time Maddy and Stella had been left motherless.

That was when they had been sent to the village of Bridge End, near Southampton, and there she had met Sammy Hodges and the parrot, Silver. She had thought she would stay there until the war ended and her father came back from the Merchant Navy and made them a new home. But his ship had been torpedoed and, as orphans now, she and Stella had been parted and sent to their different children's homes. And from there, Maddy had found her new home and family in Burracombe.

I wonder where Stella is now, she thought, suddenly missing her sister more than ever before, and a great wave of sadness swept over her as she allowed herself, for the first time, to face the possibility that she might never see her again.

*

And at the same moment, back in her own children's home in Winchester, Stella was wondering just the same thing. Was Muriel happy and well looked after, wherever she was? Was she thinking of Stella, and hoping that one day they would find each other?

We will, Stella vowed. As soon as I am grown up and can start to search, I will find you. We *will* be together again ...

A Child in Burracombe

AUTHOR'S NOTE

Sometimes, especially when writing a series, an author finds certain characters tugging at her hem, demanding that their story be told. And when that character also begins to tug at the heart, it is only to be expected that one day the author will give in.

This is what happened with the Simmons sisters, Stella and Muriel (later to be known as Maddy). They first appear in *The Girls They Left Behind*, the second of my April Grove series, set in and around Portsmouth during the Second World War and published in 1995. Bombed out of their home in one of the first major raids of 1940, they find themselves with their mother Kathy and other homeless families in a crowded church hall, waiting to be rehoused, with nothing left of their home and possessions; and when they are allocated a new home, it turns out to be a squalid little house with no electricity, previously occupied by an old woman and her cats. With only five pounds to buy new clothes and furniture, and the house itself needing to be scrubbed from top to bottom, Kathy Simmons, pregnant with her third child, is in despair until Jess Budd, from nearby April Grove, comes to offer help.

From that day, the two little girls are caught up in all the horror of war. Terror grips them almost every night as the air raid sirens wail and the bombs fall all over the city – for, as a front-line naval port, Portsmouth was bombed without mercy. Their brother Thomas is born in the air raid shelter at the bottom of the garden, with only the local air-raid warden to bring him into the world as the bombs explode about them. And then tragedy strikes again as Kathy and Thomas are killed during an horrific blitz which lasts seven hours and almost destroys the city.

That could have been the end of the story. At this point, I could have sent Stella and Muriel away, perhaps to other family members, perhaps to evacuation, never to be heard of again. But already they had become too important to be abandoned. Their father, all too often facing his own danger at sea with the Merchant Navy, is able to come home for a brief visit to the little house in April Grove where Jess Budd lives and has taken the sisters in. And, almost before I knew it, Jess was suggesting that they be sent to the village of Bridge End, where her own two boys are billeted with the elderly vicar – a thin, spidery-looking man who rides round the parish on a rattling old bicycle, takes early morning services with his pyjamas still on underneath his cassock, and organises games of cricket or snowball fights on the vicarage lawn with his young evacuees.

Somehow, I was never quite able to send these two little girls to the outer fringes of the story. Muriel, in particular, insisted on being in the thick of it. She makes friends with Sammy Hodges, who appears in three books of his own – *Tuppence To Spend*, *A Farthing Will Do*, and *A Penny A Day* (also set partly in Burracombe). And you can be sure that if these two get into mischief, Muriel will be at the heart of it, from getting stuck up trees to almost losing Ruth Hodges's parrot Silver on a picnic. Like all good characters, she developed a personality of her own, without my having much to do with it. She was tugging at my hem, and beginning to tug at my heart.

But there is still a war on and the country idyll – living with a vicar who buys the children's sugar ration at a halfpenny a spoonful and his housekeeper who is a second mother to them all – could not last, for these two are marked for tragedy. Their father is lost at sea and they are now orphans. They come under a different 'authority' and it is deemed more appropriate now for them to be removed from normal evacuation and placed in homes for orphaned children.

Note 'homes'. Not one home, where they can still be together. Stella and Muriel, still under the age of eleven, were to be separated and sent to different Children's Homes, with no contact between them. Their past was to be cut away. It was to be as if none of it had ever happened and they had never had any family at all.

I think this was the point at which my heart was truly captured by the plight of these two little girls and all children who, like them, had been treated in this manner. I have known personally of a brother and sister who, years after the war and because of a family tragedy, had been parted and denied all contact. I had never forgotten their story and I had heard others, telling similar tales. The unthinking cruelty of it had touched me and would not let go. And although Stella and Muriel were fictional characters, not based on anyone I knew or had heard about, I felt their distress and pain as acutely as if it were real, and wanted to know what happened to them. Would they ever find each other? Would I ever be able to write their story? The questions were always at the back of my mind.

But it was not the time then to explore further. I had to let them go and continue with the stories of the Budds, of Sammy Hodges (in his first two books) and then, leaving April Grove and Bridge End, stories of others caught up in the Second World War – the Lyons Corner House 'Nippies' in the Corner House trilogy, the VADs of Haslar Hospital in *A Girl Called Thursday* and *A Promise To Keep*, the partly post-war Devon stories *Love & Laughter* and *Wives & Sweethearts*, the story of the Dartmoor airfield *A Song At Twilight*, and – what I always think of as my best wartime book of all – the story of Dunkirk in *Three Little Ships*.

April Grove and its inhabitants did appear in some of my other books – *Dance, Little Lady* and *Under the Apple Tree*. But Stella and Muriel were gone, far away, and I still had no idea what had happened to them or if I would ever find out and write about it. Until, one day when I felt that I had written enough about the war, my editor suggested a series set in a Devon village in the 1950s.

The 1950s! Stella and Muriel would be young women! Perhaps they would have found each other – perhaps they were still searching. Was this my chance to catch up with them and find out what had happened during those lost years?

If you have read the first of the *Burracombe* series, *The Bells of Burracombe*, you will know some of the answers. (And if you haven't – well, they are still available, either to order through your bookshop or to download on to your e-reader. And I hope that you will enjoy reading them, and the wartime stories mentioned above, as much as I have enjoyed writing them.)

And yet ... there was still a huge gap in their lives, still a story to be discovered. And that story has finally been told now, in the book you have just read: *A Child in Burracombe*.

*

People often ask me where I get my ideas and how I develop them. Quite honestly, I am not really sure. An idea can come from a stray snippet of conversation and lurk in my mind for months or even years before being used. It may, like many of the events in the Second World War books, be triggered by my own memories of that time, even though I was only six years old when it ended. Or it can simply develop from things the characters I am writing about do or say at any particular moment, for the characters often seem to have their own agenda in how the story will develop.

Writing, to me, is not so much a matter of sitting down to work out a plot, step by step – although that does happen at certain points – but more like opening a door into a different world and writing down what I see happening there. A psychotherapist friend of mine once said that I probably go into a trance-like state, and I think that is very likely true. I know that I often raise my eyes from the screen and look out of the window at the familiar view of the fields and woods across the valley, and blink a bit, and wonder what time of day it is. Have I had lunch? Is it tea-time? (I always know, however, if it is time for the dogs to have their walk, because they come and tell me!)

And some characters, as I have already said, just won't leave me alone. Sammy, for instance, who first appeared as a lonely little boy living in a poor home with a rough elder brother, a sickly mother and a father who might have been violent and demanding but was in fact as lost as his son. Sammy was never originally intended to have three books but he was another who caught at my heart and also, I think, the hearts of many readers. And he was also deeply involved with Muriel/Maddy's story. (I'm sorry, by the way, about what happened to Sammy. I was sobbing myself as I wrote that, and I know many readers did as they read it. They told me so! But it was still the right thing to do – anything else would have been ducking the point of the story.)

And while on the subject of Sammy, who could forget his parrot Silver, who – after Muriel – becomes Sammy's closest friend and confidante. Silver was first written into the story of Thursday, the VAD in *A Girl Called Thursday*, but was in danger of taking over, so was removed, set aside and saved until he could appear in his rightful place – which happened to be Ruth Purslow's cottage in Bridge End.

So it was that Stella and Muriel insisted on having their story told. The Burracombe series made this possible and when, a couple of years ago, I decided that it was time to end the series, they made it clear to me that this was their moment. They were not to be abandoned again.

I had plenty of questions to ask. Just what *did* happen to them, after they were torn so cruelly from the vicarage that day, by the woman who looked like a 'brown settee'? How *did* Maddy end up in Burracombe, adopted by the actress Fenella Forsyth and living with Dottie Friend? There are clues all through the series, but we never hear the full truth. So, having decided that the story of Burracombe must – sadly – go on without me, and without my readers, I knew that there was one more part to write, and that this part would link the two series – the April Grove and other wartime books, which I began to write back in 1994, and the Burracombe stories which end with *Farewell To Burracombe*, written in 2016.

A Child in Burracombe is a little different from the others and, I think, a little special. It tells the story of something that happened to many children, both during and after the war, when it was thought that you could part families and nobody would suffer; when children were believed to be 'resilient' and able easily to forget those they had loved. I don't suppose anyone has any idea how many adults today were treated like this as children, or what it did to them in later life. I can only hope that today we know better and care rather more about the bonds of childhood.

In *The Bells of Burracombe*, you can read how Stella and Muriel's story continues. And I am happy to say that the brother and sister I knew myself found each other again, although they can never regain those lost years. But there must be many whose lives were very different, who have memories, some vague and some very clear, of the family they once had and have never been able to find. To all of them, I would like to add an extra dedication in the form of this book, *A Child In Burracombe*.

May you find your own happiness.

Make sure you've read all the books in the heartwarming Burracombe series . . .

1 The Bells of Burracombe

When Stella Simmons comes to the Devonshire village of Burracombe to start her teaching career, she is alone in the world. Orphaned as a child and brought up in a children's home, she was separated from her sister Muriel and has never been able to trace her.

Stella is soon caught up in the life of the village, and especially in the plans for celebrating the Festival of Britain. As headmistress Miss Kemp and vicar Basil Harvey try to keep the peace between villagers, who all have their own ideas for the proposed pageant and fair, Stella tries, with the help of artist Luke Ferris, to find her sister. But Luke has his own troubles ...

2 A Stranger In Burracombe

Like the rest of the nation, the Burracombe villagers are shocked when King George VI dies suddenly in 1952. But in the midst of their grief, the arrival of a stranger in the village on the very same day goes almost unnoticed, as the villagers have their own concerns.

Farmer's daughter Val needs to find a home before she can marry her sweetheart; Hilary is struggling to come to terms with her new responsibilities, and Stella is still getting to know the sister she thought she had lost during the war. While the children at the village school are as lively and inquisitive as ever, there are still conflicts and feuds among the long-standing residents of Burracombe.

Then a search for a family draws the whole village together, and more than one person is led to question their own ideas about families and what they mean.

3 Storm Over Burracombe

Hilary Napier is upset and angry when her father brings in a new manager for the family estate which she has been running for the past year. Even though she cannot help liking Travis Kellaway, she resents his presence. But before long, she begins to appreciate Travis's strength and compassion, and she finds herself drawn to him.

Meanwhile, life in the village is enlivened by the new drama club, formed by energetic young curate Felix Copley. Almost the entire village becomes involved in the pantomime he decides to organise – with results they didn't quite plan for!

Then tragedy strikes, making everyone realise exactly what is important in their lives ...

4 Springtime in Burracombe

The village of Burracombe is looking forward to the Coronation, but 1953 is to prove to be a year of heartbreak as well as celebration. While Stella begins to plan her wedding, her sister Maddy is only just coming to terms with the loss of her own fiancé; Val and Luke are wondering if they will ever become parents, and Hilary's chances of marriage seem at first to come closer, then to recede.

The Tozer family also face anxiety. As grandmother Minnie fights for her life, Tom and Joanna's premature twins battle with their own crisis and Jackie, working in Plymouth, is determined to live her own life.

Meanwhile, the life of the village goes on, with all its ups and downs, its feuds and differences. Bossy Joyce Warren tries to organise everything and everyone, Miss Kemp and Stella plan yet another event for the school, Jacob Prout strives to keep Burracombe looking its best for the festivities – and romance comes from a quite unexpected direction ...

5 An Heir for Burracombe

It's a summer's day in 1953 that turns Hilary Napier's life upside down. When Marianne, a beautiful French woman, knocks on her door, Hilary can't help but be struck by Robert, the young boy with her. He has the same eyes as the brother she lost in the war. As she listens to Marianne's sad tale, she realises that her soldier brother lives on in the son he never met. But this is only the first revelation ...

As the village of Burracombe tries to make sense of the strangers in their midst, there is also much to celebrate. A wedding is being planned, a birth is imminent and a courtship just beginning. Yet, as always, life is complicated, and some people must learn cruel truths about the world ...

6 Secrets in Burracombe

A seemingly sleepy Devonshire village, Burracombe is in fact full of intrigue and drama. Family secrets, budding romance, cruel twists of fate and amazing friendships all play out against the backdrop of the beautiful countryside.

It's autumn 1953. The village is delighted when Joe Tozer – who left Burracombe as a young man in 1919 – returns to visit his family. His life since emigrating to the States has been a world away from rural Devon, but coming home, he falls in love with the place (and one particular person) all over again. With him is his eldest son, Russell. He sets hearts fluttering in the village – but will there be anyone on his arm when he catches the boat back to America?

7 Snowfall in Burracombe

In the village of Burracombe, nothing stays secret for long and behind the peaceful, rural charm there's always a scandal to uncover, a newcomer to the village to set tongues wagging, a happy occasion to celebrate or friends to help their neighbours through the tough times.

It's December 1953 and for Stella Simmons, recovering from a car crash, the winter wedding that she and her sweetheart had planned seems impossible.

Elsewhere in the village, Jackie Tozer is dreaming of America and Hilary Napier, who thought the war had robbed her of her chance of happiness, has to ask herself if she could ever imagine leaving her life at the big house for the sake of love and adventure. The darkest time of the year finds everyone asking questions with no easy answer.

As snow falls softly on the village, Burracombe proves once again that there's always a surprise just around the corner.

---

8 Weddings in Burracombe

Devon, 1954. The villagers of Burracombe pull together to help each other through the tough times but now it's summer, and a time to celebrate love and new life. Even so, there are still a few surprises to come . . .

At Burracombe Barton, Hilary Napier is doing her best to keep the estate ticking along, all the while longing for a man she cannot have. She welcomes help from young Patsy Shillabeer – but Patsy is more headstrong than she first appears, and there's trouble brewing.

And all is not well in the village school, where a strict new teacher appears to be making the lives of the little ones a misery. And almost everyone is missing their beloved teacher Stella, still in hospital after the accident that nearly killed her.

As the first crocuses bring colour and the promise of change back to Burracombe, the villagers help each other through the hardships.

For, while the course of true love never did run smooth for anyone, in Burracombe there are weddings to plan and it won't be long before everyone in this very special village comes together in a joyful celebration of love, life and the things that matter most.

9 *Celebrations in Burracombe*

It's the late 1950s, and change is in the air. For the Napier family, up at the big house, the old ways are shifting. Hilary must discover if reaching out for a chance of happiness must mean breaking away from the life expected of her, while Patsy, their young housekeeper's help, is facing motherhood without her own family around her.

Down the hill from the Napiers, villagers young and old are setting out on adventures – Stella and Felix begin married life, change comes to the village school and the Tozer family continue to find surprises in their midst.

10 *Surprises in Burracombe*

Hilary Napier has had enough of secrets. Her engagement party is a chance for her and David to finally celebrate their good news. But with obstacles springing up on all sides, there may be more than the dress and venue to arrange before she can consider walking down the aisle.

Frances and James are doing their best to ignore their feelings for each other as they organise the school play. Can Frances find a way to let herself love again?

Amid all the drama, old friends are always on hand, and when Dottie falls ill, a familiar face comes back to Burracombe to lift her spirits and perhaps change her life.

With surprises around every corner, life is never dull in this beautiful Devonshire village ...

11 Farewell to Burracombe

The day that Hilary and David have been waiting for has finally arrived and as the church bells ring out for the arrival of the bride, everyone's fingers are crossed for the day to go without a hitch. The festivities set the tone for the year ahead and there's more love in the air in Burracombe as planning continues for both Dottie and Joe's and Frances and James's nuptials. There's nothing like a wedding to bring the village together.

Times are changing in Burracombe and as young and old embark on new adventures it's time to say goodbye. But with friends like these, a goodbye is rarely for ever, so instead we'll say a very fond farewell.

And read about the wedding that unites villagers of April Grove and Burracombe in

A Penny A Day

December 1952. A wedding is being planned in April Grove, Portsmouth, and Jess and Frank Budd want to bring together all their friends and neighbours. They even invite Stella Simmons and her sister Maddy, who now live in the Devonshire village of Burracombe.

Dan and Ruth Hodges attend, together with Dan's son Sammy, who immediately falls in love with his childhood playmate Maddy. But Stephen Napier, son of the Squire of Burracombe, proves a strong rival and Maddy is not yet ready to make such a momentous decision about her life.

And don't miss these seasonal short stories with your favourite villagers. Available exclusively in eBook

A Burracombe Easter

On Easter day in 1918, as the Great War entered its closing stages, Frances Kemp looked out at the little thatched village in the valley below and promised that, one day, she'd come back ...

For long before Miss Kemp became headmistress of the village school, when she was just a teenager, she had reason to know and love Burracombe. Sent to stay with family in the village, young Frances treasured her summers there and the friends she made.

But as she grows up, she admits that there is someone there who is more than just a friend. Yet just as they realise their childhood bond is deepening into something else, war is declared and life will never be the same again.

A Burracombe Christmas

Autumn 1918 has brought young Alice Whiddon to the Tozer's farm to work as a maid. Alice soon falls in love with the little village and with life on the farm. But that's not all she's falling for. Youngest son, Ted Tozer is half promised to young Ivy Prowse, daughter of a neighbouring farmer, yet Alice and Ted feel a powerful bond forming.

But while the first peacetime Christmas in years beckons, romance must wait as influenza comes to the farm and threatens to bring tragedy with it, just as the Tozer's eldest son Joe returns from the front to Burracombe and his sweetheart, Dottie.

As Alice and the family wait and hope for the new year to bring long-awaited joy and peace, no one knows whether the bells will peal in sorrow or in celebration as the year turns.